CR

As In Funny Ha-Ha, Or Just Peculiar
A Murderous Ink Press Anthology

****

Murderous–Ink Press

CRIMEUCOPIA

As In funny Ha-Ha, Or Just Peculiar

First published by
Murderous-Ink Press
Crowland
LINCOLNSHIRE
England

www.murderousinkpress.co.uk

Paperback Edition ISBN: 9781909498266
eBook Edition ISBN: 9781909498273

Acknowledgements

To those writers and artists who helped make this anthology

what it is, I can only say a heartfelt Thank You!

It's a Wrap first appeared in *STOPOVER and Other Stories for a Rainy Night* (2014).

**125, 135, 509 first appeared at https://www.intrinsick.com/ 30/05/2020.

***The Big Favor* first appeared in *Wrong Turn* (Blunderwoman Productions 2018).

****Saving Mrs. Hapwell first appeared in the March/April 1997 edition of the *Dogwood Tales Magazine*.

And to Den, as always.

Contents

They Don't Write 'em Like That Anymore…   vii

Dirty Pictures – Jesse Hilson   1

Long Live the King – Gabriel Stevenson   13

Who Let the Llamas Out? – Maddi Davidson   19

Don't You See? – Brandon Barrows   29

Danny DeLuca's Bridge – Robb T. White   41

It's A Wrap – Regina Clarke*   71

Harry's List – Martin Zeigler   77

Louie's Turn – K. G. Anderson   97

Mobster Thermidor – Andrew Hook   105

Less Than a Rental Car – Ed Nobody   119

Jack's Plan – Jody Smith   127

I Could be an Albert Tillman – Michael Grimala   137

Lemonhead – W. T. Paterson   153

The Natural Wonders of the State of Florida
    – James Blakey   171

125, 135, 509 – Emilian Wojnowski**   181

Conversations on the Plurality of Worlds
    Andrew Darlington   187

The Big Favor – Lawrence Allan ***   201

Listen To My Pitch! – Ricky Sprague   221

Fireball Rolled a Seven – Bethany Maines   251

Saving Mrs. Hapwell – John M. Floyd****   271

Lockdown's A Killer – Julie Richards   277

The Usual Unusual Suspects   285

But first, here are these massages from our sponsors...

Advert Break

...*That's Egyptian Nazi Sharks Week, all next week, here on Fux.*

Have you been attacked by a shark? Then why not call CLAMS DIRECT on 1-800-555-55-55 for some of the best and most aggressive No Win No Fee bi-valves around.

CLAMS DIRECT – Sponsors of the Egyptian Nazi Sharks Week here on Fux

And now, back to our regular deprogramming...

After Monday and Tuesday, even the Calendar says WTF...

(An Editorial of Sorts)

There comes a time when the amount of unusual submissions gets you to thinking: How can we use this stuff?

The answer is, of course, when you get enough to put together a collection of short fiction that will hopefully make you go *Hmmmmm*.

Yet that doesn't mean every piece in here has been written with a psychotic eye for Avant-garde detail. Okay, maybe *some* have – the Law of Percentages would dictate for one thing – and there is also the fact that writers are, well, to put it bluntly, often overly surreal in their inventiveness at times.

But that's certainly no reason to just leave these stories on the side in the hope that they will wander off of their own accord.

Of the 21 writers within these pages, it would be fair to say that none wrote their pieces specifically for this anthology. However, if it had not of been for them taking a gamble, then this collection would not be seeing the light of day.

The first that came over the windowsill was W. T. Paterson's **Lemonhead**. After that, Andrew Hook's **Mobster Thermidor** and Emilian Wojnowski's **125, 135, 509** joined Gabriel Stevenson's **Long Live the King** and Ed Nobody's **Less Than a Rental Car** – which, to us, has a touch of Beat Generation style – sort of Burroughs without the dystopia.

Jesse Hilson's **Dirty Pictures** has the classic hook of a '*So where is this going?*' opening, and Jody Smith's **Jack's Plan** has both humour and a fast pace, which is balanced by Robb. T. White's more downbeat **Danny DeLuca's Bridge** – one of the three pieces here to make reference to the Covid-19 pandemic.

It would be hard to pin a 'label' on Martin Zeigler's **Harry's List**, or Andrew Darlington's **Conversations on the Plurality of Worlds**, so, by way of a contrast, Michael Grimala's **I Could be an Albert Tillman**, along with Lawrence Allan's **The Big Favor** and James Blakey's **The Natural Wonders of the State of Florida** are about as close to NOIR as this anthology gets.

Maddi Davidson shows that llamas are not to be messed with in her humorous offering of **Who Let the Llamas Out?**, and Regina Clarke's **It's a Wrap!** helps explain why actors don't like working with children or animals.

Brandon Barrows' **Don't You See?** and John M. Floyd's **Saving Mrs. Hapwell** take us back in time, before Ricky Sprague's **Listen To My Pitch!**, and K. G. Anderson's **Louie's Turn**, bring us home with a more modern setting.

Bethany Maines presents **Fireball Rolled a Seven** – the second CV-19 piece, and closing out this anthology is Julie Richards and her **Lockdown's a Killer** – something we hope will raise a smile before you start to read about the writers who have made you laugh, groan, pause for thought, or made you willing to step out of your comfort zones to read and enjoy something totally new.

In the spirit of the Murderous Ink Press motto – "*You never know what you like until you read it.*"

Dirty Pictures

Jesse Hilson

A spring weekday in 1954, Syracuse, New York.

Dr. Aristide Hoover was fifteen minutes into Francine Rowan's session when she pulled a small pistol from her purse and pointed it at him.

"It's loaded," she said.

"Put that thing away," Dr. Hoover said after a tense moment. He was trying not to communicate any fear.

"I just bought this gun three days ago," Francine said. "I barely know how to use it. It could go off at any minute, I have no control."

They sat there for a minute, looking at each other. Francine had dark circles under her eyes, no makeup. She did look unhinged, even more so with the gun as a threatening prop.

"What do you want from me?" Dr. Hoover asked. His forehead and upper lip were sheened with sweat.

Francine stood up from the couch and, keeping the gun trained on Dr. Hoover, walked to a point between him and the door, to prevent escape.

"You're going to pick up that phone," she said. "You're going to call that pervert, convince him to come here and confess. Then I'm going to shoot him, then I'm going to shoot myself."

"My one o'clock appointment will be here in—" He carefully checked the clock positioned behind the couch. "—in forty minutes. You can't be here when they arrive."

"Then you haven't got much time, Doctor. Besides, I'll be dead if it all goes according to plan."

"What's his number?"

She told him. He raised his hands to show her he wasn't threatening, got up and went to the phone. His pulse was throbbing and he had to tell himself it would be alright. In his training Dr. Hoover had dealt with many unstable patients. But none of them had ever pointed a gun at him. This would be quite a story for Hennings if he ever made it out of there alive.

"Don't call the police or you're done for."

He picked up the phone from its cradle and dialed the number she gave him on the rotary dial. He tried not to let his hands shake, not to let her see.

What if Mr. Rowan wasn't home? Surely there must be some sort of pathway out of here. Some element of her plan would come to grief and she would collapse into tears and give up.

"Hello, Rowan residence."

"Ah, yes, Mr. Rowan. This is Dr. Hoover. I'm your wife's therapist, I believe we've met."

Silence. "If this is about money then I'm sure the mistake is on your end as I've been paying you all along, for the past two months."

"No, there's no problem with billing." Hoover looked at Francine, at the gun in her hands. "I'm afraid there's a situation. With Francine."

"Is she okay? Is she at the hospital again?"

"No, she's here. She can't quite come to the phone. She's very upset and confused. She wants to see you, Mr. Rowan. She wants you to come to my office."

"There?" The man sounded astonished.

"For...couples therapy."

"What's that?"

"It's a technique for getting to the heart of problems that lie in marriage. With both parties present."

"What's she been telling you about me?"

Dr. Hoover had half a mind to tell him on the phone that his wife said he was a pervert, but instead said, "I think it would be best to talk about it when you get here." Dr. Hoover felt the failure of his words as he wished he could have communicated to the man that his life was in danger.

A long silence. Mr. Rowan didn't answer. Dr. Hoover made a theatrical shrug in Francine's direction to let her know that it wasn't going anywhere, he was doing what she asked but nothing came of it.

"What's your address again?" Mr. Rowan asked. He sounded dejected. "I can't seem to locate your business card." To Hoover it seemed as though Mr. Rowan knew something of what this was about, of his wife's fragility. It sounded like there had been a long strain on the man.

"It's 3800 Oppenheim Street, Office B."

"I'll be there in about twenty minutes."

Dr. Hoover hung up the phone. He looked at Francine. "He's coming. Now don't you think you should sit down, give the theatrics a rest, and tell me what's going on?"

Francine held the gun on him for two minutes, then returned to the couch.

Dr. Hoover said, "I want to tell you that this is a very dangerous course of action, not merely physically and legally, but involving me in the situation of killing your husband will have terrible implications for your course of therapy. There will never be resolution. If you go much further down this pathway you may never get back to a place where you can get relief from the issues and neuroses which are plaguing you."

"I'm not plagued with neuroses," Francine hissed. "And it won't matter, will it? When I'm dead?"

"I refuse to give up on you, Mrs. Rowan," Dr. Hoover said. "I think you're going to come back out of this state you're in and you're going to see how foolish your prior positions on things were."

"You're the fool."

Dr. Hoover took up his pen and his notepad. "Tell me more about what's going on with your husband."

"You know all of it. Mostly."

"You told me he has some questionable friends. You said he gambles, which we agreed is a clear indication of a wish to return to childhood. You said he comes home bloody."

"I told you how he was good around the house?" Francine asked.

He thought for a moment, trying to remember. He had so many patients. "You said he kept busy with repairs, and with the tenants in your house."

"That's right, we have two other apartments in our house. Ms. Betson lives in one, and the Salheims live in the other. The Salheims are nice good people but Ms. Betson is suspicious. We don't know anything about her past and I would have loved it if Dick had just put her out on the curb."

"Why is that?"

"She's a fallen woman," Francine said.

"Does she bring men back to her apartment?"

"If she does, I would have noticed. But she stays out late and sometimes doesn't come home at all. She's a tart."

"And your husband, Dick...he...?"

"He's never done anything. Or so I thought." Francine's grip on the pistol did not change, which made Dr. Hoover very nervous. "He was always fixing things around the house, in the basement and the attic. He said he was trying to fight the bats that get in. He was up in the attic a lot blocking up holes. I didn't question him because I knew he'd get cross."

"So you left him alone. What happened?"

"One day when no one was home I went up in the attic for something or other, I forget now. It was a shock. There were holes in the floor of the attic. I tried to work out where they would have been and I was pretty sure they were above the bathrooms of the two apartments. He's been spying on them in the bathrooms."

"My, my." He scribbled on the pad.

"Yes. I found photos, in the attic, of Ms. Betson in the shower. And the worst part of it is, there's no darkroom in our house. At least that I can see. You'd think you'd notice it, all the chemicals. I think he waited till she was in the shower to take the pictures so no one would hear the noise of the shutter. And worst of all, Mrs. Salheim having bath time with her baby daughter."

"Both in the tub?"

"Yes. So I found photos of the Betson woman and Mrs. Salheim and her baby but no darkroom. These photos had been developed somewhere else."

"Where?"

"That's just it, I don't know, but I suspect Dick has a friend who not only would develop the negatives but would buy them. Ms. Betson is a very well-developed woman, if you know what I mean. I think Dick runs around with some really disgusting violent criminal types who would find a way to make money from those photos of her. And of Mrs. Salheim."

Dr. Hoover stopped writing. "Why don't you go to the police?"

"I couldn't live with it. The shame is so great I want to die. But I want to make him pay first."

"It's fine to be angry," Dr. Hoover said. "But why resort to this? There must be a way out that doesn't involve violence. You couldn't kill somebody."

"I could kill you before he gets here. You made the phone call to get him here, that's all I wanted you for. You're of no use to me now."

"But why here, at my office?"

"It would catch Dick off guard."

Dr. Hoover paused, gathered strength. "I think you are doing this here because this is a site of therapeutic catharsis for you. It's here that you unburden yourself of your fears and you want Dick to know about it. You want an eruption of insight that will overpower him."

Francine was grimacing, perhaps under the weight of Dr. Hoover's words? He couldn't tell but went on.

"Your motives in this are your own business, but you have recruited me in this. Partially because you want me to witness your statement to Dick about the seriousness of your revealed feelings, but also because it's a cry for help. You see me as a potential intervention into your violent actions. You could have shot him at home, at the store, in the countryside. But you chose to confront him at the location of your healing. This is about your therapy more than it is about your willingness to murder."

Dr. Hoover hoped his speech was eroding Francine's rage and bringing her back to reality.

"Let's not go too far," she said.

"Weren't you telling me some weeks ago about how your father, before he passed away, never really gave Dick the respect he felt he deserved? And that you joined Dick in feeling that resentment? It caused a schism between you and your father."

"It did."

"But now with this new information you are seeking to in some ways reconcile with your father's judgment about Dick. You see me as a kind of paternal authority figure that could offer a new judgment."

"Yes, how did you know?" Her sarcasm was thick but underneath it Dr. Hoover knew there lurked a wounded truth.

"You may not be conscious of this, but patients often cast their therapists into other roles, including surrogate parental ones."

Francine paused, wiping away tears. "So you're like my father?"

"Not your father but in this therapeutic situation I embody certain traits of your father image, namely, the person you turn to, to seek justice, to enact it. There's not much else explaining why you're doing this here."

Dr. Hoover sensed that while he was getting through to Francine, things were still highly dangerous. The gun was still pointed at him.

The buzzer from the front door went off.

Francine, her face red and running with tears, flicked the gun towards the door, indicating Dr. Hoover should get up and answer it. He put his notepad and pen aside, realizing that although he and Mr. Rowan had met months ago when Francine's therapy had started, he had forgotten what the man looked like.

At the front door, Dick Rowan's eyes were hard to see as they were hidden in the shade of the brim of his hat. His jaw was set, rigid. The city street behind him roiled with traffic. Dr. Hoover had an urge to warn Dick, to tell him to run, and to run away himself leaving Francine in his office with her gun. But he didn't. He felt like he was getting somewhere with Francine and that he could really help her out of this hole. He brought Dick inside.

The man did not seem alarmed to find himself staring down the barrel of his wife's pistol. "What's that supposed to be, a fly-swatter?" he said.

Dick stood by the door. Dr. Hoover went back to his chair. The dynamic slightly shifted as Dr. Hoover stopped being a primary target.

"Dick, tell Dr. Hoover about the pictures."

"What pictures?"

"The pictures in the attic."

"There's no pictures in the attic. Is that what she told you?" Dick asked Dr. Hoover.

"She told me that she found holes in the attic leading onto the bathrooms of your tenants."

Dick sighed with exasperation and took his hat off. "Doc, you know as well as I do that Francine isn't well. She gets these ideas in her head. She latches onto one detail then blows it all up into a big scenario."

"He's lying," Francine said.

"We should really take you to a hospital," Dick said.

"What about the pictures in the attic?" Dr. Hoover asked.

Dick looked at Dr. Hoover with horrible wisdom and patience. "I admit that there's something in the attic. But it's not photos of any tenants. I do have a couple boxes of men's magazines up there, you know, lingerie catalogs and...worse. Francine must have found them and constructed this whole dirty plotline."

"No," Francine said, weeping again.

"She exaggerates," Dick said. "And she elaborates. You know once she thought people were following her? We were driving to the Grand Canyon and she swore some people from a rest stop a hundred miles back were popping up everywhere we went."

"They were there," Francine said, grave.

Dr. Hoover suppressed a shiver. He said, "Francine, we need to get you help. I can help you. But the first thing you must do is give over the gun to your husband. You have no business handling a gun. It needs to be in safe hands."

Francine cried and shook her head.

"You know this has all been a fabrication, and you know that the only way to safely resolve the situation is if we're all out of danger. Give Dick the gun."

"I thought I saw dirty pictures in the attic," she said. "I could have sworn it was Ms. Betson. I guess I don't know what I was looking at."

"I'm sorry about the girly magazines," Dick said. "It's not decent. But there's nothing going on with our tenants."

Francine cried out and Dr. Hoover had seen this anguish before, in other mental patients. It was the anguish of being confronted with proof of one's own delusions. She held out one hand, palm up, with the pistol in it. It was a small pistol. Dr. Hoover decisively reached out and took it, quickly passing it into Dick's hand. Dick put the gun into his deep coat pocket.

"Should I call the hospital?" Dr. Hoover asked.

"No, I'll just take her right there," Dick said.

"You're going to be feeling much better very soon," Dr. Hoover told Francine. "You've made the healthy choice.

Doesn't it feel good to turn away from violence toward understanding and sympathy? There's nothing wrong with your husband's urges. Make peace with reality."

Francine put her head in her hands. "I've been sick for so long," she said.

"Come on, darling," Dick said, gesturing to Francine. She got up from the couch as though trying to shake off an iceberg. Dick came to her and took her by the arm. Dr. Hoover tried to help but Dick gently held him back.

"We're going to the hospital. Thank you, Doctor." They shuffled toward the door.

"Tell them to keep me apprised of Francine's condition," Dr. Hoover said. "I'm happy to share my notes with the psychiatrist."

"Sure thing."

They went out the door together.

The relief Dr. Hoover felt could have tranquilized a flotilla of nervous old biddies. He reached for a cigarette and lit it with shaking fingers. He checked the clock: 12:50. Ten minutes until Ms. Jarvis arrived and he would be hearing about her dramatic clashes with the neighborhood ladies' auxiliary. He touched his face and felt sweat on his fingertips. He had a little time to splash some cold water on his face and calm himself.

He heard the buzzer while he was in the bathroom. Ms. Jarvis was early.

He went to the door and opened it to see Dick Rowan, pointing the gun in at him.

"We're not going to the hospital," Dick said. His voice was changed. "I thought about it. We're going home. And Francine

11

will go to her room until she learns not to go through my things."

"So it's true, about the attic..."

"Who cares what's true. I should never have brought her to you, she's got a big mouth. But I guess that's all you do here, is get big mouths to spill their guts about their spouses and their families. You must be swimming in secrets. I bet a lot of husbands would be glad if you never heard anything ever again."

Dick shot Dr. Hoover twice in the chest. He fell to the floor, knocking over his chair. Dick stepped over him and looked through the desk for money. He flipped through the notepad, ripping out the pages from his wife's session. With his last wheezing breath, Dr. Hoover said, "You won't get away...with this, they'll know...it was you..."

"Maybe. Maybe not. But whatever happens, that'll be one less bill I have to pay every month. So it's a good day, all in all," Dick said, and left.

Long Live the King
Gabriel Stevenson

I should've counted myself lucky to land that renaissance fair gig, and for a while I did. After all, I was fresh out of the pen, and where else do a phony English accent and a bitching beard get you hired without so much as a background check?

All I had to do was prove I could stay in the saddle for one lap around the lists—that's what they call the field where they joust—and I was in like Flynn. I grew up on a ranch in West Texas before my pops got busted for meth and the feds seized the place, so I can ride drunk or sober. Mostly drunk as of late.

Boss don't care, though. I play King Arthur, so I don't joust. I just say, "Let the tournament begin!" and then sit there for an hour while the young bucks whale on each other with phony spears and blunted swords and the chumps in the audience hoot and holler and eat their greasy-ass turkey legs.

You know what they didn't have in the Middle Ages? Turkeys, that's what. But where was I?

Oh yeah. So I'm King Arthur. I just sit there and wave every once in a while. And of course Queen Guinevere sits by my side. Guinevere is—well, used to be—my real-life old lady, name of Candi, with an 'i'. If you think that sounds like a stripper name, you ain't wrong. We found her at the Itchy Kitty in West Hollywood, where wannabe movie stars go to die, so the renaissance fair was a step up for her, just like it was for me.

When Candi came on board, all the boys were sniffing round her. But for some reason she picked me. Said she used to be a method actress, so maybe she really thought she was the queen and me her king. Or maybe she just had daddy issues, and the gray beard turned her on. I didn't ask. I just took what the Good Lord gave me.

So everything was copacetic for a minute, me and Queen Candi sitting on our thrones, holding hands and waving at the fake knights and the chumps in the stands, and then getting high and rutting like animals behind the lists when the show was over. When the fair hit Vegas, we even went to that little love chapel and got hitched.

But like pops's ranch, good things don't last forever. We'd barely finished our honeymoon when Lance showed up.

Of course there had always been a Lancelot character, but the old Lancelot got busted for statutory outside of Flagstaff and they had to find a new one fast.

So this dude had just quit the rodeo and, I won't lie, he was the best rider in the fair. I never knew his real name, but he made everyone call him Lance. He was a handsome son of a bitch, a real Captain America type with blue eyes and a jaw you could crack nuts with… I can tell by your smile you know what comes next.

Candi fell for him, hard. I bet you think it's funny, don't you? Guinevere and Lancelot, just like in the old legend, and poor King Arthur don't know what's going on.

But I did know what was going on, and it wasn't funny. Not one damn bit.

Let me tell you, brother, there's a reason I was in the pen, and I ain't gonna get into it 'cause that's a whole 'nother story, but suffice it to say that I ain't the kind of man who puts up with some punk-ass cowboy or no two-timing skank. So while Lance and Candi were sneaking around like teenagers, I was figuring a way to get even.

Just about that time, we were tearing down in Tucson, and it was all over the news about what happened over in Tombstone. Not the O.K. Corral bullshit. That's old news. No, some re-enactor pretending to be Doc Holliday loaded up with real bullets and plugged Ike Clanton five times right there in the middle of the street in broad daylight.

And I knew right then that's what I had to do. Sure, I coulda snuck into Lance's trailer and put some rat poison in his whiskey, I coulda smothered Candi with a pillow and tossed her body over the fence into Mexico, but no, I wanted something more. I wanted the whole world to watch it happen.

How to do it, though?

You can load an old Colt with live ammo, but what do you do with a lance or a sword? Especially when the riders wear real armor during the jousts?

That's when I remembered Hormiguito.

Hormiguito was a vaquero from Juarez, who used to play the Black Knight because he looked kind of like an Arab. He'd wear black armor with a turban wrapped around his pointy helmet and he rode a black horse, and he used a scimitar when he fought on foot. But then this four-eyed professor type came round and convinced the boss that the Arab was some other dude named Palamedes, and the Black Knight was just a white dude in black armor.

Maybe Hormiguito was banging the professor's girl. He was banging the boss's girl, no doubt, so the boss was happy to call ICE and send his ass back to Old Mexico. Course Four Eyes got the Black Knight gig.

Me, I kept in touch with Hormiguito 'cause after he lost his job he went back to work for the cartel. They'd have him bring powder across the border on horseback, a kilo at a time, and he'd sell me a gram or two cheap.

So I told Hormiguito I had a killer idea to get back at Lance and Four Eyes both, but I'd need his help. And a week later, I was out in the desert west of El Paso, waiting for Hormiguito.

He was late as always, but eventually he rode up on that black horse, wearing his vaquero get-up and holding a medieval lance like Don Fucking Quixote.

It cost me my left nut, but that lance was perfect. All black, of course, for the Black Knight, identical to the ren fair lances in every way. Even the rubberized tip looked just like it was supposed to.

Anyway, I took the lance back to the fair, and then, after Candi excused herself to "go for a walk," I snuck out to the lists to make some other preparations.

The next day was the big day at the El Paso County Fair and Rodeo Grounds. The stands were full of fat, pasty chumps, chowing down on turkey legs and historically accurate funnel cakes. We rode our lap around the lists, waving at the crowds, and then dismounted to go up onto our little balcony, me and Candi.

There were a few jousts—Gawain, Tristan, Percival—and then Lance knocked Percival off his horse and fought him on foot and finished with the old, "Do you yield?"

And Percival yielded and the crowd was cheering, and then it was the moment you've all been waiting for.

Four Eyes rode up in his Black Knight get-up and called

Lancelot out.

Candi got up and said her little bit about, "Defend our royal honor, good Sir Lancelot," and I just sat there and looked pissed, which wasn't too far from the truth.

Lance got back up on his white horse and went to his corner, and the Black Knight went to his, and Candi dropped her hanky, and they charged.

When they met mid-list, instead of the normal clang of lance on armor, there was a boom like a fucking cannon.

See, Hormiguito's boys down in Juarez had fashioned that spear into a shaped charge like the Iranians used to use over in Iraq. 'Explosively formed penetrator' they call it. The rubber tip concealed an impact fuze, with a length of det cord running down to a titanium base full of Semtex covered by a soft copper plate. When the lance hit Lancelot's breastplate, it triggered the fuze, which detonated the Semtex, which melted the copper plate into a blob of superheated metal and propelled it straight forward with enough force to punch through tank armor.

It punched through Lance's armor alright, blew a Coke can-sized hole through his chest, through his backplate too, and kept on going through the whole plywood Camelot behind him. Eventually embedded itself in the engine block of a Mack truck a hundred yards back.

"Lance!" Candi screamed and jumped up off her throne.

She leaned over the parapet to look down at his dead body, but it didn't hold her weight, seeing as how I'd removed all the bolts while she and Lance were boinking.

The balcony's only about twenty feet up so she barely had time to scream before she landed on the rack of melee weapons somebody had left right under the loose parapet.

Landed right on the business end of a pole-axe. Those

weapons ain't too sharp, but when you fall on one from twenty feet up, they're damn well sharp enough. The pointy part went right through her but the axe part got stuck in there somewhere, tearing her up inside 'til she stopped flailing around.

The Black Knight had been knocked off his horse but wasn't much worse for wear otherwise. The crowd was going nuts. Cops came out within twenty minutes and locked up old Four Eyes.

Turns out he'd been some kind of engineer for the military too, so he had the know-how to make something like that.

I figured the cops'll work it out eventually though, so I ain't sticking around with the ren fair. Gonna head down to Mexico with Hormiguito to train racehorses for the narcos. Like Hormiguito said when he got canned, "Fuck this *pinche feria*. Time to go make some real *feria*."

Looks like the boss'll need a whole new cast before San Antonio, but that ain't really my problem, is it?

Who Let the Llamas Out?
Maddi Davidson

The voice of the Lost Falls, Idaho police dispatcher crackled on the airwaves. "Control to Unit Nine. We have an 80-33. Woman reporting loose llamas, SR10 south of Basque Road." Sitting in his truck intently listening to a portable police scanner, Jackson felt a warm glow of satisfaction. He rubbed his perennial five o'clock stubble reflexively, a Grinch-like grin spreading across his mouth and curling up the sides of his face.

"*Cómo se llama?*" he said, snickering.

"What?" In the passenger seat, a narrow-eyed, round-headed, young man resembling the Charlie Brown character fondled a red monkey perched on his lap.

"Nothing, Colt." Jackson said. "Just talking to myself."

"Can we go now?"

"Not yet. Be patient."

Not for the first time, Jackson wondered if he'd made a mistake by including Colt in his plans. He needed a second pair of hands for the heist and reasoned that Colt, who was more than a few neurons short in the brains department, would be unlikely to notice when Jackson appropriated the greater share of the loot. On the other hand, he hadn't anticipated that Colt's childlike infatuation with animals would be so difficult to manage.

Earlier, around midnight, the two men had paid a visit to the local zoo. As the masked men approached the thirty-acre park, a cloudbank drifted over the gibbous moon, plunging the miscreants into dark shadows. Musky animal odors and the pungent smell of fresh dung bombarded their olfactory organs. The leopard's chuffing, low growls of the lions, and periodic piercing calls of unknown animals unsettled Jackson.

Their first stop was the petting zoo where Jackson snapped the locks on the gate. He was elated when the two-dozen sheep, goats, and camels made an immediate break for freedom.

At the large enclosure housing American bison, zebra, and various deer species, the men cut a wide gap in the fence. An Ankole-Watusi, a 1,500-pound behemoth, was the first to lumber through. Its horns spreading nearly seven feet from tip to tip barely cleared the opening. The zebras and a few deer followed, but the lone bison appeared uninterested in escape.

"I'll get him." Colt started in the direction of the bison when Jackson grabbed his shoulder.

"You don't want to do that!" he whispered loudly. "See those horns? Every year, a few tourists in Yellowstone get too close and are gored."

"But animals *like* me." Colt shrugged off Jackson's hand and took two steps toward the bison. It began pawing the turf, snorting, and bobbing its head.

Jackson snagged Colt by the collar, and pulled him back. "How about you let the monkeys out instead?" Colt nodded vigorously so Jackson pointed him in the direction of the monkey house and handed him a large bolt cutter.

With Colt out of his way, Jackson continued to open cages. He released an Asian elephant which thumped excitedly toward the exit. A crooked smile passed over Jackson's face as he imagined the beast stomping on his ex-wife who, weighing more than 200 pounds, couldn't outrun a gimpy turtle. "Go on, Dumbo, she's two miles down the road in Pine Ridge, 2479 Bitterroot Street."

Jackson skipped the tigers, and had opened the cages of several other species less likely to consider humans as a tasty snack when Colt caught up with him. The young man cradled a small, long-hair, red monkey in his arms.

"No. Just no," Jackson said. "It's a complication we don't need. Let it go."

Colt was petulant. "But he likes me. Curious George and I are going to be good friends."

Jackson sensed that this was not the time to fight that battle. He'd deal with the monkey later.

"I think we've created enough mayhem. It's time to leave."

*****

The Lost Falls policeman responding to the 80-33 stared dumbly at a trio of llamas, grazing along the side of the highway while a short mile away the frenzied barking of Klaus, a four-year old Miniature Schnauzer, was rousing Josh Beally.

"What is it this time?" Beally said. He was used to Klaus being alert to the movement of game animals on moonlit nights, but not the current level of ferocity he was exhibiting.

Beally rose from his bed, scooped up the dog, and glanced out the back window.

"Damn, Klaus. What have you found?"

A few minutes later Jackson's scanner crackled again as the dispatcher called for another patrol car to check out a report of a giraffe at 544 North Conway Street, Beally residence.

"Now?" Colt asked.

"I told you, be patient. Wait until--"

"Control to units Four, Six, Seven, Eight, and Nine." A tense voice issued from the scanner. "We have a report of multiple animals escaped from Lost Falls Zoological Park. All units proceed to zoo. Sixty-six zoo director to assist in recovery."

Jackson and Colt exchanged grins and slapped a high five. Curious George examined his anus.

The two men donned their masks and exited Jackson's rusted, black Ford F150. They moved quickly down the alley, hugging the back of single-story commercial buildings and dodging piles of trash and the occasional rat. They soon arrived at their target, a jewelry store with a conveniently located central air conditioning unit at the back of the building. Jackson climbed up on the A/C unit, then pulled himself onto the roof. After handing Jackson several tools, Colt clambered up and the men went to work opening a hole in the roof.

Later, sitting on the ceiling joists with Colt, Jackson grunted in satisfaction. He'd borrowed the idea of entering through the roof by reading about a successful burglary in Tennessee. Since this building was identical to the other small stores along the block including the bike shop where Jackson had once worked, he knew just where to cut to avoid the rafters.

"I figure we've got no more than five minutes after we hit the floor," Jackson said. "Three minutes to fill the trash bags with all the jewelry we can grab and two minutes to get out of the building. When I call time, we head out. Got it?"

Colt nodded in impatience and jumped. He landed nimbly on the floor amidst a scattering of broken pieces of the drop ceiling. The alarm sounded and triggered an automatic notification at the security company.

The alarm company in turn called the owner of the jewelry store, Josh Beally. Immediately, Beally threw a jacket on over his pajamas, grabbed the keys to his SUV, and with Klaus in tow headed for town. Encountering an elephant blocking the road at the entrance to the Pine Ridge development, he honked his horn. The elephant responded with a loud, indignant trumpet, forcing Beally to back up and take a detour, delaying his arrival at the store by several minutes.

The Lost Falls Police Department also was notified of the potential break-in. Although the station was located a mere two blocks from the jewelry store, at the time of the call the nearest available officer was four miles north helping one of the zoo keepers to capture a mountain goat. The obdurate beast, unwilling to be taken into custody, had sought refuge atop the police cruiser. Upon being told he had more urgent business, the patrolman jumped in his car and turned on the siren, deafening the goat and inducing it to abandon its perch. He then sped into town, arriving at the store simultaneously with Beally.

They were both too late. The burglars had already escaped with nearly $20,000 worth of jewelry and gold.

Jackson was jubilant. The only sour note to the escapade was the stench of urine and feces permeating the truck. He'd insisted that Colt secure the monkey in a canvas bag during the break-in and Curious George had responded less than graciously. When they reached Jackson's cabin, a quarter-mile down a dirt road remote from neighbors, Colt took the loot and monkey inside while Jackson opened all the truck's doors and windows and tossed the now useless but fertilizer-rich bag into the pine-filled woods.

Colt fed his new friend bananas while Jackson sat in an old, stuffed chair, hovering over his police scanner and listening to the unfolding drama of the animal hunt. The havoc was more than he could have hoped-for. The Lost Falls Police had requested help from the nearby Coeur d'Alene Police Department, the Idaho State Police, and Idaho Fish and Game. Jackson's only regret was that he hadn't burglarized a few more stores.

Eventually the sun peaked over the horizon. Not all the animals had been rounded up, but Jackson was yawning nearly continuously and Colt was asleep on the couch with Curious George in a box by his side. Jackson retreated to his bedroom, slipped off his boots, and was crawling into bed when a deep-pitched roar filled the small cabin.

"What the hell!"

Jackson raced into the front room. Colt, standing on the couch, stared down at Curious George. Before Jackson could say a word, the tiny creature opened its mouth and let forth an incredibly loud bellow.

"Shut it up before someone hears it!" Jackson yelled.

Colt dove for the monkey. It eluded his grasp, roaring and racing around the room.

Thinking perhaps the monkey wanted out, Jackson opened the door and windows before joining the chase. His relief when George escaped through the window was short-lived: the creature's outcry continued. Colt picked up a banana and raced outside, screaming for George to return.

"That monkey could wake the dead," Jackson growled. Coincidentally, his nearest neighbor was an old pioneer cemetery.

Jackson grabbed a chainsaw out of the shed, started it up, and went after an old, felled lodgepole pine in back of the cabin hoping that the roar of the saw would drown out the calls of the mad monkey. By the time Colt corralled George, Jackson had cut up enough wood to heat the cabin for weeks.

After the monkey's escapade, Jackson wanted to wring its neck and chuck it into the lake, but Colt protested vehemently. The men finally agreed that Jackson would search the Internet to find out why the monkey had roared and what to do about it. Internet connectivity being spotty at his cabin, Jackson drove into Lost Falls to use the public library computers. What he found was not good. Curious George was a howler monkey. Both mornings and evenings, male howlers established their territories by loud calls that could be heard over two miles away.

"Maybe I can change him," Colt said when Jackson conveyed the information.

"Into what? A great horned owl? Nobody looks twice around here at one of them making a racket!"

After more than an hour of battling Colt's intransigence, Jackson devised an acceptable compromise: Curious George could live, but he'd be returned to the zoo where Colt could visit him. "Just in case anyone heard him this morning," Jackson said, "we'll tell the zoo that we found him in the woods by the cabin."

That evening, Jackson sprawled in his chair drinking Budweiser and occasionally watching the football game on the television. Colt, lying on the sagging couch, was working his way through their ill-gotten gain, fingering each piece and admiring it in the flickering light of the TV. With naught but an afternoon nap and the consumption of three cans of beer, Jackson was half asleep when he heard vehicles approaching the cabin. Headlights flashed through the front window. Nervously he peered outside.

"It's the police! Hide everything!"

Colt shoved several pieces of loose jewelry under cushions and into his jean pockets while Jackson kicked the bags of stolen goods under the sofa.

Insistent knocking brought Jackson to the door. He opened it to a man built like an ex-football player running to fat. He introduced himself as Detective Foxx and was accompanied by two uniformed officers of the Lost Falls Police. Foxx handed Jackson a search warrant.

It took no time at all for the policemen to discover the loot and place Jackson and Colt under arrest.

"How did you know?" Jackson said.

"The zoo director was suspicious about your monkey story," Foxx replied as Jackson was handcuffed. "Howlers like to stay together. The others were found six miles east of here. Ergo, you must have snatched your monkey from the zoo."

Jackson swore. "I told you, Colt. I said that monkey was a mistake."

Foxx nodded. "Yup, a real howler."

Don't You See?

Brandon Barrows

The front door slammed so hard that I felt the vibration in my office, all the way on the other side of the house. Ashley was home and from the way she entered, I expected another battle.

I went out into the hallway. She stood in the foyer wearing her *Cashmere by Sofia* coat and carrying the blue velvet handbag that cost as much as I made in a week. Both were stained by half-melted snow and neither was suited to the winter weather. Fashion was all Ashley cared about. And as it was her money, which she reminded me over and over again throughout our marriage; she could spend it on whatever she damn-well wanted.

Now, though, it was clear that neither fashion nor money were on her mind. There was a lost look in her eyes and her perfect little teeth nibbled at her lower lip. She made no move to take off her shoes or coat.

"Welcome home," I said.

She looked up finally and the dam burst. Tears trickled from her eyes and she moved down the hallway towards me, ignoring the trail of slush and dirt she left on the polished hard wood floor. "Nathan... Nathan."

I went to her. Part of me wanted to throw my arms around her, but I didn't know how she'd react. In the early days, we hugged and touched and caressed each other often. Now, a hug was a big deal and taking one without invitation might just make things worse. "What's wrong?" I asked, compromising with a hand on her shoulder.

"Oh god," she cried and fell against me. I put my arms around her, holding her lightly, wary of how she might still react and the cold snowmelt soaking through my clothing. "I must have been crazy, Nathan. I don't know why I did it, I just don't. It was like a game at first and then it was, it was— "

She choked off, the tears turning to sobs. I was really worried now. This wasn't like my wife. She was usually cool, aloof. Cold, if you were to be really analytical. We'd been married fourteen years, but sometimes, she treated me like a passing stranger on the street. Even in the good, early days, I couldn't remember her ever being this emotional.

I directed her towards the living room, making soothing noises. "Come sit down." I maneuvered her to the couch and went to the small bar in the corner. I poured a snifter half full of *kirschwasser*, the Swiss cherry brandy she adored, and made her drink it. Once she did, she was gasping for breath, but the crying stopped.

I sat down next to her. "Okay, so what's going on?"

She looked up, the glass clutched in both hands like a child with a sippy-cup. Her eyes were red-rimmed and her makeup was smeared. She looked human, though, and vulnerable. "I didn't mean it," she whispered. Then louder, "I didn't really understand what was going on, that it was *real*, until it was too late."

"Okay." I rubbed her back through the damp coat. "Start from the beginning."

"I hired someone to kill you."

Unsurprisingly my mouth went dry and something pulsed in my forehead. "What?"

She nodded, her throat working. She seemed to be having trouble swallowing. I got up, brought back the bottle of brandy and refilled her glass. She sipped it then said, "It was a joke. Just a sort of… I was so angry at you one day, and I was telling Lilly"—her best friend since sorority days—"and it just sort of became a bitch session. Somewhere along the way, I brought up divorce, and she said 'a hitman is probably cheaper'. We laughed and I felt better, but then later, it came to mind again after you and I had another fight. And every time you annoyed me or we argued, I thought of it. So I looked around online and someone on one of those internet sites showed me how to get onto the 'dark web' and one thing led to another and I found someone who said they'd do it for five thousand dollars in bitcoin and… and…" She started crying again, softly this time.

"Why are you telling me this?"

"Because, look!" She dug in her purse and pulled out her cellphone. She brought up her text messages and showed me the most recent. It read simply "TONIGHT". The sender was anonymous, the name field blank.

I shook my head. "Someone's joking with you. Lilly, probably."

"No!" She grabbed my arm, her eyes wild. "This is what he said would happen. After I sent him the money, he asked me for a bunch of information about you. I told him about the school and how you spend half the night in your office working and the big picture window in there, how easy it would be. He said when he was ready to do it, I would know. This is it. Don't you see?"

My blood went cold. She wasn't joking. "Why did you do this?" It wasn't what I meant to say, but that's what came out.

"It's wrong, I know that. I knew it all along, but it didn't seem *real*. Please, *please*, believe me, it was a joke, a game, just a way to take out the stress and anger. I don't know if I love you anymore, Nathan, but I don't hate you, either. The way you treat me, the way you talk to me like I'm one of your students and how everything else is more important to you than I am, infuriates me, but I don't want you dead. Not really." She pressed her face against my shoulder and I could feel her body convulse with sobs.

My brain started to churn. There must be a way out of this and if not, I could find a way through it. I had a master's degree in education and prided myself on problem-solving.

"You can't call it off?" I asked.

"I tried," she mumbled, voice muffled by my shirt. She looked up. "When I got the text, I tried going to the site I contacted him through, but it was gone."

That made sense. Once everything was arranged, there was no point leaving anything that could be traced back.

"We should call the police," Ashley said.

I thought about it. Ideas raced through my head, putting together this and that, trying to make individual pieces fit into something workable. I shook my head. "No, I don't think that's a good idea."

"Why?" she practically shrieked. The panic was coming back.

"We don't know for sure that this man you've hired will even go through with it. It could still all be an elaborate scam of some sort. You paid him money?"

She nodded. "Half in advance, the rest when…."

"Then maybe he's just giving you a little theater for what you paid him." She opened her mouth and I held up a hand. "Besides, if we called the police, there's no way to keep this from getting out. What do you think Sacred Heart would do if they found out the granddaughter of the school's founder had hired a hitman to kill her faculty-member husband? And even if you don't care about that, what would your family think?"

Ashley looked at me, eyes wide. "We'd be ruined." Then she covered her face again and sobbed, "What do we do?"

"Can you guess when this man will be coming?" I asked.

Ashley began to shake her head, but paused. "I told him you're hardly ever in bed before one and that you spend hours after dinner in your office. I guess it'll be some time around then."

"So let's say after midnight, when the neighbors will be asleep. How does he plan to do it?"

"We…never talked about that part." She pulled away from me, as if keeping me at arm's length, as if separating herself from the coming violence she herself initiated. "What are you going to do?"

I looked at my wife. Even mussed from crying and the weather, she was lovely. She came from a very rich family and when we married, before we even finished college, everyone told me how lucky I was. A beautiful, rich wife with connections to a prestigious institution in the field I planned to go into – how perfect.

But Ashley and I didn't really know each other when we married and the more we learned, the less we liked each other. She wasn't a bad person, but money and influence had always been her armor, her shield against having to consider anyone else beyond what they could do for her. She wasn't built for sharing her life with another person, especially not as intimately as marriage required. I found the only way I could deal with her was to treat her in the same calm, detached, vaguely patronizing way I treated the rich students I dealt with day in and day out. It hurt at first, but it was better than constant skirmishes. Even so, we fought. We weren't bad people, neither one of us. We were just poorly matched. Until this moment, though, I never truly realized how poorly or how firmly we were chained to one another.

"I'll take care of it." I reached for her and drew her close, feeling the slim body beneath the layers of cashmere and silk.

"But what can you *do*?"

"If he shows up, he'll be an intruder, presumably armed. A man has the right to defend his home, doesn't he?"

She pushed away, looking at me in shock. "What do you mean?"

"Don't worry." I drew her close again, kissed her forehead, and wrapped my arms around her. "I know what to do. I'll take care of everything."

A shudder went through her entire body.

*****

Ashley had another drink and I joined her. Afterwards, I took her coat and shoes and sent her upstairs for a long, hot bath. It wasn't quite seven o'clock, so there was plenty of time.

When she was through in the bathroom, I suggested she try to get some rest. She protested, but I insisted – she had been through a great deal of stress.

She put her arms around me, looked up into my eyes. Her face was clean of makeup, her hair still damp. She smelled sweet and fresh and she felt warm and soft against my body. "I'm sorry, Nathan. I must have been crazy."

I kissed her. I agreed with her, but I couldn't say that, so I didn't say anything.

She asked, "Are you sure you can't call the police?"

"I'll be fine," I told her. I smiled for her benefit, not really feeling brave, just so desperate I'd gone beyond fear. Aside from my marriage, I liked my life very much. I liked my job, I liked my home. I didn't want to give any of it up. I wouldn't let anyone take it away from me, not by my death or any other way. "I have my father's revolver and I did some competitive target-shooting in school, remember?"

She nodded and moved to the door of the bedroom. Turning back she smiled wanly and said, "I love you, Nathan."

"Get some rest," I told her.

I went downstairs to my office. I turned on every light so it would be clear from outside that the room was occupied, drew the curtain on the big picture window and positioned my chair near the door, out of line with the window. If this hitman, if he existed, wanted to kill me, he would have to come into the house to do it.

I went to the safe in the corner of the room, beneath a removable square of the carpet, and took out the chamois-wrapped .38 revolver I inherited from my father several years earlier. He'd kept it in his nightstand for nearly forty years and never fired it outside of a target range. But he cleaned and oiled it regularly and it was like new when it came to me. I held the weapon in my hands. The familiar weight and solidness was reassuring and for a moment, something sang in my chest, a little trill of excitement. I liked my life very much, but it wasn't a very stimulating one. As insane as Ashley had been in hiring someone to kill me, a demented little part of my own brain was grateful.

I opened the cylinder, checked the loads, and then locked it back in place. I went to the chair, facing the door, and sat.

For a time, I tried to think of nothing at all, just focused on keeping myself calm. My heart would begin to hammer in my chest and my breathing would shorten and I would have to remind myself that panic wouldn't solve anything. I thought of Ashley upstairs, lying in bed, probably as awake as I was, if she didn't take a sleeping tablet. I thought of the strange marriage we had, the way we lived together but apart for so long. She said she didn't love me anymore, but that was fine. I hadn't loved her for a very long time, either.

I imagined possible futures. I wondered if I shouldn't call the police after all, my career and status be damned. I wondered what this hitman looked like. I wondered how often he did this. Was I his first "job"? His hundredth? I hoped, whatever happened, it would be over quickly. I didn't like drawing things out if there was any way to avoid it. I knew this man wouldn't hesitate and I couldn't either. Shoot first, think later.

Somehow, I fell asleep. It seems incredible, with everything happening, with my mind churning the way it was, that sleep would even be possible, but the body does what it needs to whether we like it or not. I woke up suddenly, jerking in the chair, unsure of where I was. I almost dropped the revolver, but its shifting weight in my lap brought everything back all at once. I heard a sound and realized what woke me up: slow, heavy footsteps on the hard wood flooring in the hallway.

The footsteps stopped. I held my breath. I glanced at my watch; it read 00:47.

After a long moment, the door of the office began to move slowly inward. Then it was open and framed in the doorway was a fat young man of about thirty, unshaven, his hair close-cropped, wearing a heavy black sweatshirt, black sweatpants, and white sneakers. There was an automatic in his hand, a short stubby tube screwed onto the barrel. His eyes went wide when he saw me and his gun came up, but I was quicker. The .38 jerked three times in my hand and three holes appeared in the young man's chest. He went to the floor with a grunting noise.

I moved over to him and looked down, the gun pointed at his chest, ready to shoot again, but it wasn't necessary. Blood spread across the black fabric of his clothing, leaving darker patches, and his eyes were already empty. The hand that clutched the automatic opened when he fell and the weapon, a 9mm, I thought, lay on the floor.

My chest ached with tension and the pounding of my heart. I'd chosen an incredibly risky, and possibly suicidal path, and won out. I felt exhilarated and intensely alive.

Stepping over the body, I went out into the hallway and to the bottom of the stairs. "Ashley!" I called. "Ashley!"

She appeared at the top of the stairs a moment later, short, blue nightgown barely covering her hips. From the angle I had, I could look directly up the gown. A little tremor of regret went through me knowing that even though I made it through the mess she created, it was finished between us.

"Is it over?" Ashley asked.

"Almost. Come down here."

She clung to the top of the bannister, as if for support. Lit from beneath, by light from the downstairs hallway, her face seemed to have a yellowish tint in the semi-darkness. "I don't want to."

"You need to see this. I *want* you to see."

She hesitated, then nodded, as if accepting this as punishment for the terrible thing she did. "Okay, Nathan." It was meeker than I'd ever known her to be.

Slowly she padded barefoot down the stairs. With the revolver still in hand, I gestured for her to go ahead. She moved down the hall, towards my office. She stopped in the doorway, staring down at the dead young man. The look on her face was hideous, twisted in fear and horror.

"Go inside," I told her.

She glanced at me then, grimacing, stepped daintily over the body. Inside, she went to my desk and leaned a hip against it, trying to look anywhere but at the man she'd hired to kill me.

"Look at him," I commanded.

Her eyes met mine, then she forced herself to look to the body at my feet. "My god, Nathan… you did it. You killed him."

"Yes." I put the revolver into the back pocket of my slacks, then stooped to pick up the automatic the would-be killer dropped. "I told you, I know my way around a gun. You did a terrible thing, but it's worked out. Worked out very well, in fact."

Ashley's expression changed to confusion. "What do you mean?"

"I mean that neither of us has been happy for a very long time, but neither of us could do anything about it. Your family is very Catholic, as we both know, so they'd never forgive you if we divorced. And even if we did go through with it, I'd lose everything. This house, my job at the school, whatever little money you let me have for my own interests. It all belongs to you. We were both trapped. But this is perfect. This intruder," I gestured to the body with the automatic, "whoever he is, came into our house and shot you."

I raised the automatic and fired, just once. Ashley's slim body seemed to fold around the bullet as it entered her chest and then collapsed to the carpet like a bloodied, string-cut marionette.

I walked over to her and said, "Don't you see, Ashley? I'll have our home, my career, your money, and the sympathy due a widower. It's perfect. I really can't thank you enough for this opportunity."

But she couldn't see anything. She was already quite dead.

Danny DeLuca's Bridge
Robb T. White

I hadn't seen my friend Dan DeLuca in 5 years. That's how long I was out in California banging my head against a wall trying to make a living. I'd just about made it, too, with a seafood restaurant on the beach in Santa Cruz. I'd invested every cent I'd brought with me plus the money I'd made since along with a lucky bet on the Rams in the playoffs that sealed the deal. Then the virus came to town—everybody's town—and my seaside diner went belly up overnight like thousands of small businesses all over the country. I dreaded going back to Northtown, Ohio like that proverbial dog returning to his vomit.

We used to be best friends in high school. Dan saved my diploma for me by helping with a project that kept the teacher from failing me, and he would have given that our contempt for each other was mutual. In truth, he did the entire project from scratch the weekend before it was due—something on *wave-propagation and bridge design,* which was nothing I was capable of. The science teacher tried to goad me into admitting it, but I held firm and spat out the few theorems Dan made me memorize. In the end, I received a compromise grade of C+ and called it a victory.

He was born to become an engineer. He had a mathematical gift and a spatial sense that was uncanny. He could look at a sunbeam and tell you how long it would take the dust motes to hit the floor based on wind resistance, temperature, gravity, and the curve of the Earth for all I knew. His brains guaranteed him with a reputation as a pariah, a nerd. When he overheard me leaning against my locker badmouthing the teacher, he volunteered to help out the blue. Before then, we'd never exchanged five words in 4 years of school. I'm nothing if not loyal and we started hanging out from then on. We double-dated to the prom. I remember telling him he was destined to go to Cornell—his choice of college—make a ton of money and live happily ever after. "On your deathbed, you'll be handing out stocks and bonds to your grandkids," I said, "while I'll still be scratching for a living in Northtown."

Half of that prediction came true. I was back, tail between my legs and cadging money from my siblings for beer money and sponging off my mother.

Dan never went to Cornell, never went to college. He married the girl he took to the prom. Becky was pregnant then, although no one knew it. That baby was followed by two more in the next five years I was in California.

Danny's luck kept going downhill. Becky's father got him a job on the railroad but he had an accident falling out of an engine cab, shattering his leg in three places. They put it together with titanium pins but he had a noticeable limp and had to take disability.

I wasn't sure what he would be like since we last spoke. I wondered if his disposition had taken a sour turn as his dreams, like mine, had come crashing down around his ears. I left a message and asked him to meet me at the Wyandotte Club in the harbor if he had any free time that night.

I was half-drunk at the bar by the time he came in. Backlit, he approached the bar. I didn't recognize him because of his shuffling limp.

"You lost your hair," I said.

"You should talk," he said; "you've got a stomach like a Ben Franklin stove."

He pointed at the pot belly hanging over my belt.

"Blame California," I said, laughing. "The good life."

"Pull the other leg," Dan replied. "I've heard about prices out there."

He took a seat beside me and ordered a club soda. Dan was never much of a drinker.

"Married?"

I expected the question.

"Girlfriends. None I wanted to marry."

What little of Becky I remembered from high school was unpleasant. A beautiful, spoiled girl from a well-off family, she always seemed on the verge of hysterical to me where others, Dan included, saw her as "bubbly." She gave me a bad vibe from freshman year on when I caught her in a vicious lie that ruined another girl's reputation. Even jocks who'd chase after a broom if it wore a skirt avoided her. She picked Dan out of the pack senior year when every other boyfriend had fallen away or skipped off like a goat once he'd gotten a closer look beyond the pretty face. Dan was smitten. I don't think he realized that it was all one way as far as the affection, her way as far as their social agenda they did as a couple. Becky called the shots. I kept my feelings about her to myself even when rumors had it that she was cheating on him. I figured prom was the last time we'd see both our dates.

We discussed the same subjects a nostalgic reunion prompts, the lies, and half-truths. I was quick to blame the pandemic for my own failure. He talked about his accident at the railroad, the surgeries, how that had changed his life, and affected his marriage.

His mood darkened when I asked after Becky and the kids, just to be polite.

"Becky wants me dead," he replied with no change of tone. "She's seeing another man."

Some things you're prepared to respond to. This wasn't one of them.

"I've never known you to exaggerate anything," I replied. "But are you—"

"Sure? Am I sure? Yes, no question about it. Ever since the accident, when the money got short, she changed. She didn't look at me the same way."

I bit my tongue. Becky was always superficial and self-centered.

"Who's the guy?"

"An estate lawyer, a hunk. Has money and looks. Played college ball, even had a tryout with the Browns."

"I don't know what to say, Dan."

"She's never admitted it, but I know she's had others. I

threatened to have a paternity test done on Belle and Jacob. But he seems to be the one she wants."

Not easy to change the subject but I tried. I told him I was "looking around" Northtown for opportunities. He told me he was working for the state.

"Doing what?"

"Bridgetender," he said. "I'm the one that pisses off the whole town when I stop traffic every half-hour."

He meant the only bridge in Northtown that mattered: the bascule lift bridge a hundred yards from where we sat drinking in a bar. We wound up closing down the Wyandotte that night. He stuck with the club sodas but I was sloshed. As we parted on the sidewalk out front, he invited me for dinner the next night.

With a clap on the back, I bade him farewell and staggered off to my Jeep. My heart was heavy. I dreaded sitting down to dinner with him and his wife. The dreams of youth are gossamer, light as snowflakes in the wind, yet when they crash to earth, they hit with a leaden thud.

*****

Becky was still beautiful. She'd lost some girlishness, the silliness in her personality. I grew weary of that California lilt girls out there inflected their speech with, like questions at the end of every statement. Becky had added several cup sizes to her breasts since the prom. Having children hadn't affected her figure. Gauging from her narrow waist, I suspected a heavy-duty gym routine. The breasts might be cosmetic but along with the stylish hairdo and expensive clothes, she'd have made an impact on males young and old. Clearly she wasn't denying herself anything motherhood might require as far as attention to cosmetics or fine apparel went.

Dan didn't do much talking during dinner, which added stress to the meal.

"How are the kids, Becky?"

"Oh, they're all fine," she replied. "My mom has them. She keeps them out of my hair a couple times a week so I can get things done."

Dan snorted. She fired a withering look at him. I kept my face aimed at my dinner plate.

By the time coffee and dessert arrived, a Giant Eagle Mississippi mud cake, I had a bad case of nervous indigestion and enough acid in my stomach to dissolve ten yards of railroad track. As Becky cleared the dishes, Dan clenched and unclenched his fist.

"I'm sorry, Neill, but I'm going to have to eat and run," she said. "I know we're all supposed to keep on with that social distance business, but I'm not living my life under a bed."

"Not under it, on it," Dan muttered.

I winced.

"It's a civic committee, not a club," she said, grimacing, firing another black look at her husband. "He acts as though it's just a hen club I'm chairing. Some ladies' book club where we all discuss the latest bestseller."

"Might do us both good if you actually stayed home and read a book once in a while."

I thought of Marilyn Monroe just before Joseph Cotton comes flying out of his cabin to smash the phonograph record she's singing along to in *Niagara*.

She glared at him. Her pretty, symmetrical face lost its composure, blood leached to the corners, and sharply narrowed, her eyes became feral like a cat's at night you catch in your headlights. It made me think of the triangular shape of a praying mantis—not a pleasant image to have of your friend's wife.

We sat at the table in silence as soon as she left. We listened to her car pulling out of the driveway.

"She's off to meet him," Dan said quietly. "There's no club meeting tonight."

I was lost for words.

"Let me show you something," Dan said, forcing a grin. "Bring your coffee if you want."

"A beer would suit me better right now."

Seeing it was something else. Dan had made a miniature mockup of the Northtown Bridge Disaster from 1876. It was the worst train accident in America in its time. Over 90 people dead when a passenger train plunged from a truss bridge and fell a hundred feet into the Northtown gulf during a blizzard. Not all died in the wreckage; many were burned alive when the oil lanterns and coal-fired heating stoves ignited the spilled coal. Everyone in Northtown knew its history. It was about the only thing we were known for as a rustbelt Midwestern city. The town hospital built on the site of the crash was where most of my generation were born.

The upended ping-pong table was a meticulously designed tableau of chaos and death. The structures and tiny figurines, all from specialty craft stores he'd ordered online and accumulated over the years, were to scale. Like an old nightmare from my childhood, stories I'd been told and read of in school. The collapsed bridge, the twisted iron, and shattered coach cars below. Tiny legs and arms stuck out from the mounds of debris. Jagged pieces of red and yellow plastic were inserted to symbolize the flames.

"Lifelike, isn't it?"

"Ghoulish," I said and immediately regretted it.

He had preserved the two concrete pillars on either bank of the gulf, and the locomotive cab, which alone with its coal tender made it across when the iron cracked beneath the locomotive and the engineer throttled it just as the 11 coach cars behind all fell into the frozen riverbank.

I picked up the locomotive and saw the delicately stenciled name on the cab: "Socrates." The sleeper cars all hade their proper names inscribed, some unreadable because of the "fire damage" or wreckage: "Palatine," "Yokohama," "Osceo," and "City of Buffalo," which lay atop the buckled "Palatine." Tiny firemen from the Northtown Fire Brigade and volunteers from town all scrambling about in the deep snow attempting to pull "people" from the burning cars.

One of the casualties was a man in a black suit; his mouth stuck open in a grimace.

"Who's this?" I asked, "He looks like the Grim Reaper without the scythe."

"That's P.P. Bliss," Dan said. "He wrote gospel songs."

"Check out the bridge," Dan said.

"What bridge? It's all smashed up."

"Not that one, over there," Dan said, pointing to a coffee table in the corner.

I feared another lecture, and I was right. I got it in spades—all about the flaws of an all-iron truss bridge and its failure to accommodate the live load of the oncoming train on top of its dead load. The failure of the angle blocks and their too few or poorly designed lugs, which failed to keep the braces and counter-braces from slipping.

"Danny, look," I said, "you're talking to an idiot. All this jazz about chords being too short, flanges on the I-beams, and shims—it's all Martian to me. Remember me, I'm the guy who took general math and business."

"Sorry, Neill, I get carried away sometimes."

"I'll be Becky loves it when you start talking about shear stress."

That touched a sore spot.

"I didn't mean it the way it sounded."

"It fascinates me. It always has."

I left his simple brown-and-white Craftsman with its secrets roiling inside. Becky's infidelity had tainted the visit. I had unwittingly aggravated my friend's pain by being a reluctant witness to it.

No more, I thought. I was through with high-school reunions, past, present and to come.

There's a saying about "famous last words" I should have remembered. I started to whistle a jukebox tune playing at the Wyandotte to lift my mood and thought better of it. In the depressing atmosphere I'd left behind, I imagined another tableau, one replete with tiny tombstones, mourners, and gravediggers standing beside mounds of piled earth.

I saw myself captured in it, sauntering past graves in

tumult.

*****

"Last night was a bit awkward."

"I don't know, Dan," I said. "I'm gearing up to leave Northtown again. Got a lot of packing to do."

I didn't have two nickels to rub together, but the last thing I wanted was another melancholy reunion.

"I think you'll get a kick out of it."

"I've seen the pretty blue lights," I said. "Good for the Harbor Merchants Association." I was feeling glummer as the conversation went on.

"No, not the city," Dan replied. "The state owns the lift bridge. It's one of two in the entire state still operating."

"I don't know, Dan. As I said, I'm pressed for time."

"I understand."

Nothing like Catholic guilt to stab you in the heart. Or the solar plexus.

"All right, I'll swing by this afternoon."

"My shift starts at four. Any time after is good."

Hot-diggetty-damn, I thought. *I get to hear all about the inner workings of a lift bridge.*

I wondered if my friend was sinking into a childish obsession to avoid having to deal with his cheating wife.

*****

The cramped bridgetender shed confined the operator for 12 hours without a break. Although the bridge had undergone routine repairs since its construction in 1925, you can't put lipstick on a pig. The tiny room was situated a dozen feet above the sidewalk and hung partway over the river to give the operator a line of sight.

I climbed a rickety iron-rung stairs built into the side to get inside. It reminded me of the tricky rope-and-chain Jacob's ladder I had to climb drunk returning to my berth after a binge-drinking session in bars around the Great Lakes. Having a bum leg and making the climb wasn't easy.

Every half-hour, the whistle of the air horn reverberated blasting everything inside the cabin. Then Dan had to activate the siren and bring down the gate to stop traffic. Then the big motor would grind and the leaf would rise a few feet at a time. Traffic lined up at both ends.

From the cabin, you could see the exasperated faces of the first half-dozen drivers who just missed getting across. Some smoked, others texted. Given the ten minutes the bridge was raised and lowered, the odds were 3:1 you'd get caught if you traveled State Route 531 by way of Bridge Street, a necessity if you wanted to head south on Route 11 to Youngstown or west on Interstate 90 to Cleveland or east to Erie. You couldn't avoid that bridge, no matter what.

"Think of those old-timers back in the last century," Dan said, "crossing with horses and buggy or wagons load with vegetables on a pontoon bridge before they built this."

"The river was clean at least," I said. "You could eat the fish you caught."

The stench of rotting fish was a constant olfactory assault except when the bridgetender's hand activated the chain-hoist mechanism that drove the pinions along the track to raise and lower the bridge span. The banana-scent of hot oil permeated the tiny cabin.

Dan extolled every aspect of the bridge's history when Northtown was an Iroquois hunting grounds and the first settlers were tough Scandinavians—mainly Finnish—and Irish dockworkers. My father told me that plenty of Irishmen were fished out of the river with a Finnish knife, the *puukko*, sticking out of their backs.

"This bridge is listed in the National Register."

"Those were the days," I said, attempting some levity, "when ships were made of wood and men were made of iron." A trite sailors' expression from my sailing days out of high school.

The airless cabin was suffocating. The blades of a mechanical fan lay atop a cabinet in the corner grimy with dust. Dan said he was fixing it. My face was slick with perspiration after five minutes.

"What's wrong, Neill?"

"I'm going to say something, and I hope it doesn't offend you."

"Go ahead."

"Why not divorce her?"

He gave me a crooked smile.

"Not that easy," he said.

"Tell me."

He'd had a nervous breakdown three years ago. Spent time in an institution. The marriage, Becky's mercurial temperament, his failure to go to college and get a degree ate at him for years.

Bridge Street is a hot spot if you're alcoholically inclined. Every male in my family tree had spent countless hours on this street in past and present bars. Some of the old taverns, like the Wyandotte Club, once a private watering hole for shipyard workers, tug men like my father and uncles—like me, God knows—stevedores for the Pinney Docks saltwater vessels coming through the St. Lawrence Seaway and heading to ports uplakes through the Soo Canals made it a busy place in the post-World War-Two era. Now it was a public tavern, and its clientele were tattooed college males and their girlfriends. Tommy Dorsey's swing band was replaced on the jukebox by electronic dance music, Billie Eilish, and Lady Gaga.

"She'll get custody, believe me."

"I see."

He wasn't worried about alimony. I knew he'd give every cent he made and beg in the streets for scraps rather than let his kids suffer. Becky was another story. She'd bleed him white regardless. Her father used his clout to get him this job and he was trapped in it for life. With a record and a handicap, an economy limping to its feet after the Coronavirus, he'd be lucky to get minimum-wage job on his own.

"I'm sorry, Dan."

The crooked smile returned.

"Forget it."

I stared out the grimy window pane at the traffic moving past. Twin snakes of chrome and glass in ceaseless motion passing each other on a bridge.

"What did you think of my models last night?"

Here we go again...

"Just great, Dan. Fantastic detail. I don't know much about the history of the crash…"

The wrong thing to say. His eyes glittered and he launched into another reprisal. I owed it to my friend to listen despite the low feelings my own bleak future presented me with.

"The two biggest errors in construction… lateral braces were placed only at every other panel connection, no wonder… and their ends were not square and so—"

I was turning into a somnambulist with a frozen face. I couldn't stand another second of it.

"Sorry, Dan, but I'm meeting my cousin Joe at the Wyandotte and I'm late now." I added a glance at my wristwatch.

"Sure, Neill. It was great to see you again, man. Look, I'm off tomorrow. Want to swing by for a drink at the house?"

"I can drop by tomorrow night on my way out of town."

"You're leaving again?"

"For good this time. I'm done with this armpit of a town."

I meant it. The wall of depression threatened to fall on me the moment I returned. I feared being trapped for the rest of my life like my friend.

"Give my regards to your cousin."

"I will."

The last I'd heard of my cousin was years ago. When the lakeboats laid off their crews, Joe went sailing on the Mississippi as a barge captain.

I'd have to endure another dismal marital performance between Dan and Becky. I considered it the price of the ticket to leaving town.

*****

Dan greeted me at the door with a drink in his hand. His face looked bloated.

I handed him the flowers I brought for Becky.

"Just what she always wanted," he said. "Supermarket flowers. You left the price tag on, Neill."

He tossed them on a table.

"Sorry."

I followed him to the kitchen. He was unsteady on his feet and it wasn't from the limp.

"Where are the kids?"

"Grandparents, as usual."

"Where's Becky?"

"Upstairs. Practicing her lines."

"Practicing?"

"Yeah, she's in a dinner theater troupe. My ever-so-talented wife. The play opens next week."

"What's the play?"

Just then a piercing scream erupted from a room overhead, the echo cascading down the stairs.

The hair on my neck prickled to life. Dan looked at me.

"A murder mystery—so she says. How about a drink?"

He poured a double-shot of whiskey neat to the top of the tumbler, spilling some as he handed it to me.

"Beer would have been fine," I said.

"You're Irish, right? You people like to drink—so drink

up!"

"Is there an occasion?"

"You mean am I celebrating something?"

"You're drinking. You're half-drunk."

"I am that," Dan replied. "I should be three sheets to wind by now. I can't seem to get drunk."

As if on cue, Becky's shrill voice broke in with a theatrical flourish. I made out phrases that sounded like a woman on the phone to 9-1-1, blurting that her husband had just been shot by an intruder and to send ambulance and police right away. It sounded like a crime show.

"Is this a bad time between you two? I'll go right now."

I had not expected this. Dan DeLuca was a gentle man with a highly developed sense of compassion. I'd never seen this acerbic, sardonic side all the time I'd known him. Boring, yes. Ill-tempered, no. Being tossed into the midst of a marital squabble seemed an act of rudeness. I swallowed the whiskey and set the glass on the sideboard.

"Give Becky my regards, I said. "I'm leaving. I'm aborting the homecoming tonight."

I extended my hand as I always did when we met. Fist bumps, elbow bumps and California bro hugs weren't my thing.

"Keep your filthy Coronaviruses to yourself," he said and turned away.

My face was hot as I trotted down the steps, partially relieved to be out of that squirmy mess and irked by the coarse send-off.

The weirdness of it troubled me. Becky's unseen, surreal performance upstairs while my friend drowned his sorrows downstairs. Television and reality blurred. So many victims shot, stabbed, betrayed, murdered—all the ways human beings commit mayhem on one another and the clichéd ways we express it to a stranger in a phone message.

*****

The alcohol affected me more than I realized. I'd expected a meal and so hadn't eaten anything. I'd spent the day arranging for the sale of all my earthly goods and hadn't found time to put anything but Ohio air inside my stomach.

I sat at the lights at Five Points—that being Northtown's bizarre array of 5 traffic lights—thinking about Dan's odd behavior when a Toyota misjudged the sequence of signals and slewed into my lane. I managed to avoid a bad collision but our fenders kissed hard enough to do damage.

At the green light, I pulled into the CVS lot across the street. The Toyota followed me and an agitated woman got out to approach me. She apologized. We exchanged licenses and insurance cards. I told her I was leaving town that night and didn't have a fixed address yet, but I gave her my sibling's address and said I could be reached through that number if needed. People were still practicing social distance; however, she was close enough to smell whiskey on my breath.

I was just past the township lines into Saybrook when I was pulled over. The officer gave me a breathalyzer and told me I'd failed.

"Your BAC count is point-oh-four percent," he said.

"And that means…?"

"It means you're legally intoxicated. Please turn around and put your hands behind your back."

Stupidly, I resisted. Not by much, I can tell you, because that cop threw me against the hood of my Jeep and cuffed me, while screaming "Stop resisting!" in my ear. That was that. My leaving town wasn't going to happen that night.

I was fingerprinted, given a buccal swab, and booked. The cell a deputy led me to was vacant, a small blessing given the way things had gone since I said my goodbyes that afternoon and headed over to Dan's for a farewell dinner.

The resulting legalities mounted from the moment I called a lawyer to arrange bail. My car was impounded and damaged by the tow truck so that I had to take it to the garage for an extensive repair that caused further delay and ate up my stock of travel money.

Maybe it was fate. Maybe I wasn't supposed to leave town. Not then, not ever. In the following days, I learned what Becky's screams portended—for her, for her unlucky husband, and for me, the unwanted dinner guest.

*****

It took me three days to find someone other than my siblings—all pretty well disgusted with me by now—who would help my mother put up the bail money. I ate bland, starchy jail food with little appetite, lost a full belt notch, and left the new Northtown jail on Main Street chastened, humiliated, and flat broke.

My name appeared in *Police Beat* in the *Northtown Tribune* a couple days later. If you had clout or the right connections, you could get it excised without blowback. Being familiar with driving drunk at night, I knew people over the years whose names should have been printed up for misdemeanor antics while intoxicated and some others whose names should have been emblazoned in red ink just below the *Trib*'s masthead for a variety of serious crimes including, if rumor had substance, a couple murders logged in as "accidental death" and "death by misadventure."

It caught my eye only because I was still stewing about my own misadventure at Dan's that night. In the entertainment section was a notice of the community theater's opening play.

My mother stood looking at me when I turned. I just caught that look you get from a parent you've terribly disappointed. It disappeared fast like that Norwegian gnome you see out of the corner of your eye and disappears the instant you look at it.

"You remember Dan DeLuca, Mom?"

"The smart one. Not like those other clowns you palled around with in high school."

"Water under the bridge now, Mother."

"So what about him?"

"There's a play opening in town," I said. "Dan's wife is in it. You ever heard of *A Night to Forget*?"

My mother read every Agatha Christie novel in print, some twice. If anyone knew of a murder mystery, she'd be the one.

"No, can't say I have."

With neither a cell phone nor a computer in the house, I had to walk to the local library, and I wasn't that interested in satisfying a petty whim in the midst of my legal and financial problems, so I let it go.

Fate wasn't willing to let it go. I called an Uber from a bar on Bridge Street to take me to the police impound lot, a sister having provided me with cash. The driver initiated a friendly conversation en route. I had no interest in talking trivia to anybody, although I acknowledged my end of the conversation by making a few comments or grunts, hoping he'd take the cue and shut up.

We passed a billboard advertising the play. The lead actors, a man and woman in Victorian costume, were looking askance at each other from each end of the massive poster with the central cast mugging it up in the center. I didn't catch Becky's face among them. The theater group was another excuse to meet her lover while she was supposedly rehearsing.

"My wife seen that play a couple years back," he said out of nowhere.

"Oh?"

"Yeah, it's a hoot."

"I thought it was a murder mystery."

"Naw, it's a comedy. Real wacky, the wife says. She likes that kind of goofy stuff."

I retrieved my Wrangler, signed the forms, paid the fee, but I couldn't get his words out of my head.

Late that afternoon, I drove to the Wyandotte. I'd planned to drop by the bridgetender's shed despite how we left things last time. I had to ask Dan about that thing sticking in my craw. Becky's scream rang in my head like a bell. It woke me up that morning with a sick feeling in my stomach, unable to make sense of it.

The bartender was a young woman this time. Nose and lip rings, tattoo sleeves of green, red, and blue adorned each arm from shoulder to wrist—flowers, crescent moons, Celtic knots, warrior women's faces peeking out from the vine leaves. A mobile Rorschach test for the bar flies to ponder. I remembered Dan saying how he couldn't get drunk. I was feeling the same distress despite the boilermakers I was knocking back.

I left a ten on the bar—me, the big spender with my sister's money—and left the air-conditioned club for the humidity of the street. I was sweating from the booze and my own misery. I passed cafes and bars, boutiques and shops selling everything from used clothing to Belgium chocolates.

Crossing the intersection between Bridge and Goodwill Drive, I looked down at the muddy-brown sludge of river. My father used to tell me Lake Erie was once so polluted that when he and his crew on the tugs made tows to bring in the steamships from the harbor they'd spot bats hanging in the pilot house rigging for the flies drawn by the smell.

Musing about my own deckhand days, a carefree young sailor with dreams of his own, I jumped when the bridge siren went off halting traffic in both directions. I thought of Dan inside the shed, doing a job a child could perform with one hand on a lever. Then a bomb went off.

My mind tried to make sense of it; it was no bomb. I raced toward the sound, echoing over the riverbanks and rattling store windows. The alcohol, my shock—whatever, I stumbled and did a belly flop in the middle of the street. Stunned, bruised, I lay there looking at the remnants of the block counterweight that had fallen to the roadway and shattered, spewing chunks of concrete in all directions. Silence after a deafening noise. Soon, people exited bars and shops to come running.

Picking myself off the street, I saw part of the road had buckled when the block slammed into it like a meteorite plunging to earth and cratering the street. I was thinking of Dan, worried he might be injured.

I raced to the shed, calling up to him but no one answered me. Before long, police cruisers arrived with sirens screaming and the crowds were pushed back beyond the guard rail; everything on both sides of the bridge was cordoned off with crime-scene tape. It seemed like a movie more than reality.

Standing around with the chattering gawkers made me uncomfortable, so I walked back to my car and drove home. My khakis were ripped and I had serious road rash to attend to. I told my mother what happened, leaving out the pratfall in the street.

"You're going to die of a cirrhotic liver just like your father."

"Thanks for that, mother dear."

The *Trib*'s headline on the kitchen table the following day nauseated me: "Bridge Disaster Kills Two."

The photos were grotesque. I had been right there and never saw a thing the camera's eye showed. Pieces of car bumper, an ooze of oil slick, broken glass and crimped metal lying all around. Beneath the block was a car pancaked with two people in it. They were identified as Christopher J. McCafferty, 39, and Rebecca DeLuca, 30, both of Northtown.

"Too much to drink last night?"

I hadn't noticed my mother come into the kitchen. I remember looking at her, noticing the lines in her face, the tired look in her eyes from a life of raising six children and handling a hard-drinking husband. In that crazy associational logic like in dreams, I recalled my mother had starred in her high-school play, *Little Women*.

"You're the spitting image of your father," she said.

"What the hell does that mean anyway?"

"It means you're the spit and image of your dad," she replied, walking away, leaving me alone with my thoughts and my own demons.

*****

Danny De Luca died a week later, although it's hard to say when exactly because he lay in his upstairs locked bedroom. A power outage from the heat wave that weekend knocked out the air-conditioning so his body was in a state of advanced decomposition. The autopsy revealed a gunshot wound to the head. A suicide but no note. The Glock that dropped from his hand was lying on the carpet beside the spent shell casing. Tavern gossip said a cloud of black flies emerged when the police broke down the door. They were called by Becky's mother, who had taken the children the day after Becky's death. The town was still passing around lurid descriptions of the bodies pried from the street beneath the counterweight. This gave extra fuel to it, adding in the scandal of a married woman in McCafferty's vehicle. Another reason why Northtown gave me dreams of being trapped in ever-narrowing sewer pipes.

Becky's funeral service was attended by dozens of mourners. Closed casket, of course. A glam shot of her on an artist easel up front. Sobbing from her mother and former classmates. A sister flew in from Arkansas. I stayed in the back and didn't speak to anyone. I was still numb.

Dan was cremated. No notice in the paper. I called his parents' house but no one answered. I left a message asking if I might come over "in the near future." My call was never returned. Dan's mother always liked me, but his father considered me a bad influence because of my drinking.

Like father, like son—another cliché life tossed around casually.

In my case, too true.

*****

I made the climb up the ladder to the bridgetender shed and saw a different operator staring back at me from the doorway.

"You ain't s'posed to be in here," he growled. "You miss the No Trespassing sign on the girders?"

He had a mouthful of sandwich; it was hard to understand him.

"My friend used to work in here."

I started to go.

"Hey, wait up!"

"What?"

"Your name, is it Neill?"

"Yes."

"He left this behind two weeks ago."

"You said *two* weeks ago?"

"Yeah, he quit right after his wife—right after the block came down. Couldn't blame him. Who'd want to—"

"Before the crash," I repeated. "He meant *before* the block fell?"

"That's right. He said to give this package to you when you showed up."

"*When* I showed up?"

"Hey, that's what he said, buddy. Here, take it."

He handed me a sealed manila envelope stuffed with papers.

I opened it inside the Jeep. The rank smell of the river's effluvia was overpowering in the heat, so I rolled up the windows and put on the a/c.

Xeroxes. *What the hell, Dan.*

Most of the pages were copies of the lift bridge's schematics. A dozen pages had to do with the latest bridge refurbishing and repair, dated two months ago. I saw Dan's signature on the last page as one of several who signed off. Others were hand-drawn illustrations that had to do with stress fracturing ratios. Several of the most detailed were exploded diagrams of the counterweight at its sealing joints to the superstructure that held it aloft. The block itself, I realized, was hollow entirely supported on its own truss that enabled the bridge tongue to lift.

A yellowed newspaper clipping fell out, a single column from some police archives. Dan had penciled a note to the bottom: From *Cincinnati Courier,* n.d.

No date?

It was titled "A Report That Engineer Was Murdered." The language was stilted, quaint. It reminded me of a Dickens novel I couldn't finish in high school. I threw it across my bedroom halfway through because it was full of ridiculous coincidences. I never inherited my mother's love of reading.

The article kept referring to "the terrible tragedy" and "the terrible catastrophe" of the Northtown train disaster so it must have been written in the aftermath of the 1876 crash. The engineer was scheduled to give important and probably damning testimony to a legislative committee formed after the disaster to investigate causes of the crash. The man was chief engineer of the railway company, which ultimately had to pay out money to survivors and victims' families. His death had been first reported as suicide when he was discovered in his hotel bed in Northtown with a gunshot wound to the head. It was first believed he'd brooded over the collapse and the railway's responsibility.

But two autopsies asserted homicide because of the suspicious nature of the death. His body lay "too naturally" on an undisturbed bed. A missing "roller" on a broken frame where a towel was hung, discovered missing, was theorized as a wrap for the roller used to knock the engineer senseless before placing him on the bed and shooting him. That explanation explained the "indentation" in the engineer's forehead. "A party of roughs" was blamed for the murder but no speculation as to who hired them to commit the crime.

Dan, what are you telling me with all this? Puzzle pieces I couldn't synthesize to see the "message," if any.

That night, my subconscious provided the answer in a lurid dream in which I was back in Dan's house on the last night I'd visited. Becky, in a blood-spattered dress from cradling her murdered husband's head, would make the call to police. I watched her lips move as she winked at me. Her lover's footsteps coming into the room told me I was next in the same way her practiced wail that night had told Dan he was on borrowed time—thus, the extraordinary drinking bout, the bristling temper.

Dan put his math and engineering skills to work to kill them before they killed him. How many times had he seen McCafferty's car passing below him on the bridge, knowing his wife was inside? How precise the timing had to be to blast the horn, start the siren to bring down the gates, to stop that car at exactly the right time—poised beneath that giant cement block where it and no one else would be harmed. Even more, to *know* he could work the levers inside that shed so that the stresses would shear and give way, the block would tumble and crush that one and only car. It was a thousand-yard sniper's shot— only the "bullet" was 10-ton block of cement. Witnesses in the *Tribune* reported that the massive bridge tongue was raised faster than anyone had ever seen before. One local reported he saw it "jiggle" several times before it reached its full height. Dan would have had seconds to see that car coming and know the exact time to stop traffic. His intricate mind—and these papers—proved he also knew the exact angle the bridge tongue had to be extended before stress and gravity would do their deadly work. The Uber driver's words rippled across my memory and sent an icy shiver up my back.

If I'd known… If I'd known—

What? What could I have done? Told Dan his wife was rehearsing lines for a phony 9-1-1 call when her lover, or whichever "rough" they hired for the murder, broke into the house, and killed him in his own living room?

Maybe he knew all along. Maybe he was waiting for it. I thought of his demeanor that night, his overwrought words, and his face as he spoke. I thought it was drink affecting him.

It could have been terror—*knowing*.

I opened the door of my Jeep and leaned out to vomit.

*****

Brain fever. It's odd how you remember some things. That despised novel I tossed had lots of it in there. Dickens threw it around like confetti. Hysterical women got brain fever, women in love got it, sometimes died of it. Men weren't immune, either. Like the Covid-19, it might kill you or you might walk around with it slightly sick. Sometimes it was both deadly and real. Dan included the final pages from a biography of an engineer named Scherzer who gave his name to the rolling lift bridge design of Northtown's drawbridge. He died of "brain fever" at 35.

They're still investigating the cause of the crash. It might take a year longer. The bridge will be under repair for months, according to the paper. The town groused about having to ride the long way around the river to get to the east side of town from Mary Street Hill.

*****

My mother died a year ago. I'm living in the house rent-free on sufferance from my siblings. I have a job unloading trucks at night. Steady work if not satisfying. I was cleaning out my mother's things, taking clothes to the Goodwill and packing away her hundreds of books. Most are old paperbacks, including her favorite, the cozy mysteries. She also possessed a few expensive coffee-table books, places to visit and must-see world destinations, which I found odd because she remained a recluse since my father's death.

One book with lavish illustrations caught my eye as I was packing up—a book of Greek mythology. In it, I found the story of Aphrodite and Hephaestus, the ugly hunchback god. She was forced to marry the crippled god by Zeus. It wasn't a good marriage and she wasn't faithful. Being a blacksmith and something of an engineer, he devised a net of thin gold threads to trap his beautiful wife and her lover Ares, the handsome god of war, as they had sex while he pretended to be gone. When he called the other gods to witness his betrayal, they laughed at him, not the trapped lovers, who continued to meet on the sly.

In that myth, Ares brought along a friend to keep watch for the sun rising so he could warn him in time to leave Aphrodite's bed before Helios, the sun god, saw them. The friend let the god down by falling asleep. I didn't ask to play the part of the friend to the betrayed husband or to warn anybody about what disaster was looming over all their heads. Yet I felt I'd let my friend down by not doing *something*.

Maybe I was too hasty about Dickens and his coincidences.

It's a Wrap

Regina Clarke

Evans watched the camera crew get ready. Across the desert floor, shadows appeared in the afterglow of the setting sun. No one seemed to find the whole thing ridiculous the way he did. The set designer and his assistant were discussing staging and sequence for the next scene. A prop girl was assigned to handle a strobe light, for special effect. *Yeah*, Evans thought to himself, *real high-powered filmmaking*. Still, he couldn't afford to say no to a role. Not these days, even when it was a third-rate indie.

The director walked up to him, holding the script. Jamison was a small man, quiet, never raised his voice no matter how much chaos was going on around him. That annoyed Evans more than anything else.

"Okay, Jess, all set? We're ready for you now. We'll get this shot over with and then it's a wrap, okay?"

In the fading light Evans skimmed through the pages Jamison had handed him. "You have to be kidding. I told you I wanted this scene re-written. There's no way I'm going to do what it says."

Jamison smiled briefly.

"Yes, you will. Without an argument." His voice was still soft, but Evans felt its impact and hesitated. What the hell, he thought. He walked over to the rock formation that had already been used in the master shot.

Jamison had settled himself in a chair just outside the circle of small boulders where the main scene was to be shot. He signaled a crewman, who used a crane to maneuver a large cage to a predetermined point on the hard, sandy ground. Someone else placed a mark on the ground five feet away from it.

"No closer than that, Jess," Jamison warned.

"I know what to do," Evans said, holding back his impatience.

The moon had risen by then, full and bright. Someone else set up a dimmed spotlight that was aimed at Evans' right side.

"You know, the writer ought to be here, see her precious imagination come to life," Evans called out.

"Your wife has no intention of watching us make this film. That was part of her contract, remember? As I recall, it was the part you liked best." Jamison spoke almost in a whisper, but in the night air, among the now silent crew, his words carried well.

"So where's the trainer, then? He ought to be out here, right? Watching over things!"

"He is," the director responded. "Hey, Bob! Let Jess see you." The whole crew laughed as the trainer popped his head up over a boulder.

They have to be out of their minds, Evans thought. There was nothing funny about any of it. A bad bargain he'd made in the hope of getting a good part, and Jamison likely to walk off with most of the money, and probably his wife. He wouldn't be surprised.

"Okay, okay," Evans interrupted, "just make sure he stays close."

"He will, Jess—don't worry, he will." As Jamison spoke the crew went silent again. There was no sound but the wind that had come up a few minutes before, not gusting but swirling the dust in small circles.

The next second Jamison called for action and the cameraman's assistant held up the digital slate. Evans began walking toward the cage, keeping the appropriate expression on his face. No fear, the script said. Just obliging interest. No problem. From inside the wooden structure there came a low, muttering sound. It was dark in the shadow of the rock, the moonlight spilling mainly on the other side, away from him. The dim light from the crew was focused on him, barely illuminating the ground around him. The muttering became a growl as he got nearer to the cage.

"You're not afraid of anything? That's what you're telling me? Neither am I, after seventeen years of being married to you! I'm a goddamned survivor!" Nora's words came to him, along with the fury in her face. It was because of Johnny, as if she hadn't contributed, hadn't helped make it all turn out the way it did. He saw, too, his son's face at their last meeting, the hate in it, the weakness—he didn't have the strength and power a son of Jess Evans should have. So the boy joined a drug outfit, overdosed, got himself killed. It wasn't Evans' fault.

There was still no sound from the crew, who he couldn't see, anyway. Walk five more steps, he remembered, counting. Gaze at the cage, and then lift the rope on the ground that will release the catch and let the thing out. All done. But it wasn't.

Evans stared at the door of the cage, a solid piece of wood.

There was no movement. Even if he went forward another foot, there was still a margin of safety. Something must have jammed. He wasn't going to shoot this again another day. He'd tell Jamison to go to hell, first. Take off to Vegas. Nora wouldn't know where to send her hate mail. She didn't frighten him. There wasn't a lawyer who couldn't make Evans' case sweet. Nora was the one who was caught in an affair, not him. He knew better than to leave traces.

The rope had undone the hinge, but still nothing was happening. The script hadn't foreseen this, but trust Jamison to mess it up. The trainer wasn't worth his overpriced commission.

Let's give them a little show, Evans thought. They all owed their luxurious lives to him, and were too selfish to acknowledge it. He'd see that Jamison never directed any more pictures with him. A word in the right place—

The door of the cage was outlined in the moonlight. As he watched, the bottom half began to lift as one black paw made a swiping motion. Interesting, exactly what the script called for, yet there was no coaching from the trainer, no sound from anyone. He couldn't even hear the camera. Just the muttering from the cage. He was supposed to pull out his knife and kneel on the ground, waiting. The stones were sharp, and he cursed them silently. The best boy had done a lousy job sweeping the area. Losers. Too many losers around him.

In the backlight the cage door rose further and the growling had taken on a guttural, menacing tone. Another moment and the thing would bound out. One throw of the prop knife and the trainer would grab it and he could relax. Suddenly the paw was withdrawn. It was afraid of him, he thought. The damn creature was afraid of him. A little improvisation, then.

Evans moved closer to the cage, far past the mark, on his hands and knees. Deliberately he made a sliding sound to draw the animal out. Curiosity killed the cat, he chuckled to himself. The light was steady. Now there was a dark hole where the door had been. Come on, kitty, kitty, he said to himself. Time for my gin and tonic. Let's get this show on the road, you stupid cat.

It lunged, a rush of black fur and glowing yellow eyes, and hit him hard, pushing him back on the ground. He felt the scrape of the claws and pain in his legs.

"Help!" he cried out, disbelieving. "Jamison! Bob! Help me!" The creature was all over him as he lay face down, the sand suffocating him. With a surge of strength he turned over only to feel the jaw of the beast at his neck.

His voice was a shriek. "Help! Someone, help me!" The fear rushed through in a smothering wave when no one came to pull the thing away from him. He heard his own sobbing, his strength gone, and an overwhelming horror at what was happening. Claws tore at his jacket, ripping it away.

"No!" he screamed, "*No, no, not this way!*"

The sudden light blinded him and a voice shouted out. Applause resounded through the desert air as he felt hands helping him up. Evans staggered into a chair someone had placed under him.

"Now that's what I call a wrap!" Jamison said, slapping him on the back. "No retakes on this one, Jess," and he laughed, delighted. "We're gonna have to cut that 'Jamison, Bob' shout, of course, but everything else is perfect. Going closer was good, real good. I wouldn't have thought of it, but hell, you're the actor."

Evans felt the crew approaching him, the pats and congratulations. He looked down and saw the tears in his clothing. But there wasn't a mark on him. Nothing.

The set was lighted all the way so everyone could pack up. Through the frame of two boulders he saw someone walking toward him in costume. The panther.... He turned to Jamison. His voice came out in a hoarse croak.

"It wasn't real. It was a fake. You didn't tell me..."

Jamison laughed again. His eyes were still shining.

"And break the spell? No way! Besides, it was Nora's idea, and I wouldn't have wanted to spoil it for her. She was pretty good, don't you think?" As he spoke Nora slowly removed the head of the animal, letting her blonde hair fall around her shoulders. She was smiling in triumph.

"You were afraid, Jess. I knew you would be. Nothing like a few claw holds to instill an unfamiliar trepidation, wouldn't you say? Let's call it a wrap ourselves, hon. Consider this our divorce settlement. In honor of Johnny."

And with the same smile, she laid the fake head on his lap and walked past him to join Jamison and the crew at the buffet table.

Evans looked down at the thing in his lap. Sand and dirt couldn't hide the black fur or the yellow eyes. An involuntary shudder passed through him. It was still real to him. He knew it always would be.

Harry's List

Martin Zeigler

Harry's sipping cold coffee, a shot of Beam for heat, waiting out the century for his laptop to boot. He's thumbing through the morning paper, the one he snitched off his neighbor's welcome mat, to see if his latest job made any kind of headline, when finally, a year and a half later, his piece of shit computer fires up.

This time, though, it ain't with the usual screen shot of the St. Valentine's Day Massacre. Instead there's a half-assed drawing of a piece of burnt toast, along with a message that says, *U R Toast.*

Real cut-up, whoever did this.

So Harry, he shakes his fist at the screen and says right back, "What, you too lazy to write out the fricking words?"

A perfectionist, that's what Harry is. And it shaves his hide, so to speak, whenever someone tries to cut corners, like not taking the extra effort to spell out the "you are" in *U R Toast.*

But what Harry really don't like about this message, what really riles his ass, is that whoever sent it to him also messed with his files.

Okay, his *file*—he only had one—but it was a real important one, at least to Harry, because it listed every job he ever done in his whole fricking life.

Like his very first one, where he ran a shiv through an assemblyman in return for a grilled cheese sandwich.

Like the one years later where he wrapped lead weights around a deadbeat's legs and elbowed him off a pier into the river.

Or the job he done a couple months ago. Hell, he must of ran the guy through that table saw a dozen times before shipping his parts off to parts unknown.

And then there's the job he pulled last night. Well, okay, that one wasn't in the file yet. But he was about to add it. That's why he just got through waiting a billion years for his computer to kick in.

And what happens? The file ain't there no more. Meaning, neither is Harry's list.

Yeah, I know what you're thinking. Why would Harry keep a list like this around in the first place, a list that goes on for some seventy-two pages?

Why do you think? So he can report his income to the IRS? Maybe claim deductions for business expenses, like for travel or circular blades or for the extra-silent silencers he uses?

Come on. Use your head. Harry's just like you and me. Okay, more like me than you, but what the hell. He's proud of what he does. He likes to think he's accomplished things and hasn't just been sitting around on his keister all his life.

That he's left a, whaddaya call it, legacy.

Except, let's face it, no one's ever gonna build a Harry Daggart Cancer Center.

Hell, Harry won't even get the cheap plaque or that flimsy sheet of paper stuck in a Walmart frame, the kind of award the slobs in your office get for thirty-five years of switching on the light at meetings.

All Harry can do is get on his laptop and bring up this list and relive those jobs all by himself, because he knows there ain't no one else in the world he can share them with.

So you can imagine how pissed he was at finding this fricking file missing.

Fricking?

Oh, Harry can use the word, all right, the word people use instead of fricking, but his business has a bad enough rep without him making it worse by using off-color language. His line of work demands a sense of, whaddaya call it, *decorum*, if you know what I mean, except he'd never use *that* word neither. It makes him sound like an interior decorator, which he's never did in his life, except maybe for that apartment hit down in Baton Rouge with the shotgun.

So, yeah, Harry's *fricking* file was missing, and the only thing he could do about it was eenie-meenie through the Yellow Pages, call up some outfit called *Nerd, Nerd, Nerd— Nerd's The Word*, and have them send some rude punk with thick glasses, dirty hair, and a nose ring over to his dump to fix the problem.

Turns out, the kid who came knocking looked nothing like that. He was clean cut, or as clean as you can get these days, with his belt above his butt and nothing pierced. And what's more he was polite. He tried to introduce himself. But Harry told him he didn't have a head for names, so don't bother.

And anyway, so what if the kid had manners and used soap, Harry still didn't trust him, not even after he went and destroyed what he called the *U R Toast Virus.*

"Good as new," the kid says.

Harry poked around his laptop. "I still can't find my list."

"That's one nasty virus," the kid says. "But I gave it the old heave-ho."

"That's great to hear," Harry says. "So then where's my list?"

"Nasty stuff. Nasty stuff. Once it latches onto your system, it can read everything. I mean *everything.* Even your private emails. How scary is that?"

Jesus, it's like talking to a glass to get the beer to pour. The kid starts jabbering away to me—I mean, to Harry—about how the *U R Toast* Virus'd ruined lives and brung Fortune 500 companies to their knees. How bank accounts all over the fricking country was broke into, credit card numbers copied, and people's identities swiped from under their runny noses.

It broke Harry's heart to hear all this. "Boohoo for them," he says, "but what about my list?"

The kid gives Harry a look like he's just heard the question for the first time. "List?" he says.

"No, my old lady's underpants."

"Uhhh...," the kid says. "Uhhh, was it important to you?"

Harry says to him, "What are you, a fricking moron disguised as Albert F Einstein, or what? Of course that list is important. My whole goddamn life is in that list."

The kid's a real piece of work, let me tell you. Next thing he says is, "Would you by any chance have a hardcopy?"

Harry's shaking his head. "Did I hear you right? Do I have a *hardcopy*? Why the hell would I keep anything like that around?"

The kid gives Harry a look that says Harry's got a screw loose. Harry gives the kid a look that says, you keep giving me that look that says I got a screw loose, and your mommy and daddy will be giving the countryside a look for your buried sorry ass.

*****

What the kid was telling Harry, now that Harry had him pinned to the wall with his forearm against his throat, was that whoever pulled off the *U R Toast* Virus could right this minute be reading Harry's seventy-two-page file.

This news didn't exactly make Harry all of a sudden want to drop everything and go visit Disney World. "Wait a minute," he says. "So if this jerk can read my file, why can't I?"

"It's...it's...it's disappeared—more or less."

"What the frick is that supposed to mean—more or less?"

"What it means is...uh...he deleted your copy but kept one for himself."

"That don't sound like more or less. That sounds like less."

"I—I guess so. And y-you're choking me."

Harry backed off, figuring his arm was covered with enough slobber for the week. "So who is this Toast Turd, exactly? Some pal of yours?"

The kid's rubbing his throat to see if it's still there. "I...I don't...I don't know who he is."

"How about if I...if I bum...if I bump you off if you don't find out?"

"Please..."

"Please bump you off?"

"No, please don't."

Harry says, "I mean, guys like you must be a dime a dozen. You don't show up for work, all your boss has to do is head down to the games arcade and find a replacement."

By now sweat's dripping from the kid like he's one of them, whaddaya call them, sculptures in a fountain.

"Well?" Harry says.

"I'm thinking, I'm thinking."

"Yeah, well all your thinking's getting my floor wet."

"But I don't know where to start. I don't know where he lives. I don't know anything about him. I don't know—"

"What you don't know is giving me a serious pain in my middle fricking intestine. Try coming up with something you do know real quick."

"But..."

Like I said, Harry can't stand whining. He pulls something out of his pocket, something of the .22 caliber variety, and puts it up to the little worm's forehead.

"Maybe—maybe there is a way," the kid says.

Harry always knew he should of been a teacher.

*****

Harry's now at the railyards, sitting in his heap, waiting. He pulled in after sundown, it's now past midnight, and he's thinking something better happen soon or else.

Because earlier in the day he had to work another job. After all, a man's gotta eat, put food on the table. Took him most of the day to find some lowlife welcher, drag him into a service elevator, and shove him off the roof of a thirty-story building.

And tomorrow it's the same thing—with a different welcher and, if Harry's got his head on straight, a different building. But Harry don't know if he can do it—work the day, work the night, then the day again. It'd be like burning the candy at both ends, know what I mean?

And right now it looks like the night part of this deal ain't panning out. And if that kid from *Nerd's The Word* was with him right now in the car, he'd slap the little shit senseless.

Turns out, the kid *is* in the car. It's just that Harry went and forgot all about him on account of he was deep in thought. And now that he sees him, Harry goes ahead and does it—hauls off and slaps the little shit senseless.

"Oww!" the kid screams, rubbing the instant red spot. "What you do that for? You promised you wouldn't hurt me if I came along."

"Nah, what I promised was I'd kill you if you didn't."

"Okay, but why'd you hit me? I've done everything you asked. I stayed in your apartment while you went out and did whatever it was you had to do, and I didn't complain, not once."

Harry says, "That's because you were chained to the toilet with duck tape over your yap."

"Y-yes," the kid says, "but when you came back, I also cut up the fake money from your old newspapers, just like you wanted me to. And I put it in a bag."

"Oh, you put it in a bag. Do you hear that? He put it in a bag."

"And just now I went and buried it out there by that switch," the kid says, like it's one more thing to be proud of. "And I didn't run away. Even after being locked up all day without food and water. I mean, I could have, I could have run away, but I—"

"Yeah, and I would of caught up. And from then on, you would of needed one of them furniture dollies."

"But I didn't. I didn't run away. See? I'm right here."

"Not for long if Toast Turd don't show up real soon."

"But—but that all depends on if he read the email I sent you. And if he wants the money that bad. And if he's able to get here. There are so many factors."

"Factors? Well, factor this. The guy's running around with my list. A list of jobs that took a lot of blood, sweat, and tears. None of it my own, but I still did all the work. Nine hundred and eleven percent. And that list don't belong to nobody but me. Takes talent to do what I do. A lot more than shoving paper scraps into a paper sack and, oooh, burying it by a railway switch."

The kid's a hundred different ways from a piss puddle, and now he's got his feelings hurt. "That's unfair," he says. "I got rid of the U R Toast Virus, didn't I? And then when I realized we needed it, I brought it back. That way the toast guy would be able to read my email to you. That way we could set the trap. That way—"

Harry can't take it. "Okay, okay, you're a regular doctor of philosopher."

"I'm just saying what I did."

"I know what you did. I was there looking over your shoulder, remember?"

"I—I guess so."

"You guess so? I had to stand there all morning and watch you type. I never seen nobody stutter with two fingers before. How many fricking t's does the word <u>the</u> have in it anyway?"

"J-just one?"

"And if I hadn't of mentioned the railyards, we'd still be back in my palace figuring where to pull this off. Because no way was I going along with what you first put down. The zoo? That was your bright idea? Stashing the loot next to the fricking hyenas?"

"It's just that I've been to the zoo. I know my way around."

"Yeah, I bet you do. Take a left at the elephant shit and you're home. But me, I know these railyards like the back of my hand. I hung around here when I was a kid, and later on when I was a cheap thug going places. And who knows? Maybe a leftover leg from a job I done two years ago might still be kicking around here somewheres."

The kid turned white, like he was about to toss his potato chips or whatever it is twerps like him live on. "But Mr. Daggart—"

First time the kid calls Harry *mister*, and it's a nice feeling, getting the respect.

"Mr. D-Daggart," the kids says, now adding a double D on Daggart, which don't sound so respectful. "It was a good idea of mine, don't you think? Pretending to owe you a hundred thousand dollars, telling you I'd bury the money because I was too afraid of handing it to you in person. Once the virus guy— the Toast Turd, as you call him—sees that in the email, how could he resist? Right?"

"But a month? You wanted to give him a whole fricking month? I saw that, and I whacked you one upside the head, remember that?"

"Well, in my d-defense, he could be anywhere in the world. The T-Toast Turd, I mean. And it takes time to get here."

"I don't care if he parks his ass in a little grass hut up at the North Pole, he gets wind of a hundred large, he'll thumb his way down and be here at the railyards in time for the dinner bell."

"I just wanted a little insurance, that's all." .

"Your mommy and daddy'll be happy you got it, this don't work out. And I don't think it will, come right down to it."

"P-lease. Just a little longer? An hour, maybe?"

"What am I, a night watchman? I gotta get up in the morning, you know."

"But Mr. Daggart..."

What can Harry say? He's got a soft spot for the word *mister*. "I'll give him ten more minutes. After that, it's twenty-two calories of good cooking through that brainpan of yours."

The kid goes all wide-eyed. "Ten minutes!"

"What, you need to be somewheres? Got a hot date?"

"Huh? Oh, yeah, sure. That'll be the day when someone wants to go out with me."

"Aw, Jesus," Harry says to the roof of his car. "Do you believe this guy? Maybe his last minute here on Earth, and he's just now figured out that drips like him'll never get laid."

*****

Harry's got a nice gold watch—took it off a guy who didn't need his wrist no longer—but Harry don't need to look at it to know the ten minutes are about up. The blubbering and wailing from the passenger seat has reached a, whaddaya call it, fevered bitch. There's enough snot pouring out of the kid's nose and running over his lips to fill all the tea cups in the state of China.

"Mr. D-D-Daggart. Please let me go. I won't say a word. I promise. You didn't chain me to the toilet, okay? I stayed as a guest. And I know what you do for a living, but that's cool. It's hard finding work these days. Everyone needs a job. Right?"

"It's more than a job," Harry says, waving his automatic. "It's a career."

"Yes...yes...a career."

"And my name's got only one D in it."

The kid's a pile of mess and he won't shut up. "Yes, yes, one D. Got it. One D, not two. Not three. One. One D. I think I got it, Mr. D-D—"

Harry's thinking: screw what's left of the ten. But just as he fingers the trigger, something out the windshield catches his eye.

"One D. As in D-Daggart. No, that's—that's t-two D's. It's Daggart. Yes, that's it. D-Daggart. No, no, that's two D's again. That's—"

"Will you shut the frick up!"

The kid goes quiet like a switch's been throwed but his snot ain't yet got the message.

"Something out there," Harry says. "See the shadow on that shack? It's moving."

"Yes, I see it. Moving. M-mooving."

Harry throws the kid a look, and the kid shuts up again.

"I see him now," Harry says. "And, oh, yeah, he's headed straight for the switch where the stash is hid."

Harry turns to the kid, lands a friendly slap on his cheek. "Looks like you done good, kid."

"Does that mean—I can go?"

"Soon as I nail this guy, yeah, you can beat it."

Now the kid's so grateful, even more snot pours out of his nose.

*****

Harry's outta the car and on the tracks in no time. That's because Harry's no slouch. He knows things. Lots more than all them tweed jackets with fancy diplomas. He knows from hanging around the yards that the rocks between the rails is called ballast, and that the ballast makes noise when you kick it up. There's no way of sneaking up on nobody when there's ballast. So Harry had to move quick and be on the Toast Turd before he knew what hit him.

"Move, I drop you," Harry calls out in the dark. "Don't believe me, then go right ahead and move."

The guy's on his knees, hunched over the railway switch, one hand up in surrender, the other one deep in a hole. Digging around for that sack of fake moolah, Harry figures.

"Pull that mitt of yours outta that rat hole nice and slow," Harry says.

"It's stuck."

"Aw, poor baby."

Harry moves in closer, stands over the Toast Turd, and gets a good look at him. Shaved head, goatee, dressed all in black. Kind of a mean look in his eye, like he knows he should own the world but was handed a bad deck.

"So," Harry says, letting the Turd spot his gun. "You're the guy's been making everyone's life miserable. Especially mine."

Toast Turd looks up at him. Even on his knees, he thinks his shit don't stink. "I do unto the banks and corporations like they do unto us."

"S'matter?" Harry says. "Your check bounce?"

"That's cute. I'm on your side, in case you haven't realized it."

"Oh, yeah?" Harry says. "That why you swiped my list?"

"There's no such thing as swiping. Swiping implies ownership. Ownership amounts to greed."

"In that case, give it back."

"Nice try, but I can't do that, I'm afraid. You would only keep it for yourself again, and that's why I took it from you to begin with. It was a secret you were unwilling to share. And keeping secrets is what's wrong with the world. Everyone has secrets and it's my duty to set those secrets free, because in a truly free society there are no secrets. Now get down here and help me get my hand unstuck."

Harry gets down, all right. He taps the Turd's ear with his

gun, then whispers into it. "How's this for a secret?" he says. "Next train's due in fifteen minutes. Right over this here switch you're stuck to. And coming in at a pretty good clip. I'm thinking, you don't give me that list, maybe you can use your free hand to wave that choo-choo right on over ya."

Toast Turd whispers right back, "And maybe you can use your free hand to go frick yourself." Except he don't say frick.

Yeah, he was a big talker, this one. Harry gets as many of those as the whiners. The crybabies are one thing. You shoot them just to shut them up. But the loudmouths you want to toy with, maybe rest your gun barrel on their bottom eyelid for an hour or two before you pull the trigger. And right now Harry'd love more than anything to see this guy's brains all over the ballast.

But first he needs that list.

He's watching the hand, the one in the hole, when something makes him look at the other hand, the one that ain't in the hole, and that one's got a good-sized rock in it, and it's getting bigger, and the next thing Harry sees is nothing.

*****

Harry's head hurts like a hangover gone postal. He don't know where he is. Then he does know where he is. In the passenger seat of his own fricking car. He's never been in the passenger seat before, so no wonder he don't recognize it.

And guess who's in the driver's seat. And guess who's got the gun. Yeah, the fine upstanding dipwad from Nerd's The Word.

"What the frick?" Harry says. You see, even in pain, Harry tries to remain, whatcha call it, civil.

"This is yours," the kid says. The .22's dangling from his fingers like a rotten pair of panties. "Shoot me if you want."

Harry takes it. "I will if you don't tell me what's going on."

"I was out of the car and about to head home, when I overheard the Toast Turd tell you that his hand was stuck. I buried the money in that hole, remember? There's no way you can get a hand stuck. And then I saw the rock in his other hand, but it was too late. So I took an even bigger rock and did unto him the way he did unto you."

"Holy shit, kid. You did that for me?"

"Hackers like him give hackers like me a bad name."

"I know the feeling, kid. There's hit men out there with no clue at all what it means to be professional."

"You know, Harry, it felt kind of good knocking him out."

One thing Harry don't like is being called Harry. "Hey, I don't care what your first name is, and you don't care what mine is, got it? And one more thing. Don't start thinking you're hot potatoes just because you whacked some mook over the noodle."

"Okay, whatever."

"Don't *Harry* me, and don't you ever *whatever* me. Got it?"

"Sure."

Harry's starting to think this kid's starting to think he's too big for his britches. "So, tough guy, after you laid the turd out, did you happen to search him? For the list, I mean?"

"Sure," the kid says again, like none of this ain't no big deal. "There was nothing on him but a wallet and car keys, and nothing in his car either."

Harry figured as much. But what could he do? He was tired, his head hurt, and he had to get up in a couple hours to throw someone off a building. He was beginning to wonder if there was a point to any of this.

"But there's a bright spot," the kid says all of a sudden.

"Yeah," Harry says, "what's that?"

"Let's take a little trip."

That's the kind of thing Harry usually said, but what the hell. He was too beat to argue.

*****

It was summertime when all this was going down. I didn't mention it before, because it didn't matter before. Now it matters.

It matters because Harry's looking out the windshield and out the passenger side, and it's snowing out. And Harry's thinking: it's the middle of summer, and it ain't supposed to be snowing out.

On top of that, Harry's dome still smarts like a son of a bitch. "Kid, where the hell are we, the fricking North Pole?"

"Hardly."

"Just get me back home, will ya? I got a fifth of painkiller waiting."

Harry can only see the right side of the kid's face on account of the little worm is driving, but he's got a smile on him like you'd see on the side of a cat. The kid says, "Welcome to Business Alley."

"What're we doing here?"

"Take a peek."

Harry looks up through the windshield at the tall buildings passing by, at all the office windows, and they're all filled with faces like the squares in comic books. There's even jokers standing out on the balconies, hollering and waving down at the street.

"The frick," Harry says. "What're they yelling about?"

"What do you think?" says the kid, that smile of his getting even bigger, to the point where Harry feels like pasting him one.

"While you were out cold," the kid says, "I took a photo of the Toast Turd, who was also out cold, and sent it to the people here at Business Alley. I also sent a very detailed text message. And it looks like they got the word."

"What word?" Asking all these questions was making Harry's head explode.

With that stupid smile still on the side of his mug, the kid says to Harry, "Remember when I told you how the *U R Toast* Virus had affected hundreds if not thousands of businesses, compromising their finances, their security, their privacy, and costing them a fortune?"

"Yeah, so what?"

"I let them all know the problem was over and that the person who solved it for them would be passing through. And now, as you can see, they're expressing their thanks."

"Yeah?" Harry feels a smile coming on himself. "All this for stopping the Toast Turd?"

"That's right. And that's not snow, by the way, that's confetti."

Harry rolls down his window and listens. From all

around—the balconies, the open windows, even up on the rooftops—Harry now hears the cheering loud and clear. "You da man! The Turd is toast! You da man! The Turd is toast!"

"Da man? Why, that must be me," Harry tells the kid.

The kid don't say nothing but just keeps smiling.

Hey, the kid can smile at whatever the hell he wants. Because Harry's feeling good. Real, real good. He shoves his head right back out the open window and belts out, "I da man! The Turd is toast! I da man! The Turd is..."

All of a sudden something starts eating at Harry, and he pulls his head back into the car like he's one of them giant turtles. "So where *is* the Toast Turd, by the way?"

The kid looks up at the rearview. Harry turns around in his seat to look out the back. Even through the confetti, he can see the rope coming out from the bumper and the body being dragged behind the car. He sees the one leg tied to the rope and the other one flapping all over like it's broke in a hundred places and about to fall off. The Turd's back is scraping pavement. And his shaved head's bouncing up and down and up and down like someone's dribbling it down the street.

Now, normally under such a, whatcha call it, circumstance, Harry'd be a little concerned. If the Turd'd been tossed off a ninety-story skyscraper in another part of the city and bouncing around like this, there'd be panic everywhere, what with everyone screaming and running every which way like the world's came to an end. And then there'd be the shrieks of police sirens, not to mention ambulances, like there'd be a hell of a lot the meat wagons could do.

But this time, it's like one big fricking party. Nobody's

going nowhere, no one's calling no cops. Instead, all kinds of things are raining down on the Turd, hitting him everywhere—staplers, hole punches, paper weights, waste baskets, metal desk drawers, office chairs—you name it.

And when each new thing comes crashing, putting another dent in the Turd, Harry hears more hoots and hollers from the rooftops. More shouts of "You da man! You da Man!"

He even hears a name he never heard before, but what's he care about names? What's more, why should he care anymore about his list? With this kind of, whatcha call it, adulation, why the frick's he need those seventy-two pages anyway?

Louie's Turn

K. G. Anderson

Tonight, it was Louie's turn.

"Go on, dude." Carmen Caldoforno tugged a black knit cap over his greasy curls and peered out of the alley. "This one looks loaded. Go on, man. You wanted to try it."

But Louie Panebianco didn't move. *Waiting for Carmen. Driving the car. It had all been so easy. Why did I ask him to let me take the gun? The moon was so bright tonight! It would be easy if it were darker.*

"Easy pickings, big man," Carmen whispered. The gym rat, light on his feet, shifted side to side. "Go for it. I wanna get home and start counting that nice, hot cash."

"Yeah. On it." Louie took a deep breath and shrugged his broad shoulders. Then the 25-year-old *pizzaiolo* stepped out of the alley. Silent in high-top sneakers, he crept toward the mark: a middle-aged woman in high-heeled boots, designer jeans and a black leather jacket. She'd just parked her late-model Subaru in front of one of the new artists' lofts.

The wide sidewalks in the industrial district were nearly deserted on a weeknight. The rumble of a freight train a few blocks away covered Louie's approach. He slipped close to the car as the woman leaned in to get something from the back seat.

"Hey! Lady! Gimme the purse."

"Huh?" The victim whirled, saw Louie, and gave an odd little shriek.

The hood of raw pizza dough draped over Louie's head and shoulders had that effect on people. What had started as a late-night, too-many-beers-after-work prank had become a criminal *modus operandi*: The perfect disguise for a holdup man. The media had dubbed Carmen and Louie "the Mozzarella Muggers," news reports categorizing their holdups as "large," "medium," and "small."

Carmen was always the mugger, with Louie driving the beat-up Mazda. But tonight for the first time they'd switched roles. A mask of soft dough hid Louie's thick moustache and soulful eyes -- and his impatient grimace. Carmen had neglected to mention that the slits cut in the dough for seeing and breathing tended to sag. Louie wanted to get this finished while he could still see who he was mugging.

"The purse." Had the woman understood the words or had Louie's growl, employed to mask his real voice, come out as more of a mumble? Slightly high on the dough's fermenting yeast, Louie raised his handgun and waggled it to encourage the woman to hand over her bag. The pistol -- stolen from Carmen's Aunt Philomena's bedside drawer -- was wrapped in a second, smaller slab of dough. Using the mini-pizza for the gun had been Carmen's idea, to make it difficult for their victims to identify the weapon.

"You were robbed by a guy wearing jeans, high-tops and

pizza dough?" the incredulous cops at the North Precinct had asked the first victims. All people could recall was the growl of a male voice, the sight of the black gun barrel, and the bitter odor of fermenting yeast as they handed over their valuables.

Man, it was so easy. And it would have been tonight -- if this broad hadn't decided to fight back. Instead of handing over her valuables, she swung the purse at him. Startled, Louie leaped back, swearing. Then he did what people waving guns on TV always do: he pulled the trigger.

There was a bang. The woman clutched her stomach, made a gagging sound, and doubled over.

Oh, shit. Carmen had told him the gun wasn't loaded!

Mouth open under the mask of drooping dough, Louie waited for the woman to fall to the ground, like on TV. Instead, the woman tottered several steps back and then a few steps forward while Louie watched. To his relief, she turned and walked away from him, staggering over to one of the big industrial buildings. She leaned one shoulder against it. Then she slid slowly down the wall until she sat on the sidewalk.

Louie held his breath, hoping for the woman to fall over. But she didn't. She just sat there. Glassy eyed. Mouth sagging open. *Dead. The woman was dead!*

"Hey, Carmen!" Louie yelled, turning back toward the alley where his partner waited. His voice echoed off the tall concrete buildings, much louder than he'd intended. He tried again, softer. "Hey! Carmen!"

No answer. Louie remembered they were never supposed call each by name on a job. *Ah, shit. Carmen was going to be pissed.*

To his relief, Carmen's footsteps sounded in the alley. Running. It took Louie another moment to realize they were going the wrong way. A car door opened, a car door slammed, an engine started and tires screeched. Louie dropped the gun, peeled off the mask of dough and ran to the alley. He was just in time to see the old Mazda, Carmen at the wheel, speed away in the opposite direction. Away from the scene of the mugging. No -- the scene of the *murder*.

Louie pulled the dough from his shoulder and stared at it hand. *DNA!* Carmen had reminded him never to leave any dough, with possible DNA, behind. He looked around for a place to dump the dough. Frantic, he dropped it on the sidewalk.

When he looked up, he realized the dead lady was staring at him. In the bright light of the full moon he could see the dark blood that oozed down the front of her blouse and pooled on the sidewalk.

Louie wanted to vomit. He swallowed hard. And swallowed again. He wanted desperately to be somewhere else. Anywhere else. Back at work, cleaning up Tony's Pizza Palace. At Carmen's place, watching a video. At home, asleep in his basement room.

A cold breeze swept the broad street and Louie shivered. *Gotta get out of here.* He headed for the alley, grateful that no cars had come by.

"Aowwwww."

It was the woman. Louie gasped. *The broad was still alive! It wasn't murder after all!* Louie pulled his phone from his pocket and called Carmen. The call went to Carmen's voicemail. Louie's eyes narrowed. His pop always referred to Carmen as "that little weasel," and now he knew why.

"Aowwwww."

In a panic, Louie called 9-1-1.

"Emergency Services."

"There's...there's..," *Don't say "shooting,"* he told himself. *What would someone just walking by report?* "Uh, there's a woman, ah, laying, ah, she's bleeding, on the sidewalk on Fourth Street South."

"The cross street, sir?" *Shit.* Louie glanced up at the sign. "Uh, North Sanderson. Near the train yard."

"Your name, sir?"

He had no choice. He'd called on his own damn phone. They'd trace it. "Louis Panebianco. I was, uh, just passing by."

Hey, if the woman died, they'd never know about the holdup. He was just someone passing by. If she lived...he'd worry about that later.

The operator hung up.

The woman was moaning. She'd toppled over, and now more blood was oozing from her blouse. Louie's stomach clenched.

He picked up the pistol, removed the dough, wiped the gun on his workshirt, and then lobbed everything, dough and gun, over a high fence. There was a loud clang as it struck something metal. Louie pawed the sidewalk, scooping up the big wad of dough that had masked him. He ran to the curb and stuffed it down a sewer grating. *Clang!* Scrubbed his big hands on his jeans. *Just passing by.*

The moon gazed down on him and reminded him of the lens of a giant camera. Recording everything that he'd done. Sirens wailed in the distance. *Just passing by,* he rehearsed.

"Aowwwww," the woman moaned.

Louie walked over to her and surprised himself by falling to his knees.

"I called 9-1-1," he said. He shuddered as the woman's chest rose and fell in rough, labored breaths. *Dying. Jeez, if Carmen were here, he'd probably finish her off.* Louie could almost hear the shot. He shuddered at the idea. He was glad Carmen was gone.

"I'm sorry, lady," he whispered. "However it goes, I'm sorry."

The siren grew louder, and a cop car screeched to the curb. Doors slammed. Louie sat back on his heels. As he did, he smelled tomato sauce. He wrinkled his nose. *Garlic. Oregano?*

"You're under arrest." A powerful hand closed on his upper arm, jerking him to his feet. Two cops cuffed his hands behind his back. They rattled off his rights.

Louie barely heard them. "Hey!"

He gaped as the bleeding woman stood up, miraculously unharmed. One of the cops, addressing her as "Detective," handed her a white towel to mop off the blood. The detective's cold eyes met Louie's.

"Bulletproof vest," she said. "And a plastic bag with goddamn Chef Boy-Ar-Dee."

She caught a patrolman by the arm. "He chucked the gun over that fence. And stuffed the dough down that grating. Evidence. Get that dough in a fridge."

An ambulance and more cars pulled up, people shouting, lights flashing, and doors slamming. Louie squinted. He stumbled as two patrolmen hustled him toward one of the cop cars. He slouched, readying himself to be shoved into the gated back seat. But the final humiliation was yet to come.

"Well, if it isn't the Mozzarella Mugger!" A toothy hipster, brandishing a smartphone, leaned in close. "Let's hear you say 'cheese.'"

Mobster Thermidor

Andrew Hook

Mordent once wore a concrete overcoat, but it was two sizes too small and a little short in the sleeves. It wasn't a garment of choice – he had wrestled to get into it – but instead a by-product of an encounter with Marcia, his mob-connected girlfriend. If Mordent had been a smarter PI he might have made that connection sooner, but there was plenty of time for reflection as he sank to the bottom of Lake Michigan. You could say he fathomed it out.

The lake's average depth was forty-six fathoms and three feet, which was forty-six fathoms deeper than Mordent had wanted. The rush of water kept his senses busy just as it muffled them. He held a breath in his lungs although preferred an air-tight container. Visibility was down to zero but sight wouldn't matter.

In Mordent's favour he knew it wasn't a practical method of execution. The mobsters had proven farcical in their attempt to replicate an essentially fictional device. Cement takes several hours or occasionally days to harden, and Mordent was banking on sufficient air remaining in the mix to aid his escape. The mobsters had also taken the term literally. Had they given Mordent a cement footbath whilst he was sat comfortably reading the morning paper they might have pulled it off. As it was, the stiffened thrift shop garment took three of them to hold and proved remarkably inflexible. The buttons wouldn't do up.

If it was a simple matter of weight then Mordent knew there were precedents. In 1941 the body of Philadelphia racketeer Johnnie Goodman had been weighed down with a concrete block, and in 1964 Ernest Rupolo had something similar tied to his legs. None of these courted the elegance of fashion, and Mordent knew if he didn't survive then he would garner sixty seconds of fame. But more importantly, sixty seconds were all that he had.

Whilst water is an essential component when making concrete, it is also the most destructive in excessive amounts. The air pockets created by the mobsters' naïve enthusiasm served to reduce the concrete's compressive strength and durability. As the concrete's surface area increased, so did its demand for moisture, until the pressure of Lake Michigan's 1,180 cubic miles tore the overcoat from Mordent's body and – still holding that vital breath – he floated to the surface anticipating a hail of bullets.

Maybe it was his lucky day: his upraised mouth breached the surface in the spume of the departing speedboat. A fortuitous facial.

Maybe it was his unlucky day: he had just been dumped by his girlfriend.

*****

Marcia had applied for a pilot's licence. She had yet to own a plane, but she did have a cockpit and Mordent was a frequent flyer. He had blown into the Windy City on an assignment which had led to a quicker resolution than anticipated, but whilst retained on expenses he decided to delay his report and make use of them. Chicago wasn't like San Francisco, which had its ups and downs, but it did hold a glut of nicknames which appealed to Mordent's sense of the dramatic:

Mud City. Second City. City of the Big Shoulders. City in a Garden. The City that Works. The Great Commercial Tree. The Heart of America. The City Beautiful. My Kind of Town.

Mordent's kind of town held a bar and a girl. He found both at the same location. Not as might be expected at The Green Mill Lounge which had been Al Capone's favourite haunt, nor at Marge's where bathtub gin used to be served in the cellar, nor fellow-speakeasy Twin Anchors where - renamed Tante Lee Soft Drinks during Prohibition - it sold alcohol alongside a secret basement escape hatch. Instead Mordent favoured The Red Lion Pub on North Lincoln Avenue where – in an alley across the street - gangster and bank robber Johnny Dillinger had been gunned down in 1934. Souvenir hunters had dipped newspapers and their skirts in the blood that stained the pavement. If Mordent kept his gaze askance he might almost imagine Dillinger crossing the street from the old Biograph Theater, having watched the gangster movie *Manhattan Melodrama*. Instead he should have kept his gaze away from Marcia, who entered stage right and sat on his left, resting her hands and then her head on the dark oak-planked bar.

"I'm beat."

"Maybe you should be." Mordent was a cack-hand at one-liners.

She lifted her head from the viscous surface, eyeing him curiously. "Not many would say that in today's age."

"I'm not living in today's age; my preference is for the 50s."

"I also like older men." Faded red lipstick framed a laugh.

Mordent placed her late-forties: an old master. Perhaps an old mistress.

"Can I buy you a drink?"

"You have to ask?"

They sipped whiskey. After a couple of sips from a couple of glasses she offered her hand which extended from a limp wrist: "Marcia."

"Mordent."

"You have a first name?"

"Not until I'm christened."

"Then let's practice wetting the baby's head."

She was grey at the roots. Wore a one-piece suit which looked cut from a three-piece suite. A ladder promised a journey at the rear of one leg. Her fingernails were chipped, like the hull of a boat which has clipped the quayside too many times. Yet her smile discarded these trivialities, lent her wry charm.

Conversation hovered towards personal lives without actually landing there. Mordent held back enquiring about her lethargy, not wanting the consequences of removing his finger from the dyke. In truth, both opposites were the case. He indulged his sexual preference for bubblewrap by imagining she was a travelling saleswoman, her trunk stuffed with the stuff. The more they drank, the more attractive they became, each to the other, fantasies not withstanding.

Marcia shelled nuts at the counter, her nails digging into the pistachios, deftly easing them out with her tongue like desiccated oysters.

"How much longer are you staying in Chicago?"

"About a week."

She counted five on her fingers, held up a hand. "I'm discounting rest days."

"You think I'll need them?"

She slid off the stool and into his arms. Quite a feat considering both dress and upholstery were velvet.

"Only if you need another drink."

There was that smile again. Flecked with pistachio husks.

*****

They used Mordent's hotel. He'd paid for a single so most times one of them was off the bed and the other on it. Either the frame pressed against his knees or the back of her head. Sometimes it got rude. If Mordent had known Marcia's background he would have understood he was in so deep that he needed protection. Not that he didn't.

The room was non-smoking. Between bouts they took to the balcony, smoke rising from their cigarettes as though steam from their bodies. Mordent wondered if they had slipped into the 70s instead of the 50s. Although he couldn't kid himself that they were esoteric literature filed amongst the pulps, there was some romanticism tied to the sordid. Either way, his joints had begun to ache. When Marcia dressed and headed downstairs for food, he showered, lathering soap over his legs as if to loosen them up.

She returned with two mother-in-laws. Every man's nightmare. Although these were tamales topped with chilli and served in hotdog buns.

"A local speciality."

"Yes, you are."

Bereft of make-up – the opportunity cost of the rut – Marcia appeared younger. Mordent wondered if he might launch a *Freshly Fucked* line of cosmetics. He sensed a fortune.

"Sometime your dialogue will get the better of you."

They ate the tamales on the edge of the bed. Chilli sauce dripped onto Mordent's penis which Marcia refused to clean.

"If I ask you something, will you forgive me?"

They had finished the tamales. She couldn't stay overnight. Previous commitment. Mordent wasn't sure if she would form part of his expenses. Perhaps it was time for her to hit him for money. Not that he was churlish. And she had given great room service. Although it would have been an unfair one way transaction considering their performance was of mutual benefit.

"Sure," he found himself saying.

"What are you in town for?"

Mordent considered his cover story. Marcia got there first.

"Only I saw your gun and identification."

Mordent looked to the dresser. He had been careless within the heat. He didn't know if it mattered.

"Divorce case. Tailing a rogue husband with a cover story of a rogue wife. I've all the evidence I need but if I bring it too soon the client gets suspicious and I don't get enough to eat."

She nodded. He wasn't attuned to her intent.

She kissed him.

"I'll be back tomorrow. And I'll be sure you get enough to eat."

Mordent locked the door behind her, watched as she hailed a cab from the street. She didn't look up to the room. He took another shower and counted his blessings until he got to lucky. Then he kept on counting and reached too good to be true.

But it wasn't sufficient to count. You also needed to add up.

He was sore from exertion. Underneath the blankets he could smell her perfume. He rested his eyes and his body followed suit. If he dreamt, he held no recollection.

*****

Days segued into nights. Marcia's role increasingly nurse to an invalid. Mordent hadn't seen so much action since a faked army career. They talked in generalities, neither interested in family or history. Sometimes she raked her hands along his torso. Often he scratched her back. They both bore indentations of old wedding rings. Each had a collection of scars. When Marcia bent to pull on her hose her skin stretched revealing fine marks along the surface. Mordent wondered how easily he might be read. Sometimes he told her of cases he worked on, oftentimes he made them up. She held an interest in some of his connections, but it wasn't all dot to dot.

On the fifth day they rested as Marcia had intimated. Mordent took to the streets. He spent time in Grant Park and visited the Lincoln Park zoo, not quite believing that – like Marcia – it was free. In the Art Institute he admired works by van Gogh, Monet and Renoir. On the City Architecture River Cruise he contemplated the Wrigley Building and all those other sky-high scrapers. In the evening he ate an Italian beef sandwich with giardiniera peppers.

On the sixth day Marcia's knock wasn't quite so forceful. Mordent married his vision to the fisheye. The distortion gave appearance that her mascara had run. When he opened the door he saw that it had. Before she could speak she was flanked by two flunkies, choreographed like showgirls in a Busby Berkeley movie. Mordent understood he would be the sole dancer.

He was silent as they were marched down to the car. She was silent during the journey. He was silent at the boathouse during the fitting of the grey overcoat. She was silent as the boat bounced the lake. He was silent at the point of no escape. She was silent as he was pushed over the side. He was silent all the way down.

The overcoat was the key to the outfit. The Chicago Outfit. Mordent was lucky there were no matching trousers.

Once surfaced, he struck out for shore. He didn't consider himself fit for swimming, but it was surprising what fear could do. Upon reaching reeds he held the appearance of bursting forth from wet plaster: an escape from a statue. That might have explained the scattering picnickers, but it didn't explain his next move.

A greyhound might run faster than his legs could carry him, but Mordent knew it would never catch the rabbit.

Without gun or identification he wired a contact home for both. As guarantor Hubie rented him a hotel room opposite his former lodgings. Mordent set up residence: meals delivered. He waited for information. Considering the amount he had to give he wasn't expecting much back. Most of it hinged on whether Marcia had been clean with her name. Some of it depended on whether the goons would brag. A slice of it was reliant on their disposing of evidence. A tad of it was tied to the flying school lead.

Betting on four horses in a five horse race was one of Mordent's specialities. Hubie's also. When Hubie told him he'd come up trumps, Mordent knew it was better than trumping up come. Hubie wasn't sure how to answer that.

"I think you've guessed it, but here's my take: Marcia is Marcia Gonzales, linked to Paul Roebuck who is so high up the Chicago mob that his barber mistakes his white hair for clouds. Roebuck's not exactly running the main show, but he does have control over the fringe. Sticking with the metaphor he's a theatrical type. That concrete overcoat gig would have appealed to his *Billy Bathgate* sensibility. Seems like his guys have been free with their mouths, so convinced you wouldn't surface that they've courted the urban myth. The story circulation wouldn't prevent a national newspaper from going under, but it's sufficient to maintain a tiny rag mostly filled with ads. Marcia's name is out of it – I got *her* from *The Flying Deuces*, a Laurel and Hardy outfit where she's been having lessons – but another name mentioned in the same breath is Sol 'Sonny' George, one of Roebuck's goons. Seems like he got himself in some trouble playing away from his wife, and that – I believe – is where you entered the picture."

Mordent lay on the bed in his underpants. He scratched the top of his thigh. "Sol is the guy I patched in the adultery case."

"Seems he's connected to a high voltage."

"High enough to wipe me out?"

"People have been killed for less."

"Wonder where Marcia fits into this. She looked cut up when they grabbed me."

"Let's hope she hasn't been."

"Coincidence she was in the bar?" Mordent thought back to the lovemaking. Four days of intimacy seemed unnecessary in the scheme of things.

"This is real life. Not everything has to add up. I think they busted you for Sol and then busted you for Marcia. Even real life courts coincidence."

Mordent thanked Hubie and considered his options. Unlike Marcia he didn't need all his fingers.

Number one: revenge.

There was no number two.

*****

Chicago had been the centre for overcoat manufacture since the early 1800s. The people of the windy city needed something to pull against the cold. Mordent spent a week crafting a persona, trusting that he wasn't enough of a celebrity to be eyeballed and fingered. Hubie mailed over a fake ID: Gregory Peck. Mordent sloughed off his *what-the-fuck* and agreed he needed an angle to get unnoticed. Something that would raise eyebrows and not suspicion. Peck was a name too stupid to be false. It was hiding in plain sight.

Marcia had been spotted. At 10,000 feet. Her flying lessons had resumed. Mordent wondered if she were too high profile to be rubbed out. Maybe one day she would have an accident, her co-pilot collateral. Mordent was sure Roebuck wouldn't want to be seen as a pushover, but then everyone had a soft spot for a dame. Perhaps he might use her. Even abuse her for old time's sake. She wore no black veil. Maybe she had been in on it.

Binoculars and a note in the hand of the doorman confirmed to Peck that Mordent had checked out of his old hotel. He wondered what became of his used underwear: off-white, once white. The goons who took it looked suspiciously like those on the speedboat. He forgave tailing those rats. Had bigger fish to fry. Maybe even deer to roast.

He made a decision to call in on the job he was supposed to be working. Sol must have fingered him just as he had that girl his wife, Angie, was suspicious about. Maybe if he thought Mordent had a partner then he'd know the game wasn't over. Maybe he'd get to wondering about his sources. Mordent sent a wire to Sol's address knowing his wife was still out of town and that it would be intercepted. He played it fancy – name-checked Roebuck – gave Sol something to think about. What if Angie had him tailed under Roebuck's instructions because Roebuck thought Marcia might be involved? Sol would know Marcia played away – Mordent was evidence of that. If Mordent could plant the seed that Roebuck had been intending to frame Sol and Marcia through casting suspicion with Angie, wouldn't that leave her a grieving widow ready to move up in the establishment. A widow indeed, because Sol would have found his own overcoat a good fit. The tailors were learning. Maybe Roebuck felt threatened by Sol, a younger buck moving up through the herd, maybe he wanted to take his doe for himself. Mordent wanted Sol to reason it that way, and although his plan stank and had more holes than gorgonzola, he knew these Mafia types worked off testosterone and instinct. Throw a bomb into the crowd and they'd run to it. Pitching them against each other would keep his hands clean.

After re-thinking it three tines Mordent almost understood it. It wasn't watertight, but it might last forty-six fathoms. The three feet weren't something to worry about.

As Gregory Peck he took to the street. Chicago seemed a different place in different shoes. When he got hungry he scrolled through restaurant menus. Lobster was too close to *mobster* for comfort, but it birthed a prick of an idea. Eventually he ate stuffed deep-dish pizza at *Uno's*, wondered how easily he might identify / be identified. This wasn't the Chicago of Capone's time. Things had moved on a pace. It was all corporate. He wondered how much came from the movies. He wondered how much of his life might be fiction.

Wandering to another telegraph office he sent a second wire to Sol's house from Peck: *Leaving town. Partner disappeared. Roebuck paid me. Wants to see you. New hotel development. Navy Pier. 22:11. Don't be late.*

Then one to Marcia: *Still alive. Want to see you. New hotel development. Navy Pier. 22:11. Don't be late.*

And finally to Roebuck: *Sol & Marcia. She gets around. New hotel development. Navy Pier. Twenty to eleven. Don't be late.*

There was a doll of a breeze. Navy Pier was illuminated in red and gold. Mordent killed time in the Funhouse Maze; navigated his way through four thousand square feet of tunnels with enough twists and turns to match the plot. When he entered the half-built seven-storey, 240-room hotel, adjacent to the south side of Festival Hall, he wondered whether this dimension was no different from the maze. He looked at his watch. It was ten-thirty.

The Thermidorian Reaction was a counter revolution which took place in France on 9 Thermidor of the Year II. Maximilien Robespierre was denounced by members of the National Convention as a tyrant, leading to Robespierre and twenty-one associates being arrested that night and beheaded the following day. Thermidor represented the final throes of the Reign of Terror.

Mordent likened Roebuck's forthcoming appearance to that of Robespierre at the Hôtel de Ville. Hidden on the ground floor, echoes of Marcia and Sol arguing filtered from above. Mordent couldn't catch a word. He wondered if he needed to be there. Roebuck entered solo. Mordent wondered again.

He counted to ten. Two shots were fired. When Marcia returned downstairs he saw she was a smoking gun.

"You can come out," she shouted. "I always liked you in *How The West Was Won*."

Mordent revealed himself. Smiled. "Smart move."

"Someone's got to clean up this town," she said. "Drink?"

"You know an alibi made of bourbon won't stand up."

"Nor will drinking with a dead man but I'll take my chances."

They walked a few paces into the cool night air. Marcia slipped her hand in his. Mordent wondered how powder burns would compare with carpet burns.

He said: "A good dish for celebration is lobster thermidor. You know where we can get some?"

"There's The Cape Cod Room on the ground floor of the Drake Hotel at the corner of Michigan Ave. and E. Lake Shore Drive."

"Does the hotel do rooms?"

"Do lobsters sing *Under The Sea*?"

Mordent considered egg yolks and brandy, cooked meat and red carapace. It was a crab in the movie, but he didn't feel pinched.

If he closed his eyes he might imagine Roebuck and Sol, warmed by a dying sun through an unglazed window, their blood pooling in fresh concrete creating a creamy sauce. In failing light maybe mistaken for mustard.

But he didn't.

Less Than a Rental Car

Ed Nobody

We're in the cramped corner of some small cafe, beige walls, dark blue siding, dull hipster art in blonde beechwood frames. She's across from me, blonde hair in a braid over white V-neck, bent over a plate of oyster salad. Her glass is mostly empty, dry lime standing up.

And she has this look about her, with her thin pencilled brows and her upturned nose and her round blue eyes and her smile: a look that says she's about to make me vanish. Her cutlery's set down on the table now, and she's just looking at the plate and...I know what she's thinking. She's thinking how it will look—when she—Don't....

She stirs, arms uncrossing, right arm in tell-tale dive to bag—Stop!—reaches on something and pulls—Ahhh!—out comes the phone, pointed to the plate and

*****

Chinese restaurant, paint smell, sound of construction. The warble of a high-pitched song. So we're standing in front of a buffet counter, metal trays, slotted spoon, beansprouts and chicken. Behind the counter is a small Asian girl, thin eyes straight hair sharp smile. To my right, peering into the counter with a glazed look, my girlfriend.

And she's poking her finger at the glass. Trying to 'tap' the food. Squinting at the food image, playing with her ponytail, pinched, restless fingers I know are gonna—Not again—but yes, swinging her purse and flipping the top, deft hand diving inside—Wait—something rumbling now, "Hold on, I think I just got a–"

*****

"What is this all about, exactly?" Middle aged man behind cheap mountain ash desk. His fingers are folded together, face screwed in a confused knot. Dusty mustache, the gleam off his glasses hiding his eyes. Looks screwy, wouldn't trust him on the street. His name is 'Paul Seymour Goodman-Bawls' which is even screwier.

And the gleam's not just on his glasses, it's like down his face, his eyes, vertical stripes like a barrel. And it's weird coz the window is *behind* him, so where is this light even coming from? Turning my head there's only the door I just came in, solid, no window.

Smell of fried bread or donuts filling in the air and I'm starving now and don't even know the last time I ate, since every time I'm about to eat, I keep on getting—

"Look," I say. Oh and on his desk there's a little plaque that says 'Existence Broker.' The hell does that even mean. And why am I here? Oh yeah. "I'm here," I say, (Paul Seymour raising his brows at me expectantly), "I'm here because I have a very real problem."

"Which is…?"

"Which is, how should I put it?" I tug at my collar, boy getting hot in here huh, must be the heat from the donut shop or whatever downstairs. "Whenever my girlfriend pulls out her phone, *I stop existing for a while.*"

"Ah." P.S. leans back in his black pleather chair, probably

like that IKEA one with the faux-Swedish name, costs $50, wouldn't recommend it, specially if you're tall. This guy's short, maybe it ain't a problem for him. He says, "Yes, I've heard of that before..."

"You *have*?" I jump back, startled. But, hey hold on, isn't the wrong guy getting surprised here? And what's that jazz music I hear, ah so it *is* a donut and coffee joint down there. Damn I shoulda gone there and eaten instead of coming up to this clueless a-wad, even if he *is* pretending to know what I mean, when like clearly there's no way he does.

"Oh yes, yes, she ignores you and looks at her phone," this Goodman-Bawls character says.

"No, no, no, you don't get it," I tell him (he's opening his mouth to interrupt but I keep going), "I mean I *actually* stop existing." The small home-office seat nipping at my sides; it'd be more comfortable to sit on the subway steps.

"Aha, I see now. So you stop existing and uhm hmhm hmm..." he trails off.

"What was that? You're mumbling."

"Sorry."

My face must read like three question marks at this point, yet this Paul Seymour here is serene as a Zen pond! His clasped hands unclasping and splaying out Last Supper style. "Well, I can help you with this."

"You *can*?"

"You want me to *verify* your existence, I presume. For the next few days or so. That would put your mind at ease, would it not?"

"Uh yeah maybe, but uh..." Okay so maybe he thinks I'm having memory lapses or something, is that it? Lost time. But it's not my time that's getting lost buddy, it's my whole like, *being.* But also he's never going to believe that unless he sees it first hand, so sure, go nuts. "You're just going to tail me around, right?"

"Well yes. I mean, it's not one of my usual activities. As you can see, I am not a private dick."

No, just the bawls.

"Excuse me?" he blinks at me. I must have said it aloud.

"Never mind," I say. "Listen, how much are we talking here?"

"Hmm, let's say $100, for two days."

"Gee, that cost less than a rental car."

"Well, business has been rough lately."

"The business."

"Right."

"The existence brokerage...business."

"Uhum."

"So listen can I pay by check?" (A clatter from downstairs, definitely sounds like a deep fryer).

"Yes, yes of course."

"Okay," I take out my chequebook, write his name, "here you go."

He peers at it a moment, looks up, face clouded with cynical recognition.

"Ahem, you've written it incorrectly," he says. I take the check back, glance at it.

"I have?" *-Paul Seymour Good-Man-Bawls-*

"Yes... my surname is not *triple-barrelled.*" He's turning red.

"Oh, my bad. You're right."

So I redo the check again, only one hyphen this time.

"Next sign here."

"Okay," hurriedly scribbling my signature on the contract so I can hop outta here, go downstairs and grab me some breakfast(?) What time is it anyway, not like I got a watch.

*****

So there I am next day out with her (sounds of people going upstairs, downstairs) and we're at the donut shop *'Joe's,'* below Paul Seymour's office. Making it easy on this 'broker' to watch me. Rough times and all that.

"And she says to me that," (this is Tera speaking now, my girlfriend) "she bought this antique clock up in Yonkers, and the guy claims it's 18th century and she pays through the nose for it, turns out the thing is *Edwardian*. You know what happened then? She takes the clock back to the guy and he says all sales are final. I mean she really got suckered by this guy."

"I guess that makes her a *clock sucker*."

"What?"

"So what are you having, my love?" I'm breathing in coffee fumes, fried dough. Heavy traffic outside on a bustling Tuesday morning (I know this because the day's special is Boston Cream, which of course they're all out of by this point since it's already 11AM. But somehow neither of us have work at this hour, which is good if I'm about to...you know...)

The guy behind the counter puts the Eye in Italian: floppy white hat, Mario Brothers moustache, curly mop of hair and so on. He makes a mean mug of joe. Funnily enough the guy's name *is* Joe, but he's not giving me a mean mug, he's all smiles; another Italian stereotype! Next he's gonna start pinching his fingers when he speaks and gesticulating all over the place and saying *ay marone...*

All this is to say the 'scene' just don't feel right to me, it's almost manufactured. Whether or not this has anything to do with my recent 'interruptions,' who knows. It would be easy to say that I'm just losing my mind right now (heavy stamping from above—geez that floor is really thin huh? Must be the same architect as that Chinese restaurant with the kungpao chicken), but uh, I don't think I am. Losing my mind that is.

So Tera says she'll 'just' have a double caramel latte and a small roll. I'm like 'just'? So because you get your calories in liquid form it don't count? But she's sensitive about her weight so I let it slide…Anyways, what I'm most afraid of at this point is this dessert she's calling coffee—like its gonna come out all glamorous and what not, drizzled in hot fudge and with a cherry on top and like sprinkles. You just know the second she sees it her hand's gonna zip inside her purse like Billy The Kid at noon, 'cept it's gonna be *me* catching a stray bullet.

"*Ay marone!*" (shout from the back, gush of steam, crash of plates to floor)

I peer into the back over the bar there but can't see nothing. We're standing there, the two of us, me and Tera. There's only two real tables in the joint and they're both full, one of those standing room venues, traditional like. But the difference is that those places only used to serve espresso—you were meant to knock it back like a shot and mosey. Not slurp on 20oz of whipped cream for half an hour while fucking around on your—

Aw jeez, I just wanna get it over with already. Or not, like maybe it won't happen, now I got this bug in my brain that I'm being watched. Like maybe can I just enjoy my bear claw over here? Anyway get it together, here comes her drink. Joe slams it down on the bar, gives it the chef's kiss—yes, really—purses his lips (probably about to say *Bellissimo!* or some shit) but gets interrupted by another customer (thank God), some

Manhattan lady with resting bitch face talks a mile a minute telling Joe how to make her non-fat half-caff triple venti extra drizz…Joe's face just goes like *madda ming*. And the lady's hair is that straight-black-bangs look like the chick from Pulp Fiction who pukes to death or is that what happens I don't remember too well.

"Okay lady," Joe disappearing into the back. (More stamping from upstairs). I look back around and Tera's uploading her latte to Pinterest and

*****

"Okay Paul Seymour, give me the scoop. What exactly *did* happen to me yesterday?" I'm back in his office, light through the blinds like slanted arrows, his face wet or greasy like he just ate a hot meal.

"Hmm, mmm, mnn…" He trails off before he even starts! That bad, huh. No, it's definitely sweat on that face of his. Looks like someone stamped on his Goodman-Bawls. Maybe that's what all the stamping was. (Sound of the blender from below—what's Joe making, Margaritas? Or I guess it's the bean grinder never mind).

P.S. is breathing out uncomfortably when he says, "Okay, yes, I um watched you at Joe's and?"

"Is that a question?"

"Hmm? Oh, no, no."

"Then what?"

"Standing at the bar with your girlfriend. Ordered your."

"Yeah, the coffees, got it. I know that part already. *Then what*?"

Gaddammit!

heart thumping so hard breathless faint shit gonna pass out heart really like stamping upstairs DUMPA DUMPA DUMPA

DUMPA chest screwed into a tight ball of gristle it'll be okay it'll be okay we'll deal with it whatever happens jeez would he just tell me already fuck I can't handle this

"Yes, you disappeared, I'm afraid."

When he says it, I'm so worked up about it that it ain't even a shock anymore, but just a kind of letting go, letting go of the tension and fading into sedated gray...but it's not like fading away, because the times when I disappear I don't even feel it, I don't feel nothing, I'm just there and then suddenly I'm not, and so I'm not afraid of *that* exactly, as I fall back and back and back, off the uncomfortable chair and into the slanted light and crashing onto the floor which I know they'll hear downstairs at Joe's, and I'm still here but my *being* is being taken from me it feels like, and now I finally understand what it means that P.S. is an *existence broker*...

You see *something* has been after my existence for a while now, snatching it up for hours at a time but never hanging on for very long. But now the *something* has hired this Paul Seymour goon here to get it instead. And what's worse is, since I've signed the contract and all, it's already settled.

He can finally take my existential ass out for good.

There's barely enough time to catch my last breath. Paul Seymour Goodman-Bawls walks over to me, tears up my check, flings a c-note onto my chest. The contract, now that I think about it, had said that *he* has to pay *me*...

Finally, he reaches into his pocket, makes to pull something out. And I know what's about to happen. For good this time. And all I can think to myself is—

I cost less than a rental car.

Jack's Plan

Jody Smith

Larry was in trouble, and by extension, so was Jack. They needed money something fierce. The cogs of life were loose and ready to fall off, but Jack had a plan. Jack always had a plan.

Larry cowered behind the drapes as the fish man rolled up the laneway. The living room was a mess, dusty and cluttered.

"You sure about this, Jack? I need the fish?"

"Sure," Jack said.

Larry took a whooping breath and stepped through a slim alley of boxes lining the walls of a hallway. The home was big and a failing roof demanded that they move of everything from the four rooms upstairs to the main floor or basement. The basement was small and it housed two generations of stuff already.

Shambles was the right word to describe the house. And just how was he ever going get enough money to fix what needed to be fixed? Selling wasn't an option. The home value exceeded the current market value, meaning they'd never get enough to break even with the bank, not by a longshot.

"Hey there, Mr. Sullivan. How's the wife?" Reggie Black, the fish man, asked. He was a tall skinny, fidgety man with a full beard and a horseshoe hairline. He wore blue overalls and black boots.

Larry tried to play cool, but he was sweating buckets, and it had zip to do with the weather. "She's fine." There was no way he'd tell the horrible, dirty truth. He'd never tell that. "She's off visiting with her mother in Chicago."

"Oh, she a Mid-Westerner?"

Larry nodded, holding his breath.

"Guess I would know that if I ever heard her speak."

He's on to us.

Reggie grinned. "It's like all those old shows. The wife is always off in Chicago, or Philly, or New York. Visiting. You don't have her in the deep freezer, do ya?"

Larry regained his composure at that. "Sure, she got too sassy and I chopped her purdy head right off her neck. She minds me now, real nice she does," Larry said, mimicking Reggie's tone.

Reggie wrinkled his nose. "What'll it be? Same as last time?"

"That's right. I want the same as last time." Larry withdrew his wallet from pocket. He did the math and decided that it was likely the final visit within the budget, at least until he figured out a new source of income. "And you know, I'm gonna take a little break from fish buying, so you don't need to come back next month."

"Real shame. You going on a trip, too?"

"Sure," Larry said.

"That's nice. Thirty-two even will do it."

Larry pulled out three tens and two singles.

"I don't like fish so much, but the wife…now she loves the

stuff. I'll put this in the freezer for when she returns. See? That's why I don't need an order next month. She can eat this month's order when she gets back in a few weeks."

"Right."

Larry waved. Reggie waved. The freezer van toured back out the dusty lane and Larry took the heavy bag of fish, his personal meat of choice, back into the aged and failing farmhouse.

"He's onto us," Larry said to his only friend in the world.

Jack wore his go-to expression: V-shaped eyebrows peaking up a long forehead that inched toward a receded hairline, piercing eyes, and a devilish grin that stretched most of the way across his face.

"Calm now, Larry my boy."

"That's what you always say."

"Don't twist your knickers. Old Reggie don't suspect a thing worth worrying. That one's just a wee secret anyhow. Where we have to focus is on getting out of this stinking money mess."

Thirty-grand would float him and fix the roof. Float him and Jack for the interim. Jack knew how to get it too. Jack always had great ideas.

"Transportation is an issue." Larry rubbed his chin, mulling over the plan.

Jack disagreed. This plan was simple. There were vehicles available, waiting for a driver. Jack would steer the getaway car after the fact, but Larry had to give him a good reason to run. Larry was not a criminal. Larry was a poor capitalist, which often made an innocent man turn to the dark side of the law.

The goofiest bank robbers in the history of Greyland County, possibly in the whole state, rode doubles on the blue Schwinn chopper bicycle Larry got for his thirteenth birthday eighteen summers earlier. In a soft guitar case, Larry carried his grandfather's Cooey .22 long barrel. The ancient bolt action with the stock sawed down offered only a modicum of confidence. It was all he had, that and Jack's reassurances.

It took nearly an hour along the back roads and secondary streets to get to Old Mrs. Ingles house. Mrs. Ingles had died two months earlier and her kids hadn't come around yet to clean out the place. Mrs. Ingles used to pay Larry twenty a week to come and tend to her yard and driveway. All four seasons.

For sixteen years Larry worked for the old woman and couldn't believe he hadn't thought of it himself when Jack suggested it. They'd bike to town with the gun, stop at Mrs. Ingles, get the keys from the hook hidden under the workbench, and take her Pinto for a getaway car.

"Wally's getting old, but he ain't changing. Man always has his lunch, then takes a crap, from twelve-fifteen to twelve-forty, like clockwork, just how your daddy joked he did. You go on in while he's indisposed and mosey up to the teller, put that big old stick in her face, and demand the bag filled. Then shout that everybody get down. Take what you can and we'll be out and back up to the business of easy street. If you gotta shoot, you shoot; remember, none of them is a real anymore, the change done come, Larry my boy."

"Right," Larry said.

There were six people in the bank. They were like ghosts. Larry recognized all of them, though not of this life, in the times before everything went to shit.

"Hey, is that Larry Sullivan?"

"Jesus, Larry's got a rifle!"

"What you doing, Larry?"

These ghosts knew him. They all knew him and that was bad. They knew him, but didn't know him. This was Larry on a mission, not Larry who stayed at home on his folks' property while it fell apart around him.

"Somebody call Wall—!" a woman shouted from behind the counter.

This thing was too quickly getting out of control. Larry levelled the old tool and fired before the woman finished her sentence. Her head jerked back and then straightened. The little hole was like a terrible mole on the woman's face. She pawed at it stupidly. The blood smeared all over her cheek.

"Holy crow," Larry whispered and then shouted, "Everybody down or you're all cooked turkeys!"

"Come on now, Larry," an older voice behind him said.

Larry spun and put a shot through the man's throat. That Cooey held true even sixty years after the manufacture date.

The remaining folks fell to the floor and Larry charged to the manager. His father used to joke how the manager of the United ran a harem, hiring only women beneath him. Year after year, the woman grew younger while the manager never changed, even if the name on the desk did.

"Put the cash in the bag!"

The manager jumped. "Don't shoot."

The cash on hand went into a cotton sack. Twelve-grand? It wasn't Easy Street, that was for sure, but it was enough to repair the roof. Larry thought he might rob the other two banks in Milo and shoot up to Brownville. Surely three more would fix up the numbers.

While Larry robbed the bank and Jack sat in Mrs. Ingles Pinto, engine running, Reggie was inside Elaine's Café making a call. A busboy carted the fish order into the walk-in.

"I think Larry Sullivan's killed his wife," Reggie whispered into the phone.

The officer on the other end spoke with surprise. "Larry Sullivan from on Hobbstown Road? Larry don't have a wife 'less he got married last week."

Reggie hung up, confused, and then heard a screaming woman as she raced up the street. "There's a bank robbery happening! Help! Help! Bank robbery! Help!"

The Pinto screeched and peeled black rubber streaks around the corner. Jack was a star behind the wheel.

Minutes away, sirens trailed in the distance and the Pinto fishtailed up the gravel lane to the old farmhouse with the caving roof. Larry hooted and hollered.

"Don't think it's over yet," Jack said.

Larry spun on the seat and looked over his shoulder. There were lights catching up in a real hurry. On the air, sirens sang the precursor to *Jailhouse Rock*. Larry hadn't thought about the middle steps, just *get money, fix roof*. Thinking was usually Jack's area of expertise.

"Shit, what'll we do?"

"No trouble, get inside and listen close to old Jacky."

"Got it."

Doors slammed. Cruiser tires cut divots in the lawn.

"Larry, we know you're in there. Come out with your hands over your head," the voice of Chief Moran said through a squeaky megaphone.

"Shit." Larry rubbed his head and peeked through the mobile clothes rack once belonging to his dead mother and then through the bedroom window behind it. There were several men pointing shotguns at the house. A few held handguns. "What now?"

"Seems as if we went about this all wrong. Insurance money is the ticket. Burn the house, create a diversion, we'll hit the road and you can collect the insurance for the house burning."

"You think they'll let me collect? I mean, I shot two ghost people."

"You said it, only ghost people. Now, let's go. Lighter fluid my boy, a little dab'll do ya."

"Right."

"Start upstairs. Do as I say and we'll be smooth sailing."

"Right."

The megaphone squeaked. "Larry, last chance or we're coming in and you'll have a hell of a lot more places to shit from than you did when you woke up this morning!"

"Jesus, fire. Chief, fire!" a pistol-pointing officer said.

The flames jumped quickly. The upper floors were bright red, orange, blue, and green swaying with the hot dance of destruction. Smoke poured and within seconds, the windows on the main floor had burst outwards with flames. Engulfed and hungry for more, the heat feasted.

"Larry!" The chief was angry all over that megaphone.

The officers rolled their cruisers back, doors open, weapons pointed in the general direction.

"Larry, if you're in there—!"

"Hey!" Another officer pointed his shotgun at the storm cellar door swinging open. "Freeze, now!"

The flames jumped from behind Larry and Jack as the rusty, leaky, nearly empty, furnace oil tank exploded. Shrapnel cut through the air like wayward, malformed ninja stars.

Larry fell and Jack fell. The sack from the bank flew, unnoticed, across the yard and into the pine trees that Larry's grandfather had planted seventy-two years prior.

Pain seared up Larry's back.

Jack screeched in a throaty growl, "Larry! Larry my boy!"

"Jack! It hurts!"

A piece of the doorframe had splintered with the explosion and fired into Larry's left kidney. The officers converged on Larry. The first in line was Wendell Henry. Wendell's cousin Marie took a shot through the cheek less than an hour earlier. Wendell lost his virginity to Marie, and he loved his cousin dearly even though they never again mentioned what they'd done that one magical afternoon when she was fifteen and he was fourteen. He stomped on that hunk of wood jutting from Larry's kidney as payback.

Larry writhed in the grass. "Jaaack!"

A second officer planted a foot into Larry's face. The lights inside vacated the man's eyes.

While the chief wrote the official report of how Larry died

from damages due to an explosion—leaving out that the officers had tap-danced on his head—the volunteer fire department doused the embers of the fallen house.

Once quiet, only the three rookie firefighters remained. It was twilight and the flames had long quit creeping, but fire was a wily thing and needed to be babysat, even after the fact.

"Way I see it, only one of us gots to stay," Leeman Henry said.

"That's right," Travis Henry seconded.

"Way I see it, you're the newest, so it ought to be you."

"That's right."

Candy Lafontaine was used to the macho bullshit, the grab-assery, and the muddy end of the stick. It was the cost of being a woman in a man's world. Since a girl, she wanted to be a fire*man* and damned if what was between her legs was ever going to stand in her way.

"Fine," Candy said.

"Good."

"Good."

The Henry brothers left in their Dodge and Candy hunkered down in the blackened grass. She stared at the former building and wondered what went through Larry Sullivan's mind. The crew told stories while they monitored the remnants, discussed how he'd always been *soft*, even a little *touched*. But folks were difficult to believe after these kinds of things happened.

From where she sat, Candy saw the sun reflect against the shiny black shoe of an old doll. She scooted across the dry grass in her bulky pants. It was heavy, wooden; a marionette without strings, paint chipping, and a fairly glaring modern modification. Where the typical Pinocchio-style face should've been was a soft bulb, like a sock-puppet's head. A silk-screened Jack Nicholson face rose from the wood like an eerie balloon.

"Hello there, Mr. McMurphy," she said, recognizing the image from the film *One Flew Over the Cuckoo's Nest.*

"Hello, Candy. Lookin' for a pal?"

Somehow, this felt *normal.* His voice was an elixir.

"Sure am, R.P."

"That's a character, I'm Jack."

"Nice to meet you, Jack."

"Back at'cha. Wanna hear a juicy bit of gossip, Candy my girl?"

"Sure do."

"There's a big bag of bank money in those trees and if you take me with you, I'll show you where to find it. Hell, I could even do ya the favor of life coaching. You'd like that, wouldn't ya?"

"Sure. I could use it."

"Ain't that just sweet. Stick with Jacky and things will always turn out sweet. Just like your name, Candy. Just. Like. Your. Name."

Jack led Candy to the bag and they rode off into the sunset in Candy's Corolla.

I Could be an Albert Tillman
Michael Grimala

The dog park has a way of turning everyone into a crone. Men and women, old and young, it doesn't matter—there's just something about the place that transforms ordinary people into unabashed gossips.

It's human nature, I guess. People are social, and for the husbands and wives in this neighborhood, they do their socializing in the same place as their dogs. I think the climate of Las Vegas makes it worse. I've lived here for three years, and the heat really is something else. It forces the dog owners to gather in the slivers of shade provided by the Palo Verde trees that line the big, grassy field at Heritage Park. And in close quarters, the groups naturally mingle. They talk. They align.

That's what drew me to Darla. Like me, she was more concerned with her dogs than the latest upper middle-class dirt. I'd been bringing my dog Runner to that park every day after work since I adopted him a year earlier, and in all that time Darla was the only other regular who didn't fit into the crowd.

The first time I noticed her she was on opposite side of the park, walking behind her French bulldog and her big Pitbull as they circled the perimeter. Her dogs generally stuck together, and wherever they went, she stayed close behind. While the two dozen other owners huddled around the shady benches near the entrance, Darla and I existed as the only two not attached to the larger group. I could hardly take my eyes off her; for the hour she was there, she didn't say a word to anyone.

She showed up every day around dusk, the same time as me. I kept my distance, content to return her nods whenever her pups and my Jack Russell crossed paths. Whenever Runner showed particular interest in the Pitbull, Darla made a point to crouch down and scratch his little ears.

That went on for a month, until I arrived on an unseasonably cool day to find that Darla and I were the only people in the park. When I clanged the gate closed behind me, she looked up from across the grass and smiled. First time. Her dogs also looked up, all three of them in unison. I remember that.

I waved. It was an impulse and I immediately regretted putting myself out there like that, but she waved back. "Hi," she called. And that was it. I walked across the park, Runner at my heels, and introduced myself.

We talked. The Frenchie was Petal, the pit was Pitty. They lived on the other side of town in Anthem, one of the city's upscale locales and easily a thirty-minute drive from this park. I mentioned my job as a digital editor. She didn't work; rich husband, I assumed. Her dogs were purebreds, both one year old, on special order from a breeder in Arizona. Mine was a rescue I scooped from a local shelter.

And that was the extent of it. Other regulars showed up,

one by one, and Darla and I went our separate ways for the next hour. Occasionally we'd catch each other's eye from across the field. That was enough. Let the rest of the crones play their game of telephone—she and I had a real connection.

We began saying hello regularly. Then we started walking together, and even talking just a little. She had a way of saying something, then tagging her statement with an additional thought—nothing more than a quick murmur—and it made me laugh every time.

Our dogs got along. Darla clearly loved Pitty. She liked Petal, too, but she *loved* that big Pitbull. On the rare occasion when another dog would approach Pitty, Darla would lock her focus on the interaction, as though Pitty couldn't take care of herself. In reality she was the biggest dog in the park, but Darla was protective. Petal was allowed to wander a little, but Darla never strayed more than a step or two away from Pitty.

Sometimes Darla brought her dogs in the morning instead, and that was the worst. Whenever I got to the park at sunset and Darla wasn't there, it felt like the entire day was a waste. I'd put in my hour with Runner, throwing his ball back and forth, but my heart wasn't in it. Seeing the assembled gossips on those days only made me angrier.

Darla eventually devised a system. Near the back of the park behind some trees there was an old pumping cabinet sunk into the ground. Sort of like a fuse box for the park's irrigation system, but a newer sprinkler set had been installed recently and this little box was now useless and forgotten. On days when Darla went in the morning, she would leave a note in the box. Kid stuff, I know, but I loved it. I read the notes (usually just a line or two, often unrelated to anything we had ever spoken about), turned them over, wrote a response on the back and returned them to the box.

Once in a while Darla showed up with bruises on her arms and legs. She didn't attempt to cover it with clothing. It was Pitty, she'd say. That dog played rough and it was fine.

Three months into our burgeoning friendship, Darla didn't show at all. That wasn't so unusual, but there was no note in the box, either. The next day, same thing: no Darla, no note. On the third day I called into work and took a sick day so I could bring Runner to the park in the morning. It must have been the most crowded day of the year at Heritage Park; most of the dusk regulars were there, while others were unfamiliar to me. But no sign of Darla.

I had no other way of contacting her. I knew very little about her. No phone number, no address, no email. I didn't even know what kind of vehicle she drove; she parked in an auxiliary lot across the street, and she never accepted any of my offers to give her a lift to her car.

On the fourth day I couldn't concentrate at work so I went home at lunchtime, grabbed Runner and brought him to the park. The triple-digit heat at that time of day ensured it would be empty, so I unleashed Runner and let him have his run of the place while I made my way to the box.

Sweat saturated my shirt after walking less than fifty yards, but as I approached the box it became apparent someone had been there. The dirt on the ground around it was scuffed. I practically dove to my knees and lifted the lid, and there it was. A sheet of notebook paper folded over twice.

"Meet me tonight," it read. "442 Astol Drive, Anthem.

7:30. Bring Runner!"

I scooped up Runner and went home to spend the next six hours alternating between relief that she was all right and anxiety about meeting her in the real world for the first time.

As I neared 442 Astol, the anxiety won out. Driving past all the McMansions made me acutely aware that not only was I meeting Darla outside the comfort zone of Heritage Park, I was in an entirely different world than the one that housed my modest one-bedroom apartment on the east side of the Las Vegas valley.

Darla stood outside on the sidewalk as I pulled up to the house. She flashed a quick smile and looked down. Petal and Pitty stopped poking around the large front yard and came to greet Runner as he leapt out the passenger window, towing his slack leash behind him.

"You're early," she said. It was low-pitched and adorable.

I couldn't think of anything to say, so the panicky truth came out.

"I was worried. Where have you been?"

Her shoulders dipped as she let out a sigh (also adorable in its own way). "I haven't been able to make it the past few days. The girls missed you."

It was true. Petal and Pitty were usually as reserved as their owner, but on that day they bumped against my legs, begging to be acknowledged. Happy girls.

I still couldn't figure out what to say. Darla clipped a leash onto Petal and walked along the driveway, across the street and around the corner. Pitty was not on a leash but never wandered beyond arm's length of Darla.

When we turned onto the next street, Darla took Runner's leash from me, brushing her hand against mine in one gentle motion. We walked around the block like that.

"Are you worried about your neighbors?" I asked.

"These people? Because they might see me walking my dog, accompanied by an unfamiliar man?" She laughed, then added a murmur. "I'll survive until the next neighborhood affair consumes their attention."

You can probably guess which word caught my attention. And the casual way she threw it out there, I had a hard time hearing anything else she said.

As we circled the block and made our way back toward Astol, all I could think about was Darla eventually passing the leash back to me. Another chance for our hands to touch. I increased my walking pace without even realizing it, that's how much I wanted to get back to 442 for the leash exchange. But Darla never broke stride; she fell behind by a couple steps and I slowed to let her catch up.

When we reached the house I made my move and reached for the leash, but Darla had already turned up the driveway with Pitty and Petal and Runner alongside her. She didn't turn back or say anything, so I followed them to the front door.

She led us all inside. Going from the desert heat to the chill of the air-conditioned house raised goosebumps on my arms. Darla unclipped the dogs and hung the leashes on a peg, then mounted the stairs to the second floor.

The house had the sparsely-furnished, undecorated aesthetic of a chain hotel. As I climbed the stairs, I noticed the ornate fireplace in the center of the expansive living room.

The mantle lay empty.

The master bedroom sat just as sterile and unlived. Petal and Runner sniffed around the closet and the dresser, while Pitty jumped straight up onto the massive bed and curled up in the middle. She never took her eyes off her human.

I stood in the corner just inside the door as Darla sat on the bed and embraced the big Pitbull, hugging her and scratching her neck and ears. When the pup was placated, Darla hoisted the hundred-pounder and lugged her out into the hallway. Pitty sat and stared into the room as Darla closed the door between them.

Darla pulled me onto the bed and we consummated the affair in a way that would have definitely consumed the neighbors' attention.

Runner and Petal busied themselves around the room, barely acknowledging our activities. Pitty barked once from the hallway but was otherwise silent. Twice during our act, Darla looked toward the door.

Afterward, Darla opened up to let Pitty back in, and with the light from the hall framing her nude body I could make out bruises on the back of Darla's legs. Deep, almost black contusions that covered her upper thighs. The dog jumped back onto the bed and nestled itself between us. That's when Darla asked me to kill her husband.

Like with most things, she was direct with her words. I didn't even ask for an explanation.

She told me to check our message box at the dog park tomorrow, and that was the last we spoke of it.

Driving home, I didn't think much about the murder I had

just agreed to commit; my mind was completely occupied with the worst thing I had ever done, in my estimation. It happened almost ten years ago, in my post-college unemployed days. While browsing at a bargain department store at the mall, I overheard a woman approach the customer service desk to turn in a lost wallet.

"The license says Albert Tillman," she said as she handed it over to the teenage clerk. "There's cash and cards inside. I found it on the floor over there."

"Thank you ma'am," the boy said. "I'll make an announcement."

The good Samaritan left and I hovered near the service desk, just out of the clerk's sight. I had never stolen anything before, or really done anything in my life that could have been considered "wrong." But something got inside of me. I didn't even need the money that badly, it was simply a matter of opportunity.

A few minutes went by without a P.A. announcement, and I couldn't hold off the impulse any longer. I didn't know what the wallet's owner looked like, but I was sure I could pass for him if I went in with confidence. I could be an Albert Tillman.

I went to the desk and looked the clerk in the eye. "Excuse me, but I think I left my wallet somewhere in your store."

He sparked with recognition. "Oh, I'm sorry to hear that. You can't buy our stuff if you don't have your wallet! What's the name? I can check the lost and found."

"Albert Tillman."

The clerk smiled and produced the wallet from underneath the counter. "You're a lucky man. A very kind woman just turned it in. She said everything is still inside."

Without even bothering to look at the photo identification, he held out the leather wallet and I pulled it from his hand. I opened and rifled through the compartments for show. There was a decent amount of cash.

"Thank god. I've got a flight in three days and I need the I.D." That lie came to me on the spot, unnecessary but a nice touch. I was reveling in it, I can see that now.

"Happy to help," he said in a way that conveyed our exchange was over. "Enjoy your trip."

If I remember, the billfold held about two-hundred and fifty dollars in cash and a few credit cards. I kept the money and dumped the rest of the wallet in a trash can on the other side of the mall. For whatever it's worth, it turns out I did look a little like the guy in the driver's license photo.

Darla was absent from the park again the next day, and the day after that. This time it was expected. I discreetly checked the box every time, and on the third day I found her note.

"Midnight to 2 a.m. tonight. He'll be home. Disconnected the security cams. Lower left drawer, take everything. Leave it here. We'll need it."

The romantic postscript read "Please burn this page."

I parked off the street in a school playground about a mile from 442 Astol and walked. I tried to appear nonchalant while also obscuring my face from the myriad doorbell cameras that were surely pointed toward the street in this high-income area.

The house stood completely dark except for one illuminated window on the second floor. From first-hand experience, I knew that to be the master bedroom.

The front door was unlocked and pushed in silently when I turned the knob. I had considered going around back or entering through the garage, but I didn't want to attract any more attention than I had to—I figured walking through the front door with confidence would be the best way to not look out of place.

As soon as the door closed behind me, Pitty and Petal came to greet me. I had forgotten about the dogs, of all things. I froze. One loud bark to alert the homeowner and I was finished. Then it dawned on me: These girls knew me. Instead of growling (or worse), the pups just nosed at my hand until I patted them on the head. Then they turned around and left me to my business.

When I got to the upstairs landing, the bedroom door stood open. The same door Darla had closed to give us privacy from her favorite dog just a few days ago. I pressed my back against the hallway wall and took deep breaths. I wasn't a killer. I wasn't even a bad person. But, I reminded myself, I could be an Albert Tillman.

On the silent count of three I readied the only weapon I could procure on such short notice—a butcher's knife I had shoplifted from a thrift store the day before—and whirled into the room.

The light I had seen from the street was actually coming from the master bathroom, and it was apparently serving as a night light. The man lay in bed, fast asleep, the soft glow from the adjacent room outlining the blanket as it rose and subsided with each breath. I looked at him and tried to imagine how someone like him could get so close to Darla. He knew everything about her, good and bad. That was all I wanted. I envied the man I was about to kill.

I did it quickly, with one long, deep slit, and rushed out of the room. I waited outside, pressed against the wall, and listened to him die.

Downstairs in the study the dogs sprawled on the carpet, nodding off. They barely lifted their heads toward me as I opened the desk's lower left drawer. It stuck a bit, so I lifted it up off its track and pulled the whole thing out of the cabinet. In the empty space behind the drawer I found four brick-sized stacks of fifty-dollar bills, each sealed in plastic wrap.

The drawer itself contained paperwork. Why Darla wanted it, I didn't know. I gathered the papers and the cash and stuffed it all into a plastic grocery bag, then replaced the drawer.

I said goodbye to Pitty and Petal—they again couldn't be bothered to look up—and exited through the front door. I was at the dog park an hour later, neatly depositing the cash and papers into the disused sprinkler box. And as a gesture to Darla, I struck a match and lit her note on fire until it burned away and just one blank corner of the page remained. I shook out the blaze and placed the corner piece on top of the cash, closed the box and went home.

The day after the plan was devised I had put in for three weeks of vacation; it was all I had accrued in my time at my job, and though it was short notice I got approved. I had eighteen days left. I loaded Runner into the car and made the three-hour drive to Barstow, just across the California border. I had chosen the city solely for the cheap hotel rates.

I spent the next seventeen nights at a two-star joint in Barstow, just "laying low" as we had planned. As difficult as it was to have no contact with Darla, I knew the stakes. I never so much as did an internet search on the murder; I didn't want to know, and I didn't want that in my browser history if something went wrong and a police technician found himself digging through every cyber-inch of my machine.

I took Runner to a local Barstow dog park twice a day. Different grass, different trees, same groups of people. I kept to myself.

When my vacation time was exhausted I road-tripped back to Las Vegas, though I still had another week to go before our predetermined rendezvous. I spent the next six days watching the clock at work; at night I stayed in my apartment, tossing Runner's miniature tennis ball back and forth. One day after work I had an incredible urge to drive past the dog park, or Astol, or anywhere I might be able to glimpse Darla, but I kept my head down and went straight home.

On the agreed-upon date I woke up early to call in sick, which really displeased my supervisor. I can't say I blamed him, as my attendance and the quality of my work had become erratic. I suppose as a novice offender I couldn't help acting guilty.

I arrived at the park before eight a.m. and Runner had the place to himself. I realized my hands were shaking when I set down his bowl, splashing water all over the place. I let five minutes pass, then strolled to the back of the park. The layer of dirt on the box's lid was disturbed.

The compartment was full. The cash and the papers were still there. The corner of note, too, was wedged up against the side of the box. Darla had been there. I knew it. The papers had been leafed through.

The plan had been for Darla to take the papers (I don't think she knew about the cash; I figured that would be a nice surprise) and leave a note telling me where to meet her once all the police attention had calmed down. That plan was now void and I left the park trembling.

I spent the next month at Heritage Park, obsessively going every morning and every evening. Some days I'd leave Runner at home—with all the exercise, I had to double his food intake in order to keep his weight up—and sit in my car alone, just watching the people go in and out. Waiting.

I was standing in the back with Runner, a full two months after the murder, when she appeared. She walked in through the gate just as natural as could be and made her way around the perimeter, just like the first day I saw her.

The little Frenchie. Petal.

Without even realizing it I jogged to the middle of the park and took in a panoramic view of everyone inside the gates. I counted about twenty people, most of them familiar but none of them Darla—and no Pitty, either. Just Petal.

I stood there, tense and sweating. Eventually a middle-aged woman in a sun dress caught up to Petal. I didn't recognize her. I retreated to the trees and tried to stay out of sight. If things had gone bad for Darla and this other woman was involved somehow, I didn't want her to see my face. As far as I was concerned, this was the last time I would ever set foot in Heritage Park.

For the next ten minutes, Sun Dress made the rounds with

Petal. It looked like they had a rapport.

The woman worked her way around the park, and then back to the benches near the entrance. She talked to a younger woman and they got into a conversation, as people do at the park. An older man leaned in and offered his two cents. Within minutes the woman was holding court for a half-dozen regulars.

It may have been a mistake, but my inner crone got the better of me. I moved toward the group, slowly and deliberately, and milled about in the shade, close enough to overhear the conversation without joining in.

"I always knew it was shady," Sun Dress said. "He never gave me a good reason for keeping the house after we moved out."

She was a natural in this setting. She spoke clearly and emoted like a woman who spent most of her adult life entertaining at parties. She had found an audience at the dog park, and now she was spilling the tea.

"They would have pinned it on me if I hadn't been out of town when it happened," she said. "They always try to blame the spouse. But now they've got no one. They talked to his business partners and our dog walker. That's it. No leads. I haven't heard from those lousy cops in over a week."

"That's so awful," said one of the listeners.

"Thank goodness for Petal," Sun Dress said. "To be honest I never cared much for the dogs. They were Jonathan's babies. After it happened, the walker offered to take the Pitbull for a few days. She knew I couldn't handle them both by myself, especially with everything else that was going on. I didn't know the first thing about taking care of a dog."

She reached down and lifted Petal into her arms, gently rocking her like a baby.

"Now I don't know what I would do without this little girl. I just wish I could get the other one back, now that I know how much I'd love her. But I can't find the walker. Her phone was disconnected. She's got our dog and I have no idea how to get in touch with her."

"That's not right," said the older man. "Have you tried a Facebook search?"

"I don't even know her last name. Jonathan hired her. I have no idea where he found her. I just know she seemed really attached to that dog."

"I remember her," said one of the regulars. "We used to see her here all the time. Nice girl, but quiet. I don't think anyone ever talked to her."

That wasn't true. I talked to her. I even walked with her sometimes.

I took a couple steps back, retreating further into the shade.

"I think she mentioned once that she has family in Florida," Sun Dress said. "But that's all I know. So I suppose it's just me and Petal now."

The listeners kept the conversation going, pledging to let her know if they saw Pitty at the park again and tastefully (or so they thought) prying for more information about the murder. But I stopped listening.

I grabbed Runner and went home, heading straight for the hall closet. I pulled a duffel bag from the back, unzipped it and let the contents empty onto the floor: four wrapped stacks of cash and about a dozen pages of paperwork.

I flipped through the papers for the first time. I had been too afraid to do it since I removed it all from the sprinkler box weeks ago.

Among other things, I found veterinary information, registration forms and a breeder's certificate for Petal. There was nothing for the other dog.

That's why Darla didn't take the money. She didn't care about it. All she had really wanted was Pitty.

And now that she had all the pertinent paperwork, from a legal standpoint that dog was hers.

I put all the papers and cash back into the duffel bag and stuffed some clothes in as well.

I typed out an email to work, letting them know I wouldn't be coming in again. I'm absolutely certain they were fine with that.

Then I did an internet search.

I tossed the duffel bag into my car, rolled down the passenger window just enough for Runner to stick out his nose, and hit the road.

According to my search, there are two hundred and eighty-six dog parks in Florida.

I'm sure the regulars talk.

Lemonhead

W. T. Paterson

Think of it like a movie from the early 2000's. It's the only way this story makes any real sense.

There's this girl named Asha. Her name is both hip and a little Russian sounding, so she's endearing and a tad villainous. Imagine that Asha is only ever filmed at a 45-degree angle. She's unstable, hence the angle. We come upon her entering the halls of a typical high school. She wears a black leather skirt, white tank, and a fluffy fur coat – looking like she's coming off of a massive hangover. She touches her pulsing head. Her finger probes an odd bruise at the base of her skull.

Asha's hair is done up in a bun, but not tight like a ballerina, a messy one like someone tried to make hair by balling hay into their fist. The morning sun spills through the windows like the touch of God as Asha slips a box of lemonhead candies into her jacket pocket. The box has something written in sharpie – a string of numbers reading 7532659. It could be an address, a phone number, or a code. A bloody fingerprint covers the lemonhead logo. The blood is dried, but the imprint is distinct.

Classmates whisper as Asha passes, but she winks and blows them a kiss. Mascara trails etch their way down her cheek like she's been crying. She beelines past the rigid principal with his wire glasses hanging off of his nose, male pattern baldness, and a sweater vest. He is stern, but checks her out when she's down the hall. It's supposed to be a little funny because such moments were considered funny in the early 2000's.

"Asha!" says a kid who jogs to catch up. Robbie: the loveable, shag-haired nerd. There's a full backpack slung over his shoulder and his short sleeved collared shirt is unbuttoned to show a graphic tee with a science design beneath. Asha wipes her eyes and fist bumps him.

"Rough night," Asha says, and Robbie takes off his backpack. He unzips the top, pulls out a folder, and hands it to Asha.

"I've got you, Lemonhead" he says. "Stayed up all night to finish." It could be homework, or a term paper, and it looks like Asha has been using the loveable nerd to get her work done.

"Robbie…" she says and kisses him on the cheek.

"You'll be there tonight?" Robbie asks. "Eight o'clock, sharp."

"Wouldn't miss it," Asha says, and we have our first ticking clock.

The school bell rings and the halls empty. Asha ducks into a bathroom, closes herself into a rickety green stall, and pulls the box of lemonheads from her pocket. She shakes the box and dumps a small blue pill into her palm. She puts the half-full box of candies into her purse.

Pill to tongue, her eyes go wide, pupils expanding like flowers opening in timelapse. Imagine a montage of smash cuts for everything that happens next. Asha answers questions about Jackson Pollock in art class, explains the breaking point of a wooden door in physics, walks into the girl's locker rooms to use a shower to wash her hands, and throws up into a trash bin at lunch. While she vomits, she gets flashes of the previous night where before there was only blank space. She sees fragments of a murder, a smoking gun in her hands, a dead body at her feet in a back alley.

Dudes at a nearby table try to look up her skirt while she's hunched over the trash bin, but Asha pays them no mind as she cleanses the palette with an actual lemonhead candy.

Somehow, when the clock strikes 3pm, she's sober and a message comes through on her pager, because that's what people had back then, and so she goes to the payphone near the gymnasium and dials a number. A voice on the other end says: "You're a lying bitch!" It's the unfortunate reality of sexist dialogue in the early part of the 21st Century. Asha rolls her eyes and digs through her purse. She pushes aside a roll of 100's – maybe ten grands worth, and finds the box of lemonheads. Looking at the string of numbers, she hovers her finger over the keypad on the phone. She pulls away. Then, she dials.

"This is Leon," a smooth voice answers, and Asha smiles with relief. She leans against the school wall, phone to ear, lemonhead rolling between her fingers.

"It's me," she says.

"You good, Lemonhead?" Leon asks.

"Let's talk," she says. "In person." Asha hangs up and heads back to class while sucking the candy.

Lemonhead

"Remember," a teacher reminds everyone, "Reports are due Monday." Asha turns around and sees Robbie. He winks and nods at the folder on her desk. The top of it reads "Project: Save Asha." She blows him a kiss.

Asha leaves school when the bell rings and jumps into her red convertible. She drives away with the top down. Post-industrial music blasts through the speakers, something electronic and lined with heavy guitars – a Nine-Inch Nails wannabe type number – played by a band she's already forgotten the name of. She drives from the burbs into the city to meet up with Leon.

Leon lives in a large brick studio apartment. He's an artist – a painter to be exact – and he's unusually muscular. He wears overalls with no shirt and his bangs are so long that he tucks them behind his ears. When Asha buzzes to be let in, Leon unlocks the door and goes back to painting.

"New piece?" Asha asks when she enters. The door to Leon's place is a large sliding metal piece like a barn door, but modern.

"Working through something," Leon says. He says it like he's got years of wisdom tucked in that paintbrush of his. He adds a stroke to the canvas, though the canvas is splattered with red paint in no discernible design.

Asha pulls out her roll of 100's. "Something happened." Leon looks at her and sighs.

"Shit," he says, and puts down his brush. "What do you remember?" There's a shower with a glass door near his bed and Leon walks to it. He turns on the hot water and runs his paint-stained hands under warm water.

"Popanski paged me earlier, and..."

"Popanski?!" Leon says, and turns off the water. He looks out the window, then rushes to his door to make sure its locked. "Did anyone follow you here?"

"No, I..."

"You need to leave," Leon says. "Now." He takes Asha under the arm and leads her to the large door. When he slides it open, a short man with a leather jacket over a red Hawaiian shirt is standing there flanked by two enormous black men in sunglasses. They're black because representation in the early 2000's wasn't that great.

"Asha, Asha, sweet little lying Asha," Popanski says stroking his goatee while stepping inside the brick studio apartment. A gold chain dangles around his neck and threatens to tangle in the almost-excessive chest hair. "I believe you have something for me."

One of the enormous guys grabs Asha's purse and dumps it. He sorts through the car keys, used tissues, box of lemonheads, and roll of 100's.

"Ain't here, boss," the thug says. Popanski puts a toothpick between his teeth and the way he chews it reflects how pissed he is.

"Where is it?" he asks.

"She doesn't have it," Leon says, and Popanksi shoots him a look. Leon backs down.

"You don't know what I can do to you, girlie," Popanski says.

"I'll get it to you. By midnight. Big Bad Wolf," she says. It's the blue pill he's looking for. She doesn't know why she knows this, but she does.

"Eight this evening, or we erase your memory the old-fashioned way," Popanski says. Coinciding ticking clocks come up on soundtrack. He points his finger at her and the two enormous black men crack their knuckles. They leave and Leon collects his things. A hairbrush, an overnight bag, and a small canvas.

"Find the Chemist," he says. "He'll know what to do." Asha pleads with Leon to stay, but he makes it clear that she's on her own.

"I'll see you at eight," Asha says. "Robbie's thing."

"Wouldn't miss it," Leon says, and climbs out onto his fire escape. He pokes his head in through the open window. "Asha, what do you remember about last night?"

Asha pulls the jacket from her shoulder. There's a fresh tattoo, a symbol that could be a swirling molecule. The proton and neutron are yellow. The nucleus is blue.

"I got this, whatever *this* is," she says, then shrugs the jacket back on and leaves through the large metal door. Leon looks worried, his face framed by the open window.

While driving to find the Chemist, Asha has sudden flashes of memory. They explode in her mind like thunder.

In the memory, Asha is younger. She's hiding in a closet. Someone enters Asha's bedroom using her name like a taunt. Asha covers her mouth to keep silent the whimpers from behind the closet door. The person sits on the edge of her bed and grabs a teddy bear. He kisses the teddy on the nose. It reads as a warning. He leaves a box of lemonhead candies on the pillow.

Asha pushes against her eyes while she's driving to shake the memory, then slams on her brakes to avoid rear-ending the slowing traffic. She sweats and breathes heavy. Another memory explodes.

She's in the closet, but the closet is enormous, endless, grotesque. A hand on her shoulder, she turns to find Leon. He is four times her size. She steps away and trips over Robbie, who is four times smaller and asleep on a miniature bed. He wakes up and wails, and Asha throws a hand over his mouth to stifle the sound. The enormous closet doors open to blinding light and Asha screams.

A neighboring car in traffic looks over at Asha confused. Asha realizes she screamed in real life, not just her memory.

"Good song," she says in a desperate attempt to cover, and turns up the radio. It's Mm-Bop by Hansen. Comic relief. The neighboring car rolls down their window all the way like they're about to give her a piece of their mind, but the driver turns up their radio also playing Mm-Bop. Double whammy. They exchange thumbs ups and Asha pulls into an offramp. At a stoplight, she sees how bad she's sweating and agonizes in pain. She peels off her fur jacket to check out her fresh tattoo. She pulls the box of lemonheads from her purse and pops one into her mouth. After a moment, she sighs a breath of relief like whatever caused the flashback had fully passed.

It's nearing sundown and the sky hums light a like the static between radio stations. For some reason, it all feels familiar, like she's done this before, like it's déjà vu, like her body remembers something that her mind does not. That's when she realizes the numbers written on the lemonhead box are an address, not a phone number. So she pulls a U-turn to go to building 753 at 26th and 59th. The Chemist can wait.

After a while, she pulls up. Her body goes tense like the memory of a headache. The residential building is boarded up with plywood across the windows and door, even though a fragile, hunched woman brushes dust and sand from the concrete steps. Across the street, a tattoo parlor door jingles with an exiting client.

"Back already," the woman says. It's warm and gentle, welcoming.

"Have we met?" Asha asks. Her cheeks burn with embarrassment for having to ask.

"Last night," the woman says. "You grew up here. Aren't you that girl?"

"What girl?" Asha asks.

"The one from the news. This was your foster home, you and those two boys. Robbie and Leon. You were here last night," the woman says. Asha tries to remember but can't place much of the past. She walks over and touches the concrete steps, feels the iron railing, and her body shrinks with terror. It remembers something that her mind does not.

"I did grow up here," Asha says like she's lost in a dream. "They called me Lemonhead because of my hair."

"Is it true?" the woman asks. "I don't mean to pry, but what they did to you here…bless your soul. If I were on that jury, I'd have tripled the amount you all received."

Asha nods. Though her mind does not remember, her body does.

"Was anyone here with me last night?" Asha asks.

"A man," the woman says. "Both of you just stared at the

boarded-up windows. Not to speak ill of the dead, but let's just say I wasn't surprised when the bodies of your foster parents were found in that alley."

"Yeah, me neither," Asha chuckles, but isn't sure why.

"The woman, your foster mother, has her brother been by to see you at all? He owns that club downtown, the Big Bad Wolf. Popanski, I think? Comes around here and there asking about you. I don't tell him anything, kind of a menacing gentleman if you ask me. But he's always curious about you and your brothers and where to find y'all."

The world scratches to a stop like a needle dragging across a record player.

"No, he hasn't. Thanks," Asha says. She goes to her car and sits down. Across the street, the tattoo parlor's window glows with a green and pink neon rose. She gets out and crosses the street. Tatted tattoo artists sit inside.

"Hey," one of them says. "Welcome back. How's the ink?"

"I don't remember much about last night, and I was hoping..." Asha says.

"You signed a waiver, lady," one of them says. "You swore up and down you were sober."

"No, no," Asha says. She pulls the arm out of the jacket to show them her shoulder where two yellow orbs circle a blue one in the center. "Why did I want this specific design?"

"You said the yellow dots were you and your little bro, and the blue one was your big bro, that combined, you were the elemental foundation of a real family."

Asha's brain unlocks more memories and they flood her senses like the distorted synth track of an industrial rock song.

Robbie hiding, Asha being pulled from the closet, Leon trying in vain to break down the bedroom door.

"Your dad ever get ahold of you? Short guy in a red shirt. Goatee. Came in like an hour later asking if we'd seen you. Said he was worried. Gave'm your number and he gave us VIP passes to Big Bad. We're not supposed to do that but, I mean, VIP."

"I've gotta go," Asha says, and runs to her car – got to find the Chemist. She peels off.

She gets to a suburban house, a single-story ranch with a minivan in the driveway. The front lawn is littered with things like a soccer ball, a tricycle, and large plastic playhouse. Asha knocks on the door. A man with coke-bottle glasses and wild hair answers wearing only board shorts and flip flops. He is tan and looks like he just came from the beach.

"Nice lawn," Asha says.

"Déjà vu," the guy says, and the moment Asha steps inside, she sees the house is filled with science equipment. Beakers, vials, Bunsen burners, lab coats, industrial refrigerators.

"I think I'm in trouble," Asha says, and the man – the Chemist – puts on a shirt.

He says, "Sit down."

Asha sits in a reclining chair, the type usually found inside of a dentist's office. The Chemist pulls over a disc light on an extendable arm and tells Asha to look at the ceiling.

"I'm having lapses in memory," she says.

"Distorted?" the Chemist asks, and Asha nods. "Shit," he says. He turns the light on and Asha's pupils dilate. She gets flashes of a violent assault, a murder, the smoking gun. In a storefront reflection, she sees herself holding the gun and standing over the body.

"I don't know what's real, or imagined, or dreamed," she whispers. The Chemist sits back.

"Acid?" he asks. Asha shakes her head no and pulls the box of lemonheads from her purse. The chemist takes the box and notices the thumbprint.

"I don't remember whose blood that is," Asha says, following his eyes. She sits back in the chair. The blinding light clicks off.

"What's happening to me?" she asks, and the Chemist with his wild hair and coke-bottle glasses tells her that there was a recent scientific breakthrough, that doctors and scientists thought they had found a gland in the brain that controls the aging process. He explains that by fiddling with that gland, they thought they could extend human life by another hundred years or so.

"But that's not what happened," the Chemist says. These doctors leaked information too early without understanding the consequences of their work and by the time they realized it wasn't anti-aging, that manipulating the gland meant extracting physical memories, they were in too deep. Mob bosses and gang leaders showed up demanding memories be extracted. They wanted plausible deniability for their crimes, a way to beat the polygraphs or convince juries. They wanted their memories gone so that if they ever got captured, their secrets would be safe elsewhere.

"These doctors found a way to place the memories into pills," the Chemist says. "Whoever takes the pills becomes the new owner of the memories."

"Dr. Stevens," Asha says, and the Chemist stiffens when he hears his name. "Where are my memories?"

"Don't call me that," the Chemist says. "And you asked me to do this."

"Say what?" Asha asks.

"Extract your memories of..." and the Chemist pauses. "It was the anniversary...I begged you to reconsider, but you were manic and threatening suicide."

"What happened to me?!"

"Cross pollination," the Chemist says, "I think." He takes the box of lemonheads and shakes them with regretful, knowing eyes. "These candies, they were the only thing I could transfer the memories into. Each piece has different details. I only had enough materials for one pill, and that had already been used."

Asha realizes that she's been chomping her own fragmented memory all day long. Pieces are still missing, blank spots like clouds against the sun. But the blue pill inside the box...?

"Sorry, Lemonhead," Leon says, stepping into the room from the kitchen. "I never wanted any of this to happen."

Asha puts it together so fast that it hurts to breathe.

Split screen moment:

Left frame - Photo shot: blue pill – voiceover "...it was Leon's memory. The gun, the murder, the bodies...his doing."

Right frame – Live action: "You killed them?" Asha asks, and Leon doesn't move. He looks at the floor. She says, "Even if those horrible people had it coming, murder is murder."

Snap back to Full Screen real time:

Leon says, "I don't remember, but that's the whole the point."

Asha immediately understands that Popanski needs the blue pill for revenge, to hand it over to the police so they could unlock the memories and see what Leon had, to restore the slightest bit of honor to his dead sister's tarnished name.

"You came here together last night," the Chemist says. "The anniversary of your emancipation. You both had things you needed to forget."

"I went first," Leon says. "Perfect extraction. You wanted next. Said if we couldn't remove the memories, you'd kill yourself. Called Robbie and left a goodbye voicemail and everything. I called him back and explained you were having an episode."

The Chemist says, "I pushed the needle too deep into the gland. Pulled some short-term memory with it. Leon marked your candy box with the paint on his thumb and meant to take it with him. I wrote the address of your old foster home on the box just in case. I wanted to see what adverse mental effects might occur if either of you returned to the source of the trauma."

Leon adds, "You were out of it, so I drove you to school and you slept the rest of the night in the car. Forgot to grab the box until I was halfway home on the 2am bus."

"Popanski wants that memory," the Chemist says. "And we have an hour before he sends out his goons."

"How did he even know you performed an extraction?"

Asha asks. The Chemist looks at the floor and sighs.

"He's one of my regulars. When you two walked out last night, he put the pieces together."

"I have an idea," Asha says. "We can give him something better."

Leon looks at Asha, then to the Chemist.

There's a time lapse of the Chemist working on something, of liquid bubbling over a Bunsen burner, of the crystallization and hardening process, and then a fading transition as both Leon and Asha approach a bumping club. People in tight leather outfits mill about outside The Big Bad Wolf laughing and holding drinks. Music blasts from inside. Asha and Leon approach the large bald bouncer in a black suit.

"For Popanski," Asha says, and shows him a blue pill. The massive bouncer uses his earpiece to radio in. A moment later, he unlatches the velvet rope and waves them through.

"Up the stairs, take a left," he says, his voice barely audible over the heavy guitars and electronic drums. Asha and Leon ascend a flight of gated-iron steps. Two more bouncers guard a door.

"Popanski," Asha says, and holds up the pill. They nod and let them through. Inside is a quieter room that overlooks the dance floor. Popanski stands observing the club's attendees.

"You delivered," he says without turning around. "I was looking forward to hunting you down. Pity."

"Take it," Asha says, holding out the blue pill. Popanski turns and sees it between the girl's fingers and his lips pull back into a snarl.

"Yes," he says. He grabs Asha's wrist and peels the pill from her fingers, then pops it onto his tongue. "The police will need proof that what I'm saying is true. I'll give them details that only those involved will know. Detective Mullins is aware of the memory extraction ring and I'll be glad to give up you and your old doctor. I know all about the Chemist, about how he used to make house calls to deliver pills that made you forget, that he was working on some new way to blackout memory. Some of my deepest secrets are gone because of him. Brilliant, misguided man. He's....wait a minute..."

Popanski stops and his face goes slack. His eyes grow large and worried. He takes a step back in horror and bumps into the large glass window that overlooks the club's floor.

"Everything your sister and her husband did to me...it's now in you," Asha says. "All the horrible details compressed into one tiny pill. My lemonheads remolded and reprocessed."

"Oh God," Popanski says, and stumbles around the room. He places his hands against his head and shakes. Whatever he's seeing, it's painful. It's like nothing he's ever seen. "They promised me they didn't do it...that they'd never...they lied to me..."

"I've carried this in silence for years," Asha says, and Popanski falls to the ground in the fetal position. "No more bullshit. It's over."

"It's over," Popanski says, and Asha and Leon leave the room, go down the grated-iron steps, and to their car.

"We have twenty minutes to drive thirty miles," Leon says, and Asha grabs his wrist. She shakes her head: No.

"Won't make it in time," she says. "Robbie will understand."

Lemonhead

The red convertible whips through the empty streets. Leon leans back and watches the stars, but Asha breaks the 4th wall and looks directly into the camera.

"I know what you're thinking: so much plot, and there are holes everywhere, and that backstory got dark quick, but this is the early 2000's. People will call it daring and gritty because it touches on something real, but because it's fronted by a woman, it won't get the cred it deserves. You're probably wondering about that roll of 100's, too. Sometimes a person needs an exit strategy, and ten grand opens a lot of doors."

Movies from the early 2000's made some unusual style choices.

Cutaway to front of property – then snap to inside:

Robbie sits behind a birthday cake in the kitchen of a different foster home. We see pictures of an older couple after they took Robbie in, posing with Robbie at a science fair, shaking hands with a senator, and a framed acceptance letter with full ride to Stanford. The candles flicker as Robbie looks around and realizes that his foster brother and sister won't show, as per usual. He blows out the candle and hangs his head.

"What did you wish for?" the kind foster father asks.

"To be with my brother and sister," Robbie says. A wrapped present gets placed in front of him, but he smiles politely and pushes it away. "Maybe later."

He stands and walks to a back sunroom and when he turns on the light, Asha and Leon blow through kazoos and shake noise makers.

"You made it!" Robbie shouts, and runs over to hug them.

"Wouldn't miss it," Asha says, and gives him a giant smooch on the cheek. When Robbie pulls away, Asha pushes him a box. Robbie lifts the top. It's the roll of 100's. Asha winks and puts her hands inside of her jacket pocket. Her face goes slack. Between her fingers, she pinches and rolls a lemonhead candy. While Leon tells an animated story and Robbie listens wide-eyed, Asha looks at the small yellow candy, and puts it back in her pocket. Her eyes go wide again. She pulls a blue pill out. Possible sequel? Depends on the success of this story. For the first time, Asha is not filmed at a 45 degree angle.

The camera moves over the shoulders of the happy laughing family, into the calm night with crickets chirping, then pans over the passenger seat. The folder marked "Project: Save Asha" is sitting on the passenger seat. The wind blows it open. It's a personalized letter from Robbie that starts, *Dear Asha, You are a good person.*

There's more, a lot more, but everything fades to black. The music swells. The initial credits roll. After the cast gets their just desserts, it cuts to a secret scene.

There's a knock on a door. The Chemist opens. It's Popanksi.

"I need a favor," he says, and steps inside. The Chemist looks around to see if anyone has followed, and then closes the door. Fade to black. Full credits.

Straight to DVD.

The Natural Wonders of the State of Florida

James Blakey

December 1985

Leo hops on the F-250's tailgate and pulls a Miller from the cooler. Five seconds in his hand and the can is slick with condensation. "How can any place be so damned hot?"

"You think this is bad, *amigo*? Try high-noon in August." Jesus smiles, his crooked teeth barely visible in the glow of the truck's taillights, and raises his can. "Welcome to Florida."

The light of a waning gibbous moon reflects off the bay. Jack Buck's gravelly voice crackles from the radio perched atop the truck's cab. "The Dolphins blocked the punt and recovered it on the Chicago six! The Bears' dream of an undefeated season has become a nightmare tonight in Miami."

"Christ!" Leo says.

"Seventeen and *cero*. No Chicago *hombres* break our record in our house." Jesus gulps his beer. "You a Bear fan?"

"No, I took Chicago minus the points," Leo lies.

"Where you from?"

"Someplace where they have normal weather."

Red emerges from the cab and kills the radio.

"Hey, I was listening to that," Leo says.

"And I need to listen for the plane." Red's accent is as thick as the Alabama backwoods.

Leo shrugs, guzzles his beer, and drops the empty in the bed.

"Pick that up," Red says.

"It's not like I tossed it in the water."

"It will blow out. The Everglades is a national treasure. Not a landfill for Yankees and tourists."

Red has the ex-Army look: crew cut, muscles tight under his camo-green t-shirt, shoulder holster. Probably was some ass-kicking master sergeant-type.

Leo crushes the can, drops it in the cooler, and grabs another beer.

Jesus says, "Red, you think Marino can take them ba—"

"Quiet!" Red holds up his hand, glances at his watch, then up.

Uncountable stars twinkle in the sky. Insects buzz. Frogs croak. The hollow echo of water lapping against the fiberglass speedboat gives way to the faint whine of a plane engine.

"Here they come. Start the generator," Red says.

Jesus scrambles into the truck bed and depresses the blue button. The generator sputters, belching black smoke. Red grabs the spotlight and switches it on. A beam bright as an A-bomb explosion shoots across the water. He adjusts the direction, pointing it upward, tracing a giant circle across the sky.

"Take over," Red tells Leo.

While Leo searches the sky, Red pulls a radio from his pocket. Holding it to one ear, he plugs the other with his finger.

Red and green nav lights interrupt the darkness. A Christmas tree in the air? More like Santa bringing presents. Leo focuses the beam on the silver DC-3, the pitch of the engine increasing. On the side of the plane, a door opens. A flash of yellow for a moment as something is tossed out. The nav lights go dark. Leo tracks the parachute with the beam. The engine dopples, as the plane turns south. When the parachute disappears below the horizon, Leo flicks off the spotlight. Jesus kills the generator.

"Into the boat with Jesus," Red says to Leo.

"You're not coming?"

"Someone has to keep an eye out for Charlie." He pulls the 9mm from his holster and racks the slide.

Leo follows Jesus down the ramp and stops at the water. "Do I need to worry about crocodiles?"

Jesus laughs. "You've been watching too much *Miami Vice*."

They slosh through knee-deep water and clamber aboard the boat, a twenty-foot Comanche. Leo scrunches his nose at the gasoline fumes. Jesus pulls the cord on the outboard. Again. On the third try, the engine roars to life.

Red unties the bowline and tosses it in the boat. Using a telescoping aluminum pole, Leo pushes off from shore. Running lights off, they head into the channel. Jesus consults something that looks like a black walky-talky, faint red light reflecting off his face. He revs the motor, and the bow rises.

Leo mans the mounted spotlight, the beam skipping across the water. The boat curves around an island of mangrove, and the glow from the F-250 disappears.

"Light off!" Jesus kills the engine.

Leo switches off the beam. The boat bobs in the water. A cormorant oinks like a pig. In the moonlight, Jesus cocks his head, listening for...what?

"You hear something?" Leo asks.

"Shh!" In a whisper Jesus says, "I thought there's another engine." He cups his hand to his ear. "Dominicans? Crackers? Poachers? Maybe nothing." Jesus chambers a round.

"I'm ready." Leo taps the grip of the .44 in his waistband.

Three more minutes of grunting cormorants, then Jesus re-starts the engine. Leo re-powers the light. Jesus re-checks the device in his hand as they wind through a maze of low-lying islands.

"We're close now!" Jesus drops the engine to neutral. The bow sinks. He checks the gizmo. "To the left."

Leo scans the surface. Nothing but black water. "Aha!" The beam illuminates the fluorescent yellow package floating in the water.

Jesus brings the boat about, throttle at one-quarter. Leo grabs the pole, telescoping it to its maximum fifteen feet. The boat eases toward the package. Leo leans over the side, trying to hook one of the nylon parachute lines.

Water splashes. The boat shudders. The impact almost sends Leo overboard. Something snaps at his arm. He pulls out his gun, dropping the pole, and fires a shot into the gurgling water. Leo falls backward into the boat, his heart pounding.

"What the hell was that? I thought you said there were no crocodiles."

Jesus cackles. "Might have been an alligator. You can tell the difference by their snouts. Gators are wider than crocs."

"Thanks for the zoology lesson." Leo jams the pistol into his waistband. "I lost the pole. You need to get closer."

"I will. But *amigo*, no more shooting. Alligators are protected. It's against the law."

"So is cocaine smuggling."

"But this is their home."

"What is it with you and Red? You guys some kind of environment freaks?"

"Like the glades is their home, Florida is mine. I grew up here. Before El Ratón. Before the developers bought off the building inspectors and sold houses made of straw to snowbirds from Brooklyn. They're ruining this land, paving it all over."

Leo shrugs, and Jesus maneuvers the boat along the package. Leo leans over the side. Jesus grabs Leo's belt, bracing his feet against the bulkhead. Leo slips his fingers around a parachute line and lifts.

"Pull me back in." The nylon bites into Leo's fingertips.

Jesus tugs on the belt, while Leo leans back. Their center of gravity shifts, Leo falls backward onto Jesus, the package on top of both of them.

Leo grunts, pushes the package aside, and scrambles to his feet. Jesus laughs, taking his spot by the motor.

The package weighs maybe sixty pounds. Leo tries to do the

math: estimate the weight of the packaging, subtract that from sixty, convert to kilos, then multiply by the wholesale price. Twenty million? That can't be right. How many kilos in a pound? Whatever it is, it'll be more than enough to never have to work again. Or worry about alligators.

Leo won't be going back to Moline. It's time to disappear. Where to? Upper Peninsula, Maine, Idaho? Any place where they don't sweat in the winter will be fine. Or maybe he *will* go back. Pull into Melissa's driveway in a brand new, fire-engine red 'vette. She couldn't say no to Leo then, couldn't stay with Wally the accountant.

"Keep alert with the beam. I don't want to be running aground," Jesus shouts over the engine.

Leo scans the water. Nothing but peaceful black glass reflecting the moonlight. No gators and no Dominicans. Ten minutes later, the Ford comes into view. Jesus maneuvers the boat to the end of the ramp and kills the engine.

Leo jumps in the water. Jesus hands him the package. Leo wades ashore like a triumphant MacArthur returning to Leyte.

Red's waiting with a towel. "Dry it off. I don't want it ruining the upholstery."

Leo sets the package down, pulls the hunting knife from his belt, and slices the nylon lines. He leaves the parachute on the ground, towels off the package, and hefts it into the backseat.

"Pick it up," Red says.

"What?"

"The parachute. It'll never degrade. End up washing out to the ocean and some dolphin will choke on it."

"You and Jesus should join the Sierra Club."

176

"This is God's country." Red's voice booms like a tent-revival evangelist. "And we don't aim to despoil it."

Leo picks up the parachute, compresses it into a ball, and tosses it in the truck. "Happy now?"

"Elated," Red says. "Let's get the boat on the trailer. I'll drive. You direct traffic." He hands Leo a flashlight.

Red guns the engine and backs up. The trailer rattles down the ramp and half submerges in the water. Leo yells for him to stop, then jumps on the tongue. Jesus, at no-wake speed, maneuvers the boat until it's floating over the trailer. Leo attaches the line to the bow-eye and cranks the winch. When the boat's lined up on the trailer and tight to the winch post, he hooks up the safety chain.

Jesus hops out of the boat; Leo off the trailer.

"Go for it, Red!"

The Ford's engine rattles like a machine gun. Tires spin in the mud, then catch. The truck lurches forward, pulling the trailer halfway up the ramp. Red kills the engine and hops out of the truck.

"Why did you stop?" Leo asks. "Let's roll."

"Not yet, *amigo*. Time to clean and drain."

"Clean and drain *what*?"

"The boat." Red pokes his finger into Leo's chest. "You don't want to accidentally transport species between ecosystems. That's why Collier County is full of God-danged lizards from Africa chowing down on Barred Owl eggs."

Jesus and Red climb into the boat. For the first time both men are in front of Leo: Red with his back to him, Jesus raising the motor. Leo draws his .44, aims at Jesus, averts his eyes, and shoots twice. Red turns, reaching for his piece. Leo fires three times. This time Leo's blinded by the muzzle flash. He crouches on the ramp. No sounds from the boat. His eyes adjust and peeks over the side. Neither Jesus nor Red are moving. Leo splits the rest of his bullets between the two, just to make sure. He ejects the mag, grabs the spare clipped to his belt, inserts it, and racks the slide.

The boat is a bloody mess. Even if Leo dumps the bodies in the water, he can't be towing this thing down the highway. Rather than clean it, better to unhook it from the trailer, letting the boat and bodies float away. Leo fumbles with the safety chain and de-winches the boat. With an assist from gravity, the boat creaks, scrapes, and slides down the trailer into the water. The tide will take care of the rest.

"*Adios.*"

Leo knows a guy who knows a guy who knows a buyer in Louisville. Sixteen-hour drive. If Leo can get some coffee, he can make it straight through.

Leo climbs in the front seat, reaching for the ignition, and— No keys. He pounds the steering wheel. "Damn it!" He knows he won't find them but searches the floor and checks the sun visor. Red must have them.

Leo scrambles back down the ramp. The boat is floating fifty feet away. He rushes into the water, ankle deep, knee deep, waist deep. He grabs hold of the side of the boat and struggles to climb aboard. The boat drifts into deeper water. He can barely touch bottom. With one mighty effort, Leo launches himself into the air, grasping at the railing, and tumbles forward, landing on Jesus' body.

Leo stands on shaky legs, taking deep breaths. He pulls out his gun. No need. Moonlight reflects in his former partners' eyes. Dead eyes. Leo reaches into the left pocket of Red's shorts and pulls out a pack of Newports. He crushes the pack and tosses it overboard. "How do you like that, Nature Boy?"

Leo searches the front right pocket; his fingers scrape metal. The pocket is tight; Leo's body twisted. He can't get the keys. He grabs Red around the chest and lifts him to a sitting position. Leo is covered in Red's blood, but the keys slide easily out of the pocket.

The boat is drifting farther into the channel. A hundred feet to the ramp. Leo shoves the keys in his pocket and tries to start the motor. He cranks and cranks, but it won't catch. Is that another engine he hears in the distance? He's not going to wait around to find out. Leo tumbles into the water. He swims the breaststroke, keeping his head mostly above water. He smiles at the memory of Mr. Nelson's lessons at the "Y" all those years ago. Should be clo-

The alligator explodes from the water, its jaws locking onto Leo's left arm. He screams, mostly from shock, the pain has yet to register. The gator tries to wrestle him under. Leo grabs the .44, fires underwater, but misses. He pulls the trigger again, but the water prevents the action from ejecting the round. The gun is useless.

Pain versus adrenaline versus panic. Leo can't move his left arm. Out of instinct he uses the gun as a club, pounding the gator in the head.

The gator clamps harder on Leo's arm and pain wins. The gun slips from his hand. His three other limbs flail. He can't reach the knife. The gator drags him under. A moment later, he's somehow free from the gator. He bursts through the surface, coughing up swamp water. He swims toward shore, but his left arm is now a stump. As he stares at where his forearm should be, the gator attacks again.

Razor-sharp teeth slice open Leo's chest. He punches the gator to no effect. The gator's pulling him under again. Only his head is still above water. Leo struggles to free himself. He's losing blood, dizzy. Moonlight dances on the water. The gator hauls Leo under for the last time.

125, 135, 509

Emilian Wojnowski

To Werko, the girl I like to wait with at a stop

Life is like traveling by bus. We get on and off it at different stops—sometimes at those we don't want to, not necessarily due to absent-mindedness—and the further we go, the more we pay. Sometimes we get stuck in traffic jams, join wrong passengers, or lose tickets. Or the bus does not come.

The above thinking occurred to me at... a bus stop. Thoughts then are mosquitoes, and heads—if free of problems, social media, and music—are camping lanterns.

It was windy, so I sat under a shelter. I was simply waiting, with my hands in my pockets and my head leaned on a rolled-up viscose scarf.

After a look around and a few smog breaths, I thought to myself that the street lights were washing that evening away for a few pedestrians only. I don't really remember what I thought next. Nothing odd about that, yeah. But in my mind— I guess I put it badly that "I don't really remember"—this spot is filled with some white liquid. Not with emptiness nor blackness, because I remember my every move—every lift of my finger—after having sat on the bench. There is just a white hole in me. Or rather a bulge that can't be pressed in and filled.

(But recently I have thought to myself that, for example, no one at the bus stop would pay attention to someone eating peanuts; but everyone would look at someone eating peanut butter like at a fool. And the same would be with strawberries and jam. But not necessarily with grapes and wine.)

So, I was sitting on the bench, hunched-up, occasionally closing my eyes and listening to a bus coming. I was looking forward to the warmth canned in it, which after the first stops, as I knew, would make me feel nauseous.

I often come home late at night, with no headphones on, no smartphone in my hand. I plunge into thoughts that advance on a bus.

On a bus filled with tired citizens, I realize: waking up passengers at the last stop is part of the driver's job. On a crowded bus: deodorant manufacturers should stop guaranteeing that their products provide forty-eight-hour protection. On a quiet bus: street fights between the homeless could be set for little money.

But let's get back to waiting at the bus stop. I stretched out my legs and curled them back immediately so that nobody accused me of trying to make a passer-by trip over. It was also helpful while waiting to look at passing cars. So I did. One pair of beams, another, another.

I felt the plank I was sitting on bend, widened my eyes, and looked to the side. First shyly, then I turned my head.

A kid. His legs were swinging and his hands were holding on to the plank bench as if it were a start bar. He had Velcro shoes and a frayed pompom of a hat tied under his chin.

"Waiting for a bus?" he asked.

It took me a while to make sure he had said it to me.

"That's right." I felt weird about some boy trying to talk to me.

"Are you an adult?"

When a stranger starts asking me, or any introvert like me, about something unexpectedly, it is enough to make me think for the next couple of hours whether the answer I gave was correct, simple, and clear. I will be feeling the wheels of some imaginary dialogue turning in my head.

"Yes," I said. For him I might have been an adult, as for most of society, but not for myself. I don't think I will ever be an adult.

"That's what I thought."

"Really?" I sensed that he would soon ask me to buy him something that he couldn't.

"Yeah." The boy neared his hands to his frozen thighs. "Here." He pulled out his little fist.

"What's that?"

"Here." He opened his fist. "Take it."

"Thank you." I looked at the candy CIUT. "I'll eat it later."

He nodded, and then smacked his lips, pushing a candy with his tongue from one cheek to another.

I should not have taken that candy, but it would have been awkward if I hadn't. Now he would want something from me in exchange.

"You have no family," he said.

"I do."

"Wife and children?"

"Not that kind of family."

"So you have no superpowers."

"I don't, you?"

"I'm not an adult." He chewed on the candy. "Nor a parent."

"Parents have superpowers?" I asked.

"Sure."

"Guess I have to agree with you," I said, having thought about my parents.

It happens sometimes that a stranger devours our minds with one sentence. Not necessarily the minds of introverts. And that's what I am getting at from the very beginning. Some words make up such strong sentences that every now and then I dream of witnessing a car accident—a car accident around which naked people are dancing and singing kumbaya, as if they were to summon an ancient demon—just to forget what I've just heard.

"What about your parents' superpowers?" I asked and began to regret it.

"My parents' superpowers?"

I nodded.

"Dad—well—hmm. I know what kind of superpowers my mom has."

"So?" I asked out of courtesy. I shouldn't have.

"I can only—" he began, and that made me feel all warm inside, "I can only eat candies."

"Oh."

"That's why I don't have as much strength as my mom."

"I don't understand," I said.

To the considerations at the very beginning, I can only add that we too often forget that not everyone is ready to take a bus. And that some should not be let in. And that not everyone can afford a ticket.

The bus pulled up and I hopped in.

"My mom can eat sugar with her nose," the boy said.

Who has the superpower to tell him? My bus had already left.

God, who will tell him?

Conversations on the Plurality of Worlds and the Face to be seen in the Orb of the Moon

Andrew Darlington

It's only afterwards that it all comes together. The supposed terrorist event, the fear, the blood. The deaths. When I think about it, loose strands click, the floating bits that meant nothing at the time, align into patterns. It occurs that for recent days I've been living a state of shock. From which a kind of sense only emerges gradually from senselessness. Waking out of nightmare, feeling as though an Orangutan has taken a dump in my mouth. Having enjoyed five minutes of quality sleep. I'm an educated fool.

The first click was meeting William Brake.

'You loving Kréta?' He uses the Greek pronunciation for Crete.

I was with Nikkita, 'Nikki'. We'd found love in a hopeless place. We sit in the bougainvillea shade half-in half-out of Spiro's, trying to do the Roger Moore eyebrow raise. I'd been practising in the mirror, both of us cracking up in hacking laughter. Roger Moore made a career out of that one unique asset, the ability to raise a single eyebrow into an expression of amused surprise. But it's a tough skill to master. I keep practising in the mirror. I've not got the hang of it yet. Maybe I should just stick with the Elvis sneer…?

And then there's William Brake. 'You were there, last night, the 'Dionysus'. I remember you.' He crosses his arms like a skinny Buddha. His hair pulled up into a tight bun. His eyebrows showing evidence of threading.

'Yeah. It was great.' It seems amazing he recognizes us. I'm unreasonably flattered. There's a flypost blu-tacked to the pillar behind us, as if to confirm it all. It says 'WILLIAM BRAKE', and beneath it 'DJ SONIC' in smaller font. With a poor cartoon of a hedgehog, surfing on a vinyl twelve-inch record. Their rivalry is the stuff of legend

Nikki's sipping a honey-gold fruit smoothie. I'm pulling at a bottle of Samaria Gorge spring-water, each mouthful sets up shimmering ripples of nausea in the back of my skull.

Bad habits?' he quips.

'Define bad,' I parry.

'Is William Brake your real name?' says Nikki, ignoring the banter. 'It sounds like a tip-tongue version of William Blake.'

'William Blake had fiery visions of heaven and hell.'

'Perhaps he used Glide too?'

'Except that I have no brakes.'

'And your famous rivalry with DJ Sonic. Is it really important? Does it matter?'

'It's *all* that matters.'

She laughs. 'Perfect. That's not at all creepy in any way whatsoever.' As though they're flirting back and forth.

Then he flips his attention to me with practiced ease. 'You've been to Knossos? You got the T-shirt. Taste and class and shake your ass.' Evenly dividing the gift of his attention between us.

'Yes, I'm here for the culture too. Knossos is a weird place. Like, the oldest palace in Europe, swarming with myth and magic. They had the Theseus labyrinth there, where the Minotaur dwelled, half-man half-bull. So they were doing GM gene-splicing back then?'

'Santorini was Atlantis. They knew weird stuff.' He's settling comfortably low into the upholstery, as if conspiring secrets. 'Have you been there, to Santorini? If you go there now, to the highest village, and look out over the sea, there's a circular island-chain that marks out the ancient crater-rim where it blew itself to pieces.'

'Colin Wilson said Atlantis was on the northern Antarctic shore during an ice-free interglacial period. There are copies of lost maps from the dawn of time that show details that it's only possible to see now with deep sonar probes through the compressed ice-sheets.'

'Plato got it wrong. Colin Wilson got it wrong too. This land – here, is the place of myths and forgotten truths.'

*****

Malia is essentially a triangle. There's the long sun-blitzed beach that runs down to tourist Stalis. There's the road that meanders towards Heraklion and the air terminal, it shimmers smooth as glass in the dancing heat-haze. There's the Malia old town where they still do that plate-smashing dance in the traditional tavernas. But there's the essential three-way strip that really counts, with the bars, clubs and karaoke. That's what it's really about. The 'Dionysus' Club. There are two high-profile DJ sets. Boom-Boom, Shake Shake The Room! DJ Sonic – Myron, fiercely jealous of his support status, ever out to seek advantage. And this man sitting across from us, William Brake.

'There's lots of anguished reality-docs on TV about Gender Reassignment. 'I always knew inside that I secretly wanted to be a woman.' And, of course, their bravery and determination is only to be applauded.' He's talking as though giving a personal performance, acting out voices. 'But what about Species Reassignment? 'I always knew inside that I secretly wanted to be an... Orangutan.' Yes, I quite fancy that. All that long auburn body-hair. That swinging around in the high branches of trees, way above the world. No schedules to keep or niggling angst about the state of the planet. Or, failing that, do they do a Dung Beetle reassignment? That might be fun too...' He scuffs his hair as if in perplexity, then shrugs the thought away and returns to his drink.

'Problem?' says Nikki, picking up on his mood.

'Hardly worth mentioning.'

'And yet you mention it.'

'It's complicated. It always is. That's just the way of it. There's a small package of some value I need to pick up.'

Nikki looks at me. I look at her. 'Where does the pick-up need picking up?'

The steering grips on my hired quadbike spin as smooth as oil to the touch. Miles reel by, hot-footing down a branch-road off the highway, little more than a dirt track, slowing for a straggle of goats that seem to resent this intrusion. Then shooting down a slight slope towards the lab, which is a villa set out in the middle of nothing, taking an equally slight rise and coming to rest outside its shade. Yet once there, and this is strange, I thought I heard – or felt… something. A kind of unnamable twitch that nudges its way into the underside of my mind, stirring my senses for the briefest moment. A Giorgio Morodor electro-quiver, a Nile Rodgers bass-figure swimming in dub. It builds and drops. Then it disappears, leaving only the unsettling feeling of loss. I glance back at the quad-bike, though why I'm looking back, I don't know.

Two men sit at either side of a shaded table around the corner, trading shots of something emerald from a bottle. A little way further there's a shimmering pool. Two more, much younger guys sprawl naked on loungers in the poolside shade.

The first seated man looks up. They call him Magic Sam. Others know him as the Mad Professor. He resembles Christopher Lloyd as Emmett 'Doc' Brown in **Back To The Future**. Or maybe Walter 'Heisenberg' White from **Beaking Bad**. His legend has it he was once a Hawkwind roadie.

'I'm here to pick up a package' I tell him.

'Ah yes. I've been expecting you.' Although he makes no effort to get up.

'You know, we used to jive around the possibilities of frequency, back when I was with touring bands in the seventies' as though he's continuing an interrupted conversation. 'There were early moogs just testing out the extremes of what sound could do. There was this joke suggestion going around. We'd exhausted the possibilities of ordinary frequencies, we need music that would play even more directly on the senses. On the nervous system.'

He leans back in the chair expansively, and swallows a mouthful of green. 'You know what the original sense of the term super-sonic was? It means 'sound beyond human hearing', and that's there to be used too. It has no natural harmonics as audible notes do, so they have to be augmented, piggybacked or coupled in with, say, quarter-tones, amplified by notes within the audible range – for example, a passage with diminished thirds, to increase the effect. But if you hit exactly the correct sine-wave configuration playing at a venue like a festival, it can accomplish the magic that opium performs on the senses, simply through harmonic vibrations. Joy, rapture, ecstasy, can all be induced. Other variations can produce less pleasant results – pain and agony, it's fraught with deadly possibilities. Or it could just loosen and open up the bowels of everyone in the audience simultaneously,' he was hacking out the story between guffaws of laughter.

Two small clockwork robots, one black, one white, shuffle across the table between them. When one reaches the table-rim, he lifts it, and turns it around so that it shuffles back in the other direction again.

'Would that work? Did you ever actually do it?' Switching my attention to the other man. I know him. I recognize him.

'Sound has that potential. Always has. We take it for granted. It's always there. But it can do weird stuff. 'When the mode of the music changes, the walls of the city shake.' Plato said that. He was right. You know that story about 'Joshua fit the battle of Jericho'? The army marches around the city, they blow their horns and the 'walls come tumbling down'. What do you suppose that was all about? Was it just a metaphor, or the confabulation of myth? Or did they know something we've forgotten, some ancient antediluvian technology? That to hit the right sound-vibration destabilizes reality?' I get the impression he's just sounding off, saying whatever comes into his circuit.

Then he looks at me. 'Are you ready?'

'No. I don't think I will ever be ready.' A slack grin.

'Such a degree of self-awareness is a pretty cool thing.' He stands, shoves the chair back with a grating rasp. As I watch, one of the young guys by the pool gets up from the lounger, dives cleanly into the pool, swims a lazy length, then hauls himself out at the far end, to slouch face-down on another lounger. I can't help but notice he's intimidatingly hung. Eye-candy. Magic Sam opens the door and leads me into the cool shade inside. Across an untidy living space with low couches and throw-pillows. It smells rich. The stink of cat-piss. His cellar must be ankle-deep in mushrooms. Simply to inhale is an intoxication.

He leads the way through a solid door beyond into the lab itself, where electronics wire banks of screens together. What looks to be a big mixing desk with numerous peripherals. Some cages where rabbits skitter inside. A couple of the cages at the end are dripping red with spattered entrails, as though the once-rabbit inside had exploded. Through a tight aisle between incomprehensible equipment, there's a work-station with flasks and retorts. Ethyl alcohol. Propane. Butane. I know this stuff can be hazardous. Health and Safety rules don't apply. There's a sense that you can't take it all in at once, it's like nothing I've seen or imagined before outside the Horror channel. He rummages around absent-mindedly, before producing a small bulging plastic bag. This is what I've come for. The Glide that he synthesizes here in the outback far from scrutiny. The chemistry that distorts reality, alters mood on the dancefloor.

'So much in life we take for granted. The sun. The sea. The trees. The correct arrangement of chemistry.' He looks me so directly in the eye that I can see the madness lurking there. 'This is for him, right? For William Brake. No-one else.'

'Absolutely.' My heart-rate is three times faster than normal. 'Was it true, what you were saying out there, about your experiments with sound?'

'Sure. I concoct drop-in samples for the Club DJs here' he shrugs casually, indicates a sheet-music program onscreen. Four groups of staves, each with eleven lines instead of the usual five, modified and annotated in ways that convey nothing to me. A curious and complicated puzzle. 'Rhythm is primal. It bounces around from heartbeat to the great cosmic pulse of expanding galaxies, it's the sound of the universe in motion. It's the very first basic impulse. The drum is our earliest tool. It's the most primitive pre-human ape-thing, beating a stone on a hollow log – WHOP! WHOP! WHOP! WHOP! You see it everywhere. Before a child can walk-talk it reacts to music on the radio, bopping up and down on its bendy itsy-bitsy feet. We dance. We've always danced. We dance in joy or in ecstasy. We dance ourselves dizzy, into a trance as part of ritual, into altered states of awareness. We tune in on rim-shots and paradiddles. We do it forever. Sufi and Dervish. To Jazz and boogie-woogie. To Be-Bop and Hip-Hop. But now we can take it further still, techno-enhanced. We've got programmed drums. Pulses triggered to the neural beat of the nervous system, to the raw neurons firing in the cerebral cortex. Attuned to the healing force of the continuum. Loud and louder, it fills the space between your ears until there's no room for anything else. Just instinct. Just primal reaction. Response. Cleansing. Purifying. I believe this. I really genuinely believe this.'

He shoves the bag across at me. Evidently our conversation is over. 'Try not to steal anything on the way out' he grins.

Back in Malia Richard Brake is not at the 'Dionysus', and the club is closed. I call the mobile number he gave me, and he gives directions. So I return the quadbike to the pound, and head down past the bars and minimarts. There are 'Dionysis' fly-posters, many of them sabotaged by fans of the rival DJs, just as the two DJs are said to sabotage each other's sets. Onto the strip of fine-sand beach, the heat burning up through the soles of my sandals. I can see all the way along the curve of ebbing surf, the pattern of sunbeds and parasols. And yes, he's there. He looks up and grins as I pace across hot sand to sit on the lounger across from him.

'You do the do?' he says, maybe just the edge of piss-take sarcasm to his voice.

'I got the small party-package of some value from Magic Sam, yes.'

At that moment Nikki rises from the shimmering tide like a goddess from myth, wearing only her bikini bottom. My heart goes BANG SHANG-ALANG! She takes my breath away. Images of her perfect body storm in my head, pitching me back to last night. Our first time.

I don't like the way they're looking at each other. Could it be that my errand served a dual purpose? To get me out the way while Brake made his move on her? A situation she seems quite happy with.

More loose strands click. First. I got a feeling, tonight's gonna to be a good good night. I know it. I feel it. Brake said he'd put us on the guest list. It's too good to believe. But I need to check, just to make certain. He might forget. It's the bleached-out afternoon heat. Nothing much moves. There's no-one working the door. The door is ajar. I slope into the club. The dance-floor seems huge in its echoing daylight emptiness. Tacky and rundown without the magic turned on. I feel like a guilty intruder, like I shouldn't be here. I'm on the point of leaving when I see movement at the DJ decks. Sonic's equipment is at one end of the dance-floor. This is Richard Brake's decks. I hunch back into the shadow of the exit corridor. It's Myron. I know that now. And he's hanging in a furtive way around Brake's equipment.

Sonic was the man across the table from Magic Sam. He holds his head high, but he's not wholly at ease. Brake's character is stronger than this younger rival. And it's as though he resents the older DJ's charisma, dexterity and dominating personality. He has what looks to be SIM cards. I can't quite make out what he's doing, but he got those SIM's from the lab.

*****

I awake on the beach with a nail through my head. Caught in the suspension of time that takes place when you step outside of your regular life-routine. A foulness washing my mouth, sand sharp and gritty on my lips, a sluggish backwash of images on the borderland of dream. A jumble of disconnected impressions that taunt with suggestions of significance. We'd talked, a conversation with Brake on the plurality of worlds and the face to be seen in the orb of the moon. About other clubs, bands and musicians, the Shadow Architects, Cyberlad and Time Traders. Thinking, hey, how cool is this?

'The object is not to win' Brake had said. Another click. 'The object is simply to keep on top for as long as you can. That's what I feed on. People are predictable. Sometimes they're unpredictable too. The skill lies in knowing at what point the unpredictable is going to kick in.'

'And those stories about you and DJ Sonic sabotaging each other's sets…?' The chemical stink-bombs. The sudden inexplicable power-loss in mid-set. The scratched white-label twelve-inch. There was enmity between the two, the jealous resentment Sonic felt for Brake, the more playful way Brake answers the threat to his status.

'HaHa. There's a word that's useful in these situations. Apocryphal. There must be plausible deniability. Don't believe me. Just watch.' He stares at me with keen blue eyes. 'You must excuse my young friend. This was my residency before he arrived. He's ambitious, headstrong. This is good. But he's a tad too impatient. That's not so cool. But he'll learn.'

I look at the sky. I look at the sea. I look along the shoreline where the tide eddies in crystal ripples. 'I've been examining my life's choices. I'm not sure that this is the answer.'

Sure, we'd talked. Me and my big mouth. I remember those strands now. At the time they were fragments. But they're linked. The floating bits that meant nothing at the time, align into patterns. I know now they are strands. He was talking right through me, to Nikki. And I was too stupid to realize. Just as it's all about to click into nightmare. Into atrocity.

We go to the 'Dionysus' that same evening, me and Nikki. No other possibility exists. The venue is already packed to capacity. As soon as we step over the threshold, as if by magic the peeling paint heals, the floor's dullness becomes polished to a gleaming sheen, the walls sparkle reflections off the lights against the encroaching night darkness outside. And the deep electro-pulse begins. DJ Sonic's set. An artful mix of retro old-skool. Motown bass, Swedish House Mafia, James Brown break-beats. We dance into and around each other, a sinuous flirtation, a seduction and a copulation all in one.

Then Richard Brake takes over the decks, his drum-track stitching it all seamlessly into flow, slip-sliding from one into the next without definition, segueing, dropping triggered samples in loops and repetitions, tailored motifs that punctuate and shape the tide into an endless soundscape. It's getting hot in here, bodies glisten and gyrate. And he's genius. Whipped by Raygun-zap strobe bursts of hallucinogenic migraine intensity. I throw my hands up in the air sometimes. Overwhelmed in weapons-grade planetary volume, EDM, lights, energy, hi-NRG. Electricity. Fine-tuned by Glide into a sonic tsunami. Leaving dancers wrecked and emotionally drained. This is how it should be. Yet there is more.

There's something hauntingly intense and inexpressible that creeps into the back of my mind, a jarring dissonance both thrilling and scary, hammering brain and nerve beyond natural limits. A roar washes overhead, like a blast of superheated air over gyrating bodies. Not only loud in a cataclysmic death-by-volume kind of way, but modulated through lethal psychic harmonic frequencies. Somebody says 'Ouch!' It catches me sideways so that I slide, staggering with wildly wind-milling arms, slipping again to fall flat on my back with a force that knocks the breath from my body. I want to cry out, to stop it, yet I know there's nothing I can do to break that exotic spell, even if my life depends on it.

Nikki is recumbent beside and partially beneath me, my mind empties, with alternating impressions of rough and smooth, sticky and gloss. It's as though my brain is fudged into the consistency of pulled toffee with the soft elasticity of a newly-rolled ball of Play-Dough. Nausea shocks through me. My blood is fizzing alarmingly like cola. I can taste my brain boiling. My hands clamp hard over the sides of my head, fingers rammed deep in my ears, forbidding myself to hear. It's also the fact that I'm floored flat that saves me. Closer to the DJ decks I see the psycho-mad fighting begin. Punching, gouging, ripping, clawing. Raw animal squeals and bestial howls. They're tearing at each other not as people fight, but raw teeth and claw beast fighting. It's nightmarish dark spiked with lasers into jerky atrocity.

I doubt Brake is even aware of what's going on. He's hunched over the decks in hard concentration, his hands never still, phones clamped in tight around his head. Tiny red lights pulse at his temples caught in the blue-wash rippling glow from his screen. He's triggering samples over the relentless electro-beat. And heads begin to explode. A welter of blood and brain-matter detonating, programmed to the rhythms. A howl barely perceptible above the wall-to-wall noise. I watch the nightmare choreography. Blood trickles like the tracks of tears, ears, nose and eyes. Some dancers are throwing up, bloody projectile vomit. Then heads simply… explode. BLAM! BLAM!! BLAM!!!

People stampede the exit, others get trampled underfoot, there's blood and mayhem. I'm still lying where I was sound-blasted onto the floor, beneath the level of the doctored sonic blasts. Someone cuts the power. Viciously amputates the sound. The screams are suddenly even more terrible. The staff and sound-people have scattered. Brake is gone in shocked terror. I look into Nikki's eyes. 'Are you alright?' My voice echoes inside my skull.

'I can't tell' she mouths. 'It all hurts.'

A rushing sound in my ears. My senses seem unnaturally acute. And through the blood-haze chaos I glance up. Isn't that DJ Sonic behind Brake's sound-desk? And isn't he erasing and deleting samples from the screen? It's a minor detail that fails to register at the time. But comes back now. It sets off a slideshow in my head. Did Sonic realize what he was doing? Hadn't he seen the exploded rabbits in Magic Sam's lab? Or did he imagine he was just keying in that bowel-loosening dose, unleashed with mischievous spite born of the competitive antagonism that exists between them? Whatever, he's nowhere to be seen since.

I practice the Roger Moore eyebrow raise. I still can't get it right. Nikki is with Richard Brake, they're comforting each other through the aftermath trauma. When love takes over, over, over, over, over...

The Police are diligently working on the mistaken Terrorist theory. Tracking down non-existent suspects, persons of interest. It's easier to understand that way. It plays well into the existing news narrative. I watch the blurred reports on TV. Everyone has their own take on what happened. The atrocity. The deaths. Waking out of nightmare, I know different.

The Big Favor

Lawrence Allan

Bound on both sides by corn ten feet tall, a grey Toyota Hyundai sped down a country road with Shane gripping the wheel, Kevin riding shotgun and a dead body in the trunk. It was a late summer evening and they were heading to small lake in McClean County, Illinois. They were in their late twenties and had been tight since high school. Kevin, tall, brown hair, blue eyes and a wrestler's physique beginning to go soft, chewed on the knuckle of his right thumb nervously. Shane, bright red hair, lean body with a Popeye tattoo on his left forearm was the brains of the operation.

Kevin broke the silence. "You know how I'd like to drown?"

Shane frowned and looked at Kevin. "What are you talking about?" He put his eyes back on the road.

"Drowning."

"Drowning?"

Kevin nodded. "I read somewhere that if you drown in the ocean, it's easier. Your body, like, accepts it because it's salt water." Shane raised an eyebrow. Kevin explained, "'Cause our body has salt water." Shane took this in. Nodded. Kevin continued, "But, fresh water. It's not the same. Your body fights it. You don't want to drown in fresh water."

As Shane thought about Kevin's theory, the car hummed and rattled as it went over the blacktop. The road curved up and down and seemed to stretch on to infinity. "You read this?"

Kevin's head shook a little. "I might've seen it on the internet."

Shane sighed. Kevin had always been trusting. He believed everything he saw and heard. That's what Shane was for, to help keep Kevin on the right path. "I don't think it's true, Kevin. It's got to be the other way."

Kevin frowned. That didn't seem right to him.

"What happens when you get salt in your eyes?" Shane was going to explain it carefully for Kevin.

"I've never had salt in my eyes."

Shane looked at him, not believing what he heard. "You've never been to the ocean?"

"Does Lake Michigan count?"

"No. Lake Michigan does not count. I mean the ocean. The Atlantic. The Pacific."

"Never been."

Shane pressed on, "Well, I have. And let me tell you. When you get salt in your eyes, it hurts like hell." He and this girl had made the drive to North Carolina a few years ago for spring break. He had a lot of fun, but, couldn't remember the girl's name. "Besides you don't drink salt water. You drink fresh water. There's no way drowning in salt water is easier. It's got to be fresh water."

Kevin mulled it over for a second. "Maybe it is the other way around."

"It is. It is the other way around. I'm telling you."

"I wouldn't want to drown though."

"Who wants to drown?" asked Shane sharply.

"It sounds like a shitty way to go. All that water above you, and you're just sinking sinking sinking. Doesn't sound good."

Shane blurted out, "Why are you even thinking about this?"

"You know." Kevin pointed with his thumb towards the trunk.

"But, he's not going to drown. He's dead. He's dead already. So, there's no drowning. We're just dumping the body."

"Ok."

"So, can we just… just stop talking about it."

"Sure."

And with that, the men fell into silence again. Shane started to smile. Eric was going to owe him big time. It's not every day you make a body disappear for a friend. This was a big favor.

And that's when it happened. That's when they both heard it. The *thump* from the trunk.

Kevin looked at Shane, his eyes going wide. Shane looked at Kevin and swallowed. They didn't want to say it. It couldn't be true. It really shouldn't be true. Sweating, Shane finally was able to say, "Eric told me he was dead."

Kevin was barely breathing. "Maybe Eric was wrong."

Shane turned his attention back to the road. "Did you see anything when we put him in the car?"

Kevin scratched his head, remembering. "No. Looked dead to me."

"Yeah. Me, too."

Quietly, Kevin said, "All that blood."

"Yes, exactly. That was a lot of blood. Like, who lives after that?"

Thump.

This time the men said nothing. Kevin started chewing his knuckle again, Shane gripped the wheel harder. "Hey, hey. Listen. It's the car. The car went thump," said Shane, doing his best to believe it. "We're not far from Lake Bloomington. We dump the body and everything is going to be cool."

Kevin looked at Shane and asked, "What if he's not dead?"

Shane looked back and forth between Kevin and the road. "He's dead. Trust me. The guy is dead."

"I just want to get this over with."

Shane agreed and pushed down the gas pedal a little more. The engine revved and the car sailed a little higher over a rise in the road.

And that's when Shane blew through a stop sign.

A siren started to scream. Red and blue lights flashed behind them. Shane looked in the mirror as Kevin turned around to see. A State Trooper was coming up fast as the sun was beginning to dip below the horizon. Shane mumbled, "Shit."

Kevin reached under his seat and pulled out a small pistol.

"What are you doing?" Shane snapped.

Kevin replied, "I don't know… just in case."

"In case? In case of what?!" Kevin didn't have an answer. "Just be cool, alright?" Shane slowed the car and pulled to the side of the road. "It's probably something stupid. We'll just take the ticket and go." Kevin nodded quickly.

The siren stopped, but the lights stayed on. Shane and Kevin barely breathed. Shane could hear Kevin repeat quietly, "Just be cool, just be cool." The gun was now out of sight. They heard the trooper's door open and close. They heard the gravel crunch as the he came closer step by step.

The trooper, 40s, serious, with an even more serious blonde mustache, leaned down and knocked on the window. Shane rolled it down. Hot humid summer air and the sound of crickets flowed into the car. "Yes, sir?" Shane did his best to look apologetic. It had worked before and he hoped it would work again.

"Evening. License and registration, please." The trooper's voice had all the authority of a manager at McDonald's. He just wanted to write his ticket and finish out his shift in peace.

Shane nodded. He reached for his wallet, pulled out his license and handed it to the trooper. The trooper continued to look at him. Shane remembered, "Right. Registration." He leaned over to the glove compartment as Kevin leaned out of his way, stealing a glance at the trooper who was watching everything.

Shane handed him the registration.

As he was looking over the paperwork, the trooper asked, "So, do you remember seeing a stop sign about half mile back?"

Shane's mouth opened and closed. He turned around and

looked back down the road. Kevin did the same. Shane turned to the trooper. "No, sir. I, uh. I didn't. I'm awfully sorry."

The trooper's eyes narrowed. "Sorry?"

Shane smiled. "That's right, sir. Sorry. I know how dangerous it can be. Out here on these country roads."

The trooper leaned forward, looking between Shane and Kevin carefully. Kevin swallowed hard. Shane took a breath. "Everything ok, sir?"

Thump.

No one moved.

The trooper slowly looked back towards the trunk. "Is someone back there?" Shane shook his head no. Kevin followed suit. "Are you two... involved in a prank?"

"No, sir. No prank."

The trooper thought about it for a second, shifting again from Kevin to Shane and back. Finally, "Do you mind popping the trunk?"

Shane felt Kevin move. Then, a flash. And finally.

BANG.

Shane's ears rang. Time slowed. He looked at Kevin, who held the small pistol in his right hand. Smoke drifted from the barrel. Shane turned to the trooper. The trooper started to frown, his eyes confused. He reached for his neck as blood began to pour out of it. Time rushed back to normal as the trooper fell out of sight below the window.

Finally, someone said something. "Shit." It was Shane. He stumbled out of the car.

Sprawled out in the middle of the road was the trooper,

arms akimbo, eyes glassy staring at the darkening sky. Kevin was next to Shane, still holding the pistol. "What do we do?"

Shane shouted at Kevin, "How 'bout we don't shoot anymore people?! Jesus. What happened to be cool?!"

Kevin took a step back, hurt, "He wanted to look in the trunk. He was going to find—"

"You don't know what was going to happen. I might've been able to talk him out of it and we would be on the road. But, no. You shot him, Kevin. You fucking shot a state trooper." Shane was sweating, breathing hard. That's when he saw it, still in Kevin's hand. "Would you put the gun away? Jesus." Kevin slipped it into his waist band. Shane wasn't done. "All we had to do was dump a body for Eric. All I wanted you to do was be cool. That was the plan. Be cool. And now... Fuck."

Silence. Again, Kevin was the one to break it. "Couldn't we dump this one with the other?"

Shane closed his eyes and rubbed his face. He took a breath. It was as good an idea as any. "Fine. Let's put him in the trunk."

Kevin didn't move. "With the other one?"

"Yes. Yes, with the other one. Do we have another trunk?" Shane moved to the trooper's arms and grabbed them. "Pick up the legs." Kevin did as he was told and the two lifted the body with a grunt. They waddled to the back of Shane's car and placed it on the ground.

Kevin reached for the trunk, then paused, his hand hovering a foot away.

"What's the matter?" asked Shane.

Kevin looked at him, worried. "What if…?"

Shane rolled his eyes. "Fine. I'll do it." Kevin stepped back, gripped the pistol in both hands and aimed it at the trunk. "What are you doing?" Shane asked.

"Just in case."

"You can't be serious?"

Kevin was.

"Put the God damned gun away, Kevin, before I shoot you."

"With what?"

"KEVIN." Kevin did as he was told. Shane shook his head and reached for the trunk. Kevin curled his fingers into fists and was ready for a fight. "Seriously?" Shane asked. Kevin nodded and Shane shook his head. He popped the trunk and stepped back. Better to be safe than sorry.

Nothing happened.

Shane and Kevin stepped closer and peered into the trunk. Inside lay a twenty something former skater punk, with tattoos and a bloody face. Shane poked the body. The skater punk didn't move. Didn't make a noise." See. Dead."

Kevin agreed.

"Come on. Let's do this." They reached down and hoisted the trooper into the trunk, dropping him on top of the other body. Shane slammed the trunk closed.

Shane put the cruiser into the cornfield so it couldn't be seen from the road. They could come back later and ditch the car properly. Before he got out he looked at the dashboard. At the camera. Shane pulled and ripped it out.

Stepping out of the field, back onto the country road, Shane headed towards his car. Kevin was already inside. As Shane took the wheel, he handed the camera to Kevin. "We'll have to smash this."

Kevin held it close to his face, looking deep into the camera. "Cool."

"Not cool. Evidence. It recorded us."

"Right." Kevin tossed it into the back seat. "We'll have to smash it."

Shane started the car. Took a breath. "Put the gun away."

"It's away."

"In the glove compartment. Where it won't be a temptation."

Kevin made a face as he pulled the pistol out and put it into the glove compartment. "Happy?"

Shane put the car into drive and spat gravel out the back as he gunned it down the road. "You're gonna have to get rid of the gun."

"It's my dad's. He'll kill me if I don't get it back to him."

Shane's mouth dropped open. "You just shot a cop, Kevin. You have to get rid of the gun." Shane turned right. The final road on the way to Lake Bloomington.

Kevin shook his head, thinking. "I don't know man."

"You don't know?" Shane snapped and took his eyes off the road. "We have two bodies in the trunk and you're worried about your dad? Kevin, keep your shit together!"

Thump.

Shane's attention shifted towards the trunk.

He saw Kevin's eyes go wide, and his arms brace against

the dashboard. Shane looked back at the road and that's when he saw him, the bicyclist.

Shane had never hit anyone with a car before. He took pride in that. So, he did his best. He did what he was taught to do. He slammed on his brakes. They screeched. But, it didn't matter. The Hyundai still hit the bike. It twisted and fell, taking it and the rider underneath the car, while Shane and Kevin were tossed around inside. The car came to a stop.

Kevin looked back through the rear view mirror. He turned to Shane, "I don't see anything." Shane slumped. He got out of the car and Kevin followed. They looked down at the front end of the car.

Sticking out from underneath was a thin bike tire and two legs wearing cycling shoes.

Kevin got on his hands and knees. "Yeah. You hit him." He pulled the leg of the cyclist. It was thin and white, almost hairless. As he pulled, the leg would straighten, but the body wouldn't move. Kevin repositioned his hands around the ankle and gave a good tug. The cyclist's shoe slipped off and smacked Kevin in the face, knocking him on his ass. Kevin grimaced and said, "He's stuck."

Shane looked under the car. Twisted around the bike was the rest of the cyclist. Also thin, white, wearing black Lycra shorts and a red and white Lycra shirt, the man's head was turned the wrong way. His helmet was lodged between the blacktop and the undercarriage of the car. The red warning light on the man's helmet flashed red on and off, on and off.

Shane stood up. He rubbed the sides of his head as it pounded. He just wanted to get this done. He just wanted to get back, tell Eric everything was good and that he owed him.

That's all that he wanted.

Kevin said, "You should've had your eyes on the road, man."

This broke Shane out of his reverie. "This is my fault?"

Kevin shrugged, "I wasn't driving."

Shane took a step forward and asked very quietly, "Is that what you're going to say to the DA?"

Kevin stepped back. "What?"

Shane replied, "It isn't going to get you a lighter sentence."

"What's not?" Kevin wasn't very good at lying.

"Putting this all on me—!"

"I'm not putting anything on you—!"

"Because you shot a cop, Kevin!"

"You ran over a guy!"

"This was an accident!" Shane slowed it down and laid it out for him, "Listen, we're in this shit together. I go down, you down."

Kevin didn't say anything. He kept his mouth shut.

Shane said, "Now. Let's take care of this and get the job done. Then we will never have to talk about it again." Kevin nodded and then looked down at the body. Shane took a breath. "I have an idea. You hold the legs, I'll drive the car." Kevin looked at him, worry in his eyes. Shane shook his head no, "I'm not going to run over you, I'm going to reverse the car, you hold the body in place."

He got back in the car but Kevin hadn't moved. Shane looked at him, impatient. Kevin nodded and got on the ground, reached forward and grabbed the legs. Shane turned the ignition and the car came to life. He put his hand on the gear shift, and put it into reverse and lightly touched the gas. The car started moving backwards, pulling the body and Kevin with it.

Kevin grunted as his feet slid. He couldn't find any purchase on the blacktop. He heard the engine rev and he started to slide faster. "No, no, no!" He could feel his feet getting hot from the friction. Finally, a pop and body gave way, the Hyundai rolled free and Kevin was thrown forward, falling on top of the bike and body.

He jumped up as quickly as he could, trying to shake off touching a dead man. Shane was out of the car and next to him. He looked down at the cyclist. "Alright. Let's get this one in the trunk." Shane reached for the arms as Kevin picked up the legs.

After they moved the cyclist to the back, they realized there was a problem. "He's not going to fit," said Kevin. The trunk wasn't spacious and was already full.

"No shit," said Shane. "Alright. I got an idea."

After much struggle, more bickering, the body of the cyclist was belted into the back passenger seat, head and helmet dangling oddly from the torso. Shane tossed the bike into the cornfield. "We'll get it later."

"Before or after the cop car."

"Get in the car, Kevin!"

They got into the car.

Five minutes later, they finally arrived. Almost. Specifically, they were at the City of Bloomington's Water Plant. A grey concrete building that processed the water from the lake for the 120,000 people to drink in the city about twenty minutes away. Behind the building was secluded access to the lake. You had to know someone to get in and Shane knew someone. His mother's brother, who liked to gamble. Especially when he was high. Shane took care of his uncle. And his uncle owed him.

The Hyundai sat on the wrong side of the gate, engine running. Shane honked the horn. Nothing.

"Where is he?" Kevin wondered.

"He's here."

Kevin shook his head. "We should just dig a hole and dump them all in."

"I'm not digging a hole."

"It's easy. You just dig."

Shane honked the horn again. "We got three bodies to get rid of. To dig a hole deep enough so no random dog finds them will take hours. We dump them in the lake, let the fish do the work." He looked at Kevin, "This is why I make the plans. I think things through."

"Fuck you, Shane."

"Don't be mad at me. That's how it is."

"We wouldn't be in this mess if you hadn't said yes to Eric."

Shane turned to Kevin. "You don't get it do you." He tapped Kevin's head with his finger, hard.

Kevin tried swatting it away but missed. "Don't."

"Eric owing us is a good a thing."

"Eric is an asshole. He talks big. But there's nothing there."

Shane shook his head, "Let me do the thinking for the two of us ok?" He stabbed at the car horn.

"I'm not stupid."

"I'm not calling you stupid."

"Why didn't you ask me before you said yes to Eric?"

Shane frowned and snorted.

"You dragged me into this. You didn't ask me. And now we're up to our necks." Kevin folded his arms. "I didn't want this."

"You think I did?!"

"We're partners, you should've asked me."

"And you would've said no? Because you knew all of this was going to happen? Are you psychic?"

"No."

"Then shut up. No one forced you to do this."

Kevin was silent. Then. "This was supposed to be simple. You told me it would be simple. I trusted you."

"It's going to be fine."

"Yeah. Sure. Whatever."

Shane pushed at the horn and didn't let up until a grey shaggy haired potbellied man stepped out of the concrete building. The uncle wore the bright orange t-shirt that City of Bloomington employees wore and it stretched over his belly. He paused to pull a box of cigarettes out of his shirt pocket.

Shane honked the horn.

His uncle waved for him to be patient. He stuck a smoke into his mouth. Dug out a lighter and flicked it to life, lighting the cigarette. He took a long drag, followed by coughing. Puffs of smoke came out each time. He stuck the smoke back in his mouth and shuffled over to the gate.

Thump.

Shane and Kevin stole glances at each other. When they looked back towards the uncle, he had stopped moving. He stood about five feet from the gate. His arms moved like they had been caught in a gentle breeze.

Kevin leaned over and asked, "What's going on?"

Shane shrugged.

His uncle's right hand moved towards his left arm. But, didn't make it. The uncle leaned forward and kept on going until he fell to the ground. He didn't get back up.

"Aw, hell." Shane uttered.

Kevin asked, "What do we do now? That gate is locked."

"We unlock it. Stay here." Shane get out of the car and headed to the chain link fence. It rattled as he climbed and jumped over. He landed on the uneven ground, twisting his right ankle. He grunted and collapsed.

"You ok?" Kevin shouted from the car.

Shane blinked away tears and held up a thumb. He stood up and limped towards his now deceased uncle. "Screw you, Uncle Reggie." Shane bent down and put his hands underneath the large body and started to roll him onto his back.

The cigarette was still in his mouth.

Shane dug into his pockets and found the keys. He stepped over the body and headed to the gate. He reached for the padlock and looked through the keys until he found the right one.

Shane went and pulled the car into the water plant's

driveway and then locked the gate behind. Finished, he got back into the car.

Kevin looked at the uncle. "Are we going to do anything about him?"

Shane thought for a moment. "No."

"No?"

"It's a heart attack. You saw the guy. No one is going to be surprised, so let's just leave him." Shane aimed the car towards the back of the water plant.

Lake Bloomington was a small lake with a few large houses, but they were on the other side. Behind the building, the city kept material and equipment to maintain the facility including concrete blocks.

Shane parked the car near a dock about ten feet from the water's edge. It was quiet, except for the chirping of crickets. Dark, except for an exterior light hanging from the top of the building. As they got out, Shane told Kevin, "You get the bodies to the dock, I'll get some concrete blocks. We'll tie the blocks to the bodies, put the bodies in the lake and get out. Simple enough?"

"Yeah. Simple enough," Kevin replied quietly.

"Start with the cyclist."

As Shane headed towards the pile of concrete blocks, Kevin opened the back door. He leaned in, reached past the cyclist and unbuckled him. The body slumped on top of Kevin, who flinched and stepped back. The cyclist fell out of the car and the helmet hit the ground with a *clunk*.

Shane looked back, Kevin put up a hand. "All good." Kevin grabbed the body by the wrists and dragged it to the dock.

Shane met him there carrying two concrete blocks and some rope. He dropped them on the dock next to the cyclist. He looked at Kevin. "I'm going to get more, we don't want them floating back up. Get the trooper."

Kevin chewed his lip and headed back towards the Hyundai.

As Shane picked up two more blocks, he felt the weight of the night easing. The end was in sight. Everything was going to be fine. It might've been a shit show, but it was going to turn out ok. He looked over at Kevin as he was struggling with the trooper's body. Shane wondered if maybe it was time for Kevin and him to part ways. Shane had carried him this far, maybe this was far enough. After all, it was his idea to do a big favor for Eric. Why should he share?

Back at the dock, Shane dropped the blocks next to the bodies. Kevin kneeling, tying the group to the blocks. "I'll do that, you go get the skater," ordered Shane.

Kevin shook his head, "I'm already doing this."

"I said I would do that."

Kevin stopped. And then stood up to his full height. "You go get the other one."

Shane licked his lips. "That's your job. Bringing the bodies."

Kevin took a step towards Shane. "I already brought two."

"Yeah, so? There's just one left."

Kevin put a finger into Shane's chest, "I'm not just the muscle." Shane slapped the finger away. Kevin took another step. They were chest to chest. "I'm tired of you telling me what to do." Kevin set his jaw, ready for a fight.

Yeah, thought Shane, this was the last time he was going to work with Kevin. Ten years had been too long. Not willing to die on this hill, Shane turned on his heels and headed towards the car. He reached the trunk and leaned down to grab the skater punk's body. This is when Shane discovered that the trunk was empty.

Shane didn't see so much as feel the tire iron. It came across his skull with a distinctive *thump.*

When he came to, he found himself on the dock. Groggy. Dizzy. He tasted blood in his mouth. Finally, his eyes focused on a person holding the tire iron in one hand and a familiar pistol in the other. The person was bloody. So very bloody. Shane figured it out. It was the skater punk. Shane mumbled, "Can we talk about this?" as he tried to sit up. He found that he was tied to the pile bodies on the edge of the dock. "Shit."

The skater punk breathed heavily and asked with a growl, "You got something to say?"

Shane started to laugh. "Yeah. I do." He smiled. "I don't work alone."

The skater punk nodded, confused. "I know. I heard you two arguing like a married couple. He's next to you."

Shane looked to his right.

"Other side, genius."

Shane looked to his left. There was Kevin. Sweet, kind Kevin. Kevin with his eyes half open. Kevin with a bullet hole in the middle of his forehead.

"Fuck."

"Yeah," the skater punk agreed. "Fuck." That's when he pushed over the concrete blocks into the water with his foot.

Shane felt the rope go tight. "Hey, man, come on. I didn't do this. This is Eric. He's the one that killed you."

The skater punk shook his head slowly. "No, man. You were going to kill me. You were going to toss me in the lake."

And with that, the skater punk pushed Shane and the rest into the water. Shane's scream was quickly covered by the cool water. Sound disappeared as he sank into darkness. Shane struggled against the ropes. He tried to hold his breath, but the pounding in his chest and the desire to breathe became too much. He opened his mouth. And that's when he realized that Kevin was right. It probably would be better to drown in salt water.

Listen To My Pitch!

Ricky Sprague

The Mountaincrest Studios lot, last remaining movie studio in Hollywood proper, stood on forty-eight acres on Melrose between Gower and Van Ness. A complete circuit, through the Big City Backlot, between soundstages and office buildings, totaled nine-tenths of a mile. At least the route I followed. Depending on how busy things were in International Marketing, I might make two or even three loops before the Los Angeles heat made this "workout" unbearable.

Studio lots are essentially large rental facilities. Especially Mountaincrest, with either failing or dormant franchises, and an underperforming streaming service, every moneymaking opportunity had to be maximized. Which was why the Craig Rice Building—once home to studio contract player dressing rooms—now housed offices of seven independent production companies with no direct connection to or deals with the studio. Despite Mountaincrest's diminishing prominence, an address on the lot still carried some minor level of prestige.

As I walked past, the door to one of these minor-prestige beneficiaries, Half Avocado Productions, opened to disclose wealthy Hollywood party boy Kyle Lester and his girlfriend, social media Influencer Becky McComas AKA Becx-22.

Bidding them goodbye was the Half Avocado Production Assistant, Tawna Norton. As Kyle and Becky turned in the direction of the on-lot parking area, Tawna gave me a knowing, ironic look. I felt a slight thrill knowing that she was letting me in on some secret annoyance. I walked toward her, smiling awkwardly. Unfortunately, I do just about everything awkwardly.

"Our newest writer," she sighed. "He wanted to impress his girlfriend."

Three weeks before, Half Avocado had made news by buying Kyle's spec script, titled *Eclectic Unicorn Witch*. It was like a Hollywood fairy tale come true. Where else but in the city of dreams could a kid be born into a wealthy commercial real estate family, grow up with massive wealth and privilege, date the most beautiful starlets and party girls, use his connections and trust fund to buy three nightclubs, and finally (with no previous experience or professed interest in writing) sell a spec script for $675K?

"Selling a screenplay is a really big deal," I pointed out.

She shook her head ruefully. "Sometimes I think Crofts doesn't know what he's doing."

"Crofts" was Stephen Crofts, the head of Half Avocado. Like Kyle, he was from a wealthy family. He wanted to get into the film industry in the worst way possible, which was just how he'd done it. Armed with his own trust fund and investors that included his family and his family's friends, he started his own production company. Believe it or not, his type littered the gilded streets of Tinseltown.

I smiled. "Well, he hired *you*, so he did one thing right."

She laughed. "Oh my gawd, are you *flirting* with me?"

"*What?*" I stammered. "Nuh-no! Not at all!" My heart was pounding so loud I was sure she was able to hear. She could certainly see the blazing red color my face had taken on.

She laughed again. "It can't be *that* unthinkable that you'd flirt with me."

"That's not what I—"

"You should really give it a try some time. Might work out well for you." She said this in an incredibly charming way.

I felt more stammering coming on. I stifled that by making an attempt at being equally charming: "Flirting isn't my strong suit. But for you I'll make an exception." Before I could say anything more the relative quiet of the lot was shattered by the sounds of squealing tires, crunching metal, and breaking glass. A car accident—an irresistible siren call to the Angeleno. Tawna and I glanced at each other uneasily then ran in the direction of the sounds—the Melrose entrance.

Then there was a scream, followed by a gunshot. At that moment I realized I had a secret motto: *Run toward a crash, and away from a gunshot.*

There was another scream, worse than before, then more squealing tires. These sounds snapped me out of whatever fog I'd drifted into. I was surprised to find that my legs were moving my body once again in the direction of the front gate. I rounded the corner between the Mountaincrest Theater and the Gorman Building just in time to see Jack Canton's car back away from Kyle's, and take off down Melrose toward Van Ness.

How did I know it was *Jack Canton's* car? What kind of

question is that? *Everyone* knows Jack Canton's car. He's the LISTEN TO MY PITCH! guy.

*****

Because the incident had occurred at a movie studio and the victims were prominent entertainers—or at least prominent gears in the internet gossip machine—the Los Angeles Police Department, among many other law enforcement organizations, arrived quickly and closed Melrose from Gower to Van Ness.

In charge of the investigation was Detective Holly Rose. I'd met her before, unfortunately. Actually, sorry, it's not *unfortunate* that I'd met her—she was very charming and capable, that's not what I mean. I just mean it's unfortunate that I've had to ever meet *any* Homicide Detectives, that's all.

Not twenty feet away from us was Kyle's 2018 Asserta, where it had crashed against the studio's Melrose wall. Inside that vehicle were the dead remains of Kyle himself, having succumbed to a bullet to the head. All around the vehicle and up and down the street was a flurry of investigative activity.

Becky, covered in her boyfriend's blood, was taken to the Mercy Hospital on Sunset where she was being treated for shock and hearing loss from the gunshot. I don't know if you've heard a gunshot before, but it's *really loud.*

"Well this is screwy as hell," Detective Rose said. To emphasize her confusion she scratched the top of her head and pursed her lips.

In response I said, "Death is… um…"

Detective Rose ignored my profundity as she ticked off what she knew at that point: "The LISTEN TO MY PITCH! car was parked on Melrose, across from the main gate here, about ten minutes before Kyle's Asserta pulled out. The Asserta made a right onto Melrose, at which point the LISTEN TO MY PITCH! car crossed the street and rear-ended the Asserta, which slammed into the concrete wall. Then, someone who appeared to be Canton got out of the driver's side of the LISTEN TO MY PITCH! car, ran over to the Asserta, and shot Kyle once in the head—*pow!*—then ran back to the LISTEN TO MY PITCH! car, which drove off down Melrose, eventually crashing into another concrete wall about a quarter mile away, on Clinton. The person behind the wheel, Brad Melton, apparently died in the crash when his neck hit the steering wheel. And in the passenger side, Jack Canton himself was slumped over, passed out, showing signs of intoxication."

I couldn't help but point out, "That description was *really* pedantic. What do you mean 'someone who appeared to be Canton'? Wasn't it *actually* him?" Maybe she was just being open-minded.

"Melton was dressed in the same distinctive get-up as Canton."

Jack Canton was famous for two things. One was his manner of dress: He usually wore a loud Hawaiian shirt and khaki shorts, socks with sandals, a straw hat, stringy long blond hair and a surprisingly expensive pair of Ray-Ban sunglasses.

The second thing: His endless self-promotion schemes, the primary example of which was his old clunker of a car—a 1984 Olds Omega he'd spent decades painting in gaudy curlicues and flourishes that perhaps made some kind of mad sense to him while he'd applied the paint through the years. And he had written in huge, pink letters LISTEN TO MY PITCH! on either side. Which seemed inscrutable to me—some producer driving past him on the highway was supposed to see that and think, *I need to flag that guy down—he might have a million-dollar idea!*

"Jack started calling the day the announcement came out," Tawna explained. "He was pretty crazy. Angry I mean. He said that *Eclectic Unicorn Witch* was his pitch—the 'pitch' referenced on the side of his car."

"Did you call the police?"

"We get a lot of crank calls. Intellectual Property theft claims are pretty common. We didn't take this any more seriously than any of the others made against us. Half Avocado, I mean."

"So Mr Canton wasn't the first to make a claim like this against the company?"

Tawna nodded. "The kind of movies we produce make us particularly susceptible. Mostly people saying *they* had the original idea to, for instance, combine a story about bird attacks with natural disasters, or to make a movie about the environment." Half Avocado's movies were generally straight to VOD; a bizarre mixture of high-concept B-movie nonsense (*Hurricanary Attack 3*) and earnest but dull message pictures and prestige vanity projects (*Nation of Hurting: A Fracking Story*). They shared a few things in common: 1) Hardly anyone saw them; 2) Those that did see them hated them; and 3) They were all plagued by embarrassing cost over-runs.

While the two of them spoke I scrolled through the internet on my phone. Brad Melton was a vacuous-looking "dude" type who hung out with Kyle. His best friend, apparently. I had to scroll through several pages of search results but I discovered that Brad had previously dated Kyle's current girlfriend Becky. I relayed this information to Detective Rose and Tawna.

"So, maybe, uh, Brad was jealous of Kyle and Becky and wanted her back, or something…" I said self-consciously.

Detective Rose said, in a tone I interpreted as judgmental, "I'm trying to hold-off speculating at this point. We should know whether it was Canton or Melton who actually fired the gun very soon. Hopefully Canton and Becky can tell us more soon."

*****

I don't know if Dan qualifies as a roommate. Roommates share in rent and expenses on at least a semi-regular schedule. Dan was someone who lived in one of the two bedrooms in my apartment, ate the food in the refrigerator and occasionally chipped in on certain bills.

As it turned out, Jack Canton was part of his immense circle of acquaintances, which included a sort of rogue's gallery of like-minded and let's just say *puckish* types flitting around the periphery of the entertainment industry.

I wasn't surprised that Dan knew Jack, but I was surprised he would want to put forth the effort required to participate in a vigil in his honor. I wanted to go because I'd kind-of witnessed his almost-death We were two of about fifty people outside the hospital holding candles, waiting for word of his health status. The candleholders were folded paper cars with LISTEN TO MY PITCH! scrawled on the sides.

Those in the vigil were surrounded by about a hundred newscasters and photogs. It was a publicity-generating enterprise worthy of Jack himself.

Being in the International Marketing department at Mountaincrest, I'd had direct experience with one of his self-promotion stunts. In 2012, he'd snuck into a Hollywood International Press Platinum Atlas Awards ceremony and gotten one of his cohort to chat with Donna Markland in the bathroom, distracting her when her award for Best Costuming for *CarBots 4* was announced. He bounded to the stage and "accepted the award" on her behalf, beseeching the crowd to help him find an agent. The audience of half-drunk celebs, execs, and journos laughed in appalled amusement at the breech of decorum and security. It seemed ridiculous to me, but my opinion was not representative in this crowd. One of them reminisced:

"Remember that Dodger game he streaked? Where he had LISTEN TO MY PITCH! drawn on his chest? I helped him with that."

"You must be very proud," I couldn't help but say.

"I am! We pretended to be part of the high school band there to perform during the seventh-inning stretch. We snuck down to the entryway from the lockers. My girlfriend distracted the security guys." His smile faded as he added: "She ended up marrying one of them."

That was the "caper" that had earned him the attention of the wacky gang at the 100.6FM *Q Asylum in the Morning*. He continued appearing on that program, mostly as the butt of jokes.

"Remember when he got onto those local newscasts in San Diego and Reno?" someone else said eagerly. "He got that cute girl to pretend to be his agent, and really talked him up as this yo-yo expert. Of course he didn't know anything about yo-yos. One of his 'tricks' was called the 'Listen to My Pitch'!"

Over the sounds of appreciative laughter I asked, "Why didn't he just *pitch* his *idea*, if he was on TV?"

Dan looked at me exasperated. "That's not the point. The point is to get the meeting, *then* make the pitch. If he'd pitched it on TV, then the idea would have been out there in the open, for anybody to take."

"Okay, sorry." I was being a Gloomy Gus, and the man, for all we knew at that point, was fighting for his life.

Dan pressed his perceived advantage. "I'm *really* disappointed in you. He's just trying to make it in an industry where you need contacts and relatives in high places to get anywhere." He got a dreamy look as he continued: "I remember the scheme I helped him with. Last year there was a billboard for the movie *Life's a Switch* on La Cienega near the 405 exit. We changed it so it read *Listen to My Pitch!* It was hilarious."

"I want to know why you've got time and energy to scale a fifty-foot billboard on La Cienega but you can't get a regular job."

"It was only forty-two feet," he said, neatly avoiding my point. "Besides, Jack did all the planning and gathering materials and stuff. His plan was as intricate as the designs on his car." He seemed pretty pleased with that observation. "We had to shimmy up that post with this pulley system he devised, carrying the paint and—wow, it was exciting! When we were done it was just after three in the morning. Jack let me drive! It was so tense. I got distracted turning onto Pico—there was construction there and I scraped the side of the car on one of those concrete barriers. A cop pulled us over and I was pretty nervous because we had all our paint and ropes and stuff in the trunk, but the cop basically said he wanted to see the car for himself, because it was famous—like he was star-struck or something!"

"That doesn't inspire confidence in our law enforcement officers," I said.

Dan waxed melancholic. "Come to think of it, I left some of *my* tools in his trunk. I should get them back. I hope they weren't damaged in the crash."

"I'm glad that your concern for Jack's welfare hasn't affected your priorities."

"Those tools are pretty valuable. Besides that, I need them for odd jobs and stuff."

"They've been missing for a year," I pointed out. Then decided it wasn't worth pursuing so I went on: "Clearly he's dedicated to self-promotion, however misguided his efforts seem to me. But I don't understand how someone capable of coming up with these ideas can have his *screenplay stolen*?"

They looked at me sheepishly.

"Even if his screenplay *was* somehow stolen—wouldn't that be easy to prove with documents on his hard drive or on file sharing sites or Writer's Guild registration or *something*?"

"Jack's old school," Dan said. "He wrote it all on a word processor in the early '90s, using Word Perfect. It was on a floppy disk."

Dan stopped, apparently finished, as if that explained it all. No one offered to continue the story so I eloquently asked,

"So?"

"He lost the floppy disk, but he had transferred it onto a jump drive some time in the early aughts. Kyle must've stolen *that.*"

"Jack didn't have it on his computer?"

"Computers can be hacked!" Dan insisted.

"Well, jump drives can be *stolen,*" I pointed out. Couldn't help it. This was ridiculous. Part of me felt Jack deserved to have his screenplay stolen, if what Dan said was accurate.

"Chris," Dan said, in a scandalized tone. "Have a little respect for the man. He might be dying!"

"Sorry," I grumbled. Again, they were right—all the judgmental glares were well deserved.

*****

That night Becky livestreamed from the hospital. She was a lemonade-out-of-lemons kind of Influencer—after a few minutes lamenting Kyle's death, she did a tutorial on how to turn head and ear bandages into the *cutest* kitty cat ear headgear.

She also uploaded footage from two videos. The first was clipped from a stream of Kyle and Becky playing video games in Kyle's enormous home two weeks before. Apparently there's an audience for that. Suddenly, through the window, Kyle noticed the LISTEN TO MY PITCH! car parked outside on the street. He shouted that he was tired of Jack accusing him of stealing his script, and the camera followed Kyle outside to confront Jack. While Kyle opened the gate, the LISTEN TO MY PITCH! car squealed off.

Given what happened outside the Mountaincrest front

gate, the second piece of video, from three days before, was worse. It showed Becky using her phone to film herself and Kyle in his Asserta, driving on the interstate, singing along to that annoying Billie Eilish song. Through the rear windshield could be seen the unmistakable LISTEN TO MY PITCH! car. Their jokes at its expense turned to vulgar complaints of its tailgating. When it rear-ended the Asserta, Kyle looked at Becky and uttered an expletive before the video cut off.

The incidents, Becky claimed, were part of a sustained pattern of harassment. It appeared that Jack had taken his self-promotional scheming to a dangerous extreme.

*****

But how does that old Hollywood mantra go? *Appearances can be deceiving.*

The police investigation uncovered evidence of a baffling plot straight out of a Hollywood spec script. A search of Brad Melton's home found sales information and title on a 1984 Olds Omega—the same make and model as Jack's infamous car—purchased on September 25. The day *after* Jack made his first Intellectual Property theft call to Half Avocado. Also found in Brad's garage: blackout curtains over the windows and paint on the floor. It appeared the newly purchased car was painted to match Jack's.

This all pointed to a plan by Brad Melton to frame Jack for harassment, and in the process win Becky back by permanently eliminating Kyle.

When Jack regained consciousness he was able to fill in some more of the story. The night before Kyle's murder, Brad met Jack at Club Disparue on Santa Monica. They hung out for awhile, Jack got a little intoxicated and Brad agreed to drive him home. The next thing he knew, he woke up in the hospital. There was ketamine in his system—Brad drugged him in order to gain access to the actual, original, *authentic* LISTEN TO MY PITCH! car and to frame Jack.

Unfortunately for Brad, he crashed Jack's car and died before he could complete his plan to slide Jack into the driver's seat then run off. Maybe his adrenaline or nerves got to him. It was apparently only his first murder.

The police gave every indication they were satisfied with the convoluted mess. The investigation was officially closed. I decided I probably wouldn't have made a very good police officer, because it seemed too bizarre to be true.

Over shawarma I expressed my skepticism to Dan, who shrugged his shoulders.

"Love makes people do weird things, in case you hadn't noticed."

"There are *hundreds* of pictures of Melton online, with lots of different, beautiful women. Was he so hung up on Becky he'd create this *really elaborate* frame-up?"

Dan's eyes widened. "'Frame up'? What are you, a shamus?"

"Jack worked on *his* car for years—Brad painted a facsimile in a *few days*? Brad is a trust fund kid who mooches off his family and friends!"

Dan stared off in the distance, not listening to me at all. "*The Shameful Shamus,*" he said, musingly.

"And what happened to the fake LISTEN TO MY PITCH! car?"

"The Ashamed Shamus," he went on. He wasn't letting it

go.

"Why is *anyone* satisfied with this explanation?"

"Occam's Razor."

"How does that apply here?"

"If enough people accept it, then it's the correct explanation."

"That's not what Occam's Razor means."

He gave me an exasperated look. "Kyle was at Jack's house multiple times. He knew about Jack's jump drive—"

"Where does Jack live, by the way?"

"Off Crescent Heights on 4th. It's actually a few blocks from Kyle's club on San Vicente. I think that's where they first met."

"That neighborhood's not cheap. Does Jack have roommates or something?"

"No."

"What does he do for a living?" I realized I'd never asked.

"A little of this...a little of that..." he said vaguely. "Odd jobs."

"So he has no discernible source of income?"

"Lots of people in LA don't," he pointed out. "I don't."

"Yeah, but you have a 'roommate' to 'help' with the rent. Who helps him with his rent?"

"I said he does odd jobs. He gets by. He did stuff for Kyle at the club."

"Like what?"

He shrugged. "Whatever came up..."

"*Criminal* stuff?"

He scoffed. "Of *course not*. He'd never do anything illegal. Or immoral."

"Don't take this the wrong way, but it occurs to me that your definition of *immoral* might not comport with mine." Then: "Did you read his script?"

He looked scandalized. "I'd never do that!"

"What I mean is, did he ever tell you what his pitch actually *was*?"

"I'm not an agent. I might have stolen it."

"Right. I understand. But did he ever actually pitch to *anyone*? He was a very minor local celebrity. Some agent must have at least *met* with him some time."

Dan was thinking very hard. "I don't know. This town's not fair…"

I had a terrible feeling and my mind was working—but what I was thinking was insane: There *was* no pitch. No screenplay. Just an *eccentric* concocter of elaborate self-promotion schemes. The latest of which had gotten two people killed.

After a few seconds Dan said, musingly, "*The Shame-us*," and popped a piece of spanakopita in his mouth.

*****

Two days later I was making my studio-lot circuit again. Nearing the Craig Rice building, my heart raced. Would it be appropriate to look in on Tawna? *Of course*, I rationalized. She and I had ear-witnessed a highly traumatic and newsworthy event. It made sense to commiserate for a few minutes. Normal people did stuff like that, didn't they?

Besides, I thought I might want to run my cockamamie theory by her. I also *didn't* want to run it by her. It was, after all, cockamamie, and I am not exactly a confident person.

The office door was hanging open, so I went up and knocked. She received me warmly but with a frazzled, incredibly tired look. "Chris! How are you? I just popped in to get my stuff. *I am out of here.*"

"You're quitting?" My heart sank.

"Yeah. I wanted to wait to tell Crofts personally, but he's been MIA, and I got this opportunity to represent Jack—"

"*Jack Canton?*"

She smiled. "Yeah. Since this whole thing happened, with Kyle stealing his screenplay and all, we've been talking. I always wanted to be an agent, so he asked me to help him deal with all the offers he's getting for his life story. We just finalized a deal with Orbital Studios." She quickly added, "Sorry—Mountaincrest just couldn't match it. We're announcing it tomorrow."

"That's—congratulations," I said unenthusiastically. "So Kyle definitely *did* steal the screenplay?"

She looked puzzled, then shook her head ruefully. "Sorry—I'm so immersed in all this. I just assumed everyone knew. Becky posted another video. She says Kyle confessed before he died."

I whistled. "Jack was telling the truth." If Becky could be believed. "How did Half Avocado come to make the original deal anyway?"

"Crofts said he'd read this amazing script he wanted to move on right away. It was too good to pass up. This wasn't the first time he'd said that about a script, so I was pretty skeptical. But I read it, and it wasn't bad. A little convoluted, but we could polish it up. The problem was the amount of money Crofts wanted to spend."

"Was he afraid someone else might buy it?

She rolled her eyes and nodded. "I guess. We'd gotten some more funding, so we were flush. And he was determined to *flush* it all away I guess."

I took a deep breath and tried to stifle my natural urge toward shame and embarrassment. If I didn't air my concerns and they turned out to have any validity at all, I would have felt absolutely miserable. Worse even than the discomfort I'd feel by talking to her about them here, now. So I hit her with a shocking revelation:

"I, um, I think that Jack Canton might not be, you know— totally on the, um, *up-and-up*."

She stared at me with a skeptical smile. "You mean, even by Hollywood standards?"

"Yeah—that's a good way of putting it. I mean, he's planned all of these bizarre self-promotion scams; he even got my *roommate* to work for him for free. He seems more concerned with that than his actual pitch."

"His script was pretty good, though," she said diplomatically.

"You *have* to say that now, you're his agent," I noted. "But anyway, my point is, he could have plotted this whole thing as a publicity stunt and then it all went wrong in the process. And if Brad really *was* jealous and wanted to kill Kyle anyway, maybe he used this as cover?"

"That sounds sort of... crazy."

"I know. I just think that this is an elaborate plot and it seems more like something *Jack* would do than Brad. And, Kyle did steal his screenplay. So what if *Jack* got *Brad* to set this whole thing up—"

"And then killed him?"

"Maybe that part was an accident. Probably, Brad decided to kill Jack so that he couldn't tell anyone that he'd planned the whole thing. That was why they were dressed the same, you know?"

"No." She gave me a punishing look that only served to reinforce my awkwardness. "This is kind of starting to sound weird, Chris. No offense."

"None taken. I understand that." I really did, too.

"Are you saying that Jack arranged for Kyle to steal his screenplay? Or that he concocted the whole thing with Brad *after* the screenplay was stolen?"

"Well..."

"Brad definitely bought the second car. The guy who sold it identified him as the buyer..." She shook her head. "I just don't see how *Jack* could have arranged it."

"Only part of it. He kind of got the ball rolling and then Brad added on the killing parts." I then pressed on with my even worse theory: "I think that Crofts might be, you know, *not on the up-and-up* either."

"How so?"

"Well—I mean, no offense, but, like, why did he pay so much money for that screenplay? It could be a..." Here I leaned forward and stage whispered dramatically. "...Money-laundering thing."

She stood speechless. "Crofts is… He's too dumb for that."

"Well, it just seems, I mean, the whole thing seems—"

"And even if Crofts and Kyle did launder money, what's that got to do with Brad killing Kyle?"

"I don't know," I admitted.

She shook her head. I thought she was going to say something along the lines of, "*You're crazy, go away*," but instead she smiled and said, "Chris, I think that you need to take a break. Why don't you ask me out tonight, to celebrate my new job?"

"Can I take you out?" I stammered.

She pretended to be surprised. "I thought you'd never ask!"

We made arrangements. We went out that night. I'll refrain from going into details now. Discretion and valor and so forth.

*****

The announcement of Jack's deal with Orbital Studios was at a "Car Crushing Ceremony" in the 100.6 FM parking lot on Sunset. The Q Asylum in the Morning crew set up an outdoor studio beside the dented and smashed remains of the LISTEN TO MY PITCH! car, which had been released by the police and hauled to the site the night before. And beside the car was an enormous portable high-speed hydraulic press car crusher, and a crane.

Dan was part of the crowd which included those who'd attended the vigil as well as Becky, who was livestreaming it all, to show moral support.

Ever since the night of the vigil Dan had been thinking

about his billboard escapade, resentment growing. It hadn't occurred to him that he'd been suckered into working for Jack's benefit, without any corresponding financial remuneration.

Plus, he wanted his tools back.

As Dan made his way around the Caution tape-wrapped velvet ropes surrounding the LISTEN TO MY PITCH! car he peeked into the backseat, noticed it was a lot cleaner than he remembered when he'd driven in it. This he took as a bad sign. If Jack cleaned the car's interior, he'd probably cleaned the trunk.

And taken his tools! Dan hadn't missed them for over a year and now he felt desperate to get them back.

"So used," he muttered, in reference to the way he felt about himself. He glared at Jack, who was standing with the deejays, yukking it up. Tawna stood with them, along with Anna Mesrine, the Chief Creative Officer at Orbital Studios.

Dan knew of Tawna because I'd mentioned her a few times, maybe. My descriptions had meant next to nothing to him because he barely paid attention to me when I spoke to him. Seeing her now, however, jogged something in his memory.

He was *hmming* in his mind when Detective Holly Rose made her way through the crowd and stopped beside him, introduced herself to him again.

"Right," he said. "You haven't seen Chris anywhere have you?"

"No. Why?"

He shrugged. "He didn't come home last night. Left me a giddy voicemail that he was going out on a date with *her*—" he indicated Tawna "—after work, and now *she's* here, and he's *I-don't-know-where*. Not at work, which is strange. He's annoyingly responsible."

"I need to talk to her and Canton anyway. This morning around four, police in Victorville found the Olds that Brad purchased. It was burned out pretty bad but they matched the VIN."

"Huh. Well—that takes care of the question of what happened to the other car."

"Yeah, but the next question is: Whose body did we find burned to a crisp beside it?"

"There was *another body*?" Dan stage whispered, shocked.

"The driver's license they found, and some paperwork remnants belonged Stephen Crofts. The way it looks, someone was trying to destroy the car but got covered in gas himself and then started the fire anyway for some reason."

"I don't even know who Stephen Crofts is and I'm shocked."

Detective Rose nodded to Tawna. "Her former boss. The one who bought Kyle's screenplay."

"But why would he drive out to Victorville to burn up the car, with no way to get back?"

"I try very hard not to make assumptions during an investigation."

"Wait," Dan said, startled. "What if it was—*Chris's* body?"

The deejays surrendered a microphone to Tawna, who stood beside the car and began speaking. For all her outward confidence there was still a touch of nervousness: "I feel like

241

one of those car show models... so dumb..." Then: "Oops. Sorry, if people still do that. Um, it's a little bit sexist but, you know, no judgment..."

Dan groaned. "She's worse at public speaking than Chris."

"I'm Tawna Norton," she continued. "I have some really exciting news to announce. The owner of this famous car, Jack Canton, has been trying to get Hollywood to *listen to his pitch* for twenty-eight years. Well, now, Hollywood *is* listening. And all it took was a murder plot to get everyone's attention."

Laughs.

"Now that we've got Hollywood's attention, it's time to look to the future and *crush* the past... huh? Amirite? Get it?"

The crowd groaned, then clapped appreciatively.

"This is a practical event as well as a—a sort of a— metaphorical one, I guess you'd say."

One of the Q Asylum-ers said, "Don't use words like 'metaphorical' on this show! We don't want the FCC on our butts!" This statement was followed by the sounds of a slide whistle and a toilet flushing, courtesy of a very classy soundboard.

Dan, who ordinarily appreciated such morning-show antics, wasn't paying attention. He was staring at the side of the car, where it had been scratched the night of the billboard caper. One of the benefits of driving such an eccentric car was that most damage could be simply incorporated into its "look." By which is meant that Jack just painted a few squiggles and curlicues over the damage and left it at that.

That damage didn't appear to be on the car parked before him. He said, to Detective Rose, "Did that burned out car happen to have a set of really nice, brand-new-at-the-time-straight-from-Craftsman quality tools in the trunk?"

"I don't know. I wasn't there."

Tawna pressed on: "Let's give it up now for Jack Canton!"

There were applause and cheers while Jack took the microphone. "It's funny to see this car in this place of honor. She and I have been through a lot, obviously. Lots of dings and dents. And surprises. And here it is the last time I'll ever see her. I mean, I can't drive her on the streets anymore, since she's totaled out... But I knew we'd get our movie deal eventually. I just never thought I'd have to get almost killed to get that deal!"

For some reason, that elicited laughter. Probably for the "almost" part.

By this time, Dan had sidled over to the back of the car. He was brimming with resentment over being tricked into working for free. And if this car was about to get crushed, he was damn sure going to get his tools out of the trunk. If this was even the *same car*.

It bothered him that it probably wasn't. It also bothered him that I was nowhere to be found, and that my body was probably burned to crisp in Victorville for some reason, and I was narrating this story from beyond the grave, like a ghost.

"I'll be honest, though," Jack said, philosophically. "I'm gonna be glad to see it crushed, finally. As much as it's meant to me—"

Dan stepped underneath the velvet ropes, went to the trunk, and attempted to wrench it open by hand.

Jack said, "What are you doing?"

"I want my tools back!"

"Uh, Dan… if you left tools in the trunk they're not there now. The trunk is empty…"

"I don't believe it! This isn't even the same car! It's the *other one!*"

Tawna said, angrily, "Who are you and what are you doing?"

"I'm Chris's roommate!" he declared dramatically. "And I know that you killed him last night and burned his body in Victorville!" Dan didn't share Detective Rose's aversion to conclusion-jumping.

Tawna's eyes widened in appalled horror. "*What are you talking about?*"

He pointed accusing fingers at her, then Jack, then at the deejays for some reason, then the crowd for some other reason, as he went on: "Chris was right! He knew that Jack concocted the whole plan to publicize himself! His script was terrible! If anyone ever actually read it they'd know that! So when it got out and everyone saw how ridiculous it was, he had to *spring into action!*"

Tawna made the neck slashing gesture, to alert the Q Asylum gang to stop broadcasting. They refused. Dan's trainwreck was too good to pass up.

"Jack had a hypnotic, Svengali-like hold over people! That's right—I've read *Trilby!*" he added defensively. "An ability to charm them into doing the most horrible things—like working! He did it to me! Think about it: Why would Brad Melton go to all the trouble of buying a replacement Olds and paint it just to set up some harassment backstory to frame Jack? Answer: Because he wouldn't!" He pointed at Jack.

"Because *you* would!"

Dan smiled with smug satisfaction at his nonsensical declaration.

Jack said, "I'm going to sue you for libel so hard..."

"It's not libel!" Dan said with rare insight. "It's slander when it's spoken, and besides, it's not even that, *because it's the truth!*" Triumphantly he kicked the trunk, which popped open, revealing my bound, gagged, and disoriented body lying uncomfortably within.

It took nearly two awkward minutes to help me out of the trunk. My joints were stiff and achy, my mind was still sleepy and I had to pee like I've never had to pee before. My left arm and right leg were completely asleep, creating a horrible feeling of disjointed imbalance. Tawna's face was a mask of compassion as she raced to my side and attempted to help.

My attempts to push her away were hindered by the effects of the ketamine and being bound and gagged in a trunk for several hours. My movements could easily be interpreted as groping, although they most definitely were not.

When the gag was removed my mouth was sore and dry, my throat hurt so that I could barely talk. My speech was charmingly slurred as I said, "Tawna was laundering money through Half Avocado. Crofts didn't know..."

"*That's* how I know you!" Dan said to Tawna. "*You* were Jack's 'agent' when he made all those yo-yo champion appearances!"

Tawna had a look of utter contempt mingled with bafflement. She really couldn't think of what to do next.

Jack's look wasn't much different. He was clearly torn by

his natural self-promotional instinct and his natural self-preservation instinct. In the end, his mind snapped.

"Everything worked perfectly until you didn't kill this guy like you were supposed to!" Jack indicated me as he shouted at Tawna.

"This plan was stupid—I shouldn't have gone along with it!"

"Then your whole *money laundering machine* would have been exposed!"

At this point they seemed to realize they were standing in front of a large crowd of witnesses, and Jack was holding a microphone which was broadcasting to a huge number of people (Q Asylum in the Morning had a 6.3 share, for some reason).

Tawna was first to recover. She stammered: "I have no idea what's—he's lying—He's obviously crazy! Look at his car!"

Detective Rose, who'd come here intending on asking only a few questions about the burned-out Olds in Victorville, ended up arresting both Tawna Norton and Jack Canton on a variety of charges.

*****

My hospital vigil was nowhere near the size of Jack's. Only Dan and Detective Rose bothered to show up. A lot of people were angry with me. Jack was a lovable local eccentric, and I'd spoiled everyone's concept of him.

I was kept overnight for observation and while the ketamine cleared my system. It was awhile before I'd stopped slurring my speech, but I never fully recovered the memory of my "date" with Tawna.

Detective Rose's smile displayed warm irony as she filled us in on what she knew: "During your dinner she tried to steer you away from the truth, but you wouldn't shut up. *Her* words, by the way. You figured out that Half Avocado was just a money-laundering operation that occasionally put out half-assed movies, and you also figured out that *she* was the mastermind, not Crofts."

"I remember some of that part," I said. "She confessed, then tried to get me to join up with her. To start an agency together."

Detective Rose nodded. "She said you pretended to go along with it, but you were so nervous and such a bad actor she could tell you were going to the police. So she panicked, started 'crying,' knocked her silverware off the table, and when you picked it up off the floor she drugged your drink."

"I guess it was lucky she just happened to have ketamine on her at the time."

To Detective Rose, Dan said dramatically, "I know *you* don't like making assumptions, but *I'm* not afraid to say that femme fatale had murder in mind, right from the start."

"Anyway," Detective Rose went on. "They're both talking, both trying to implicate the other as the real 'mastermind.' From what we can tell, Kyle really *did* steal the screenplay. About a year ago. Jack didn't notice until he saw the announcement that Kyle had 'sold' it."

"He took his pitch really seriously," I noted.

"So he called Tawna. They already knew each other from when she worked as a hostess at Kyle's club on San Vicente, and he asked her to pretend to be his agent to help him get on local newscasts as a fake yo-yo champion." She rolled her eyes. "So pointless."

"It was actually an effective commentary on how the news is produced," Dan sniffed. "As well as good promotion for him."

Detective Rose wisely waved a dismissive hand. "I don't understand the psychology and I don't think I ever will. Tawna says he was very manipulative and passive aggressive. A lot of 'It'll be bad if my allegations lead to an investigation of Half Avocado's books...' and 'Kyle does this and that, how much do you think you can really trust him...?' and so on. So, the two of them came up with this plan to create the illusion that Brad and Kyle were framing Jack for harassment.

"Tawna then called Brad and Kyle, and got them involved—she laid it all out as if she'd come up with it on her own to discredit Jack, and got Brad to buy the 'new' Olds. She said she'd take care of re-painting it. In reality, Jack switched out the VINs and tweaked the odometer, then she just gave them the *real* LISTEN TO MY PITCH! car. The 'new' one was kept in Jack's storage space in Sherman Oaks.

"The night before Kyle's murder Jack got Brad drunk, took him home, and let him sleep until morning, at which point Jack strangled him, stuffed him in his car with that ridiculous Jack Canton get-up. Tawna called Kyle into the office to sign some papers, then called Jack when they arrived. Jack framed himself for Kyle's murder, crashed the car, and took ketamine to sell the narrative.

"Tawna had been doing Half Avocado's financial paperwork in such a way as to implicate Crofts. But it would be easier to sell the illusion if Crofts wasn't alive to dispute it.

So she gave him some ketamine and handed him off to Jack, who staged the scene in Victorville. It was meant to imply that Crofts was part of the murder frame-up."

Dan smiled. "I always knew Jack's mind was admirably complex."

We ignored that. Detective Rose turned to me. "How are you feeling?"

"I feel miserable."

"You inspired someone to kill you," Dan said cheerily. "That's quite an achievement."

"But she couldn't go through with it," I pointed out. "Which is why she tied me up and stuffed in me in the trunk of the car that they were going to crush."

"So you inspired a sort of murderous ambivalence." Now his voice was more philosophical. "You made an impression. In this life, that's all anyone can ask for."

Fireball Rolled a Seven

Bethany Maines

April 2020

Fireball had only one rule for the Pandemic Drags: wear a fucking mask. So Kendra pulled on the Mira Safety CM-7M gas mask she'd stolen from her dad's military gear and exited her Honda. Tonight was her night. She was wearing knee high Doc Martens, suspenders with jean shorts short enough to show just a little bit of ass cheek, and a white tank top over a multi-strapped black bra-let. In her hair, she had a Minnie Mouse sequin bow. She looked great and Minnie, her zippy little Honda painted in red with white polka-dots, looked *pristine*. Because, after all, if you were going to show up for drag racing, you should fucking *show up*.

Kendra made her way to the racers circle. Fireball's crew had painted out the circle with the hash marks six-feet apart. Fireball had started the Pandemic Drags as soon as the lockdown orders went into effect. For drag racers, the empty streets were too good an opportunity to pass up—plague or no plague.

Fifteen-year-old Stacy Ichigawa who worked in her dad's garage and drove whatever she could sneak out of the shop was already there wearing some sort of anime-inspired face mask. Stacy was good, but tonight she was driving a Tesla and Kendra was pretty sure she could beat that. Then there was

Anatoliy Whatever-the-Fuck-Ukranian-last-name in an embroidered face mask. He drove a Honda like she did, but had his brothers and cousins to help him on the engine. She was nervous about him. Next around the circle were Douchebag Carl (as opposed to Cool Carl, who wasn't here tonight), wearing what Kendra swore was a pair of leopard print panties as a face mask.

"I got real masks in the car if you want to buy some," said Carl, when he saw her eyeing his face.

Kendra shook her head.

"What'd you do? Steal them from the hospital?" asked Mike the Dyke overhearing the statement. Mike was wearing a hand sewn mask with a print of tiny dicks.

"Nah, I just had like three boxes of N95's from work in storage," he replied, with a shrug.

"Shouldn't you give them to the hospitals?" demanded Mike.

"Only if they pay me the going rate," he retorted.

"You are *such* a douchebag," said Mike. "Also, if you've got masks, why are you wearing that shit on your face?"

Carl pulled the panties down and waggled his tongue at Mike. "Cuz I ain't gonna get the plague," he said snapping the panties back in place. "People my age don't get it. This is all way overblown."

"I don't think that's correct," said a voice that Kendra didn't recognize. Everyone turned around to see a new guy approaching with Fireball coming along behind him. The new guy wore a red fez, a bowtie and basic N95 mask. He looked about her age—early twenties—and might be nerd cute without the mask.

"The reports coming out of Italy say that everyone's getting it," said New Guy.

"Whatever," said Ferrari Jim, the fifty-eight-year-old with the black motorcycle jacket and mask made from a Punisher t-shirt. His red Ferrari was the one to beat. He had been the winner for six races running—not that he needed the money. Kendra kind of hated him for that. She thought Fireball wasn't a fan either, but Fireball never said anything because the Ferrari made the races exciting.

"You're going to catch it or not," Jim continued. "Freaking out about it isn't going to do any good."

Kendra turned back to see what New Guy made of this, but he was staring at her and flapped his arms in excitement. "Are you my mummy?" he asked, sounding gleeful.

Fireball laughed, although it was a little fuzzy through his bandana mask. His orange hair, black at the roots, was starting to fade to pale yellow on the bleached out ends. Kendra knew the cholo-looking bandana was actually custom and hid a fully tailored mask with a filter underneath it.

"Word of advice, Doc," said Fireball, "keep your sonic in your pants or she'll exterminate your ass. Kendra doesn't take shit."

"Noted," said Doc, with a nod.

Kendra didn't get the reference, so she shook her head, trying to imply that she was tired of their bullshit already. Communicating in the gas mask meant screaming like you were trying to warn your mother away from an on-coming bus.

"Sorry. Hi. Nice to meet you from six-feet away," said Doc. He gave a dorky wave.

"Doc tries to get in your pants," said Anatoliy, in clipped syllables. His blond hair was combed down with extra severity tonight.

"I just said hi!" protested Doc.

"Total pants move," agreed Mike. Kendra noticed that Mike had zipped stripes into the side of her hair and given herself a flat top that might have been cut with a level. Pandemic hair was starting to be a thing.

"Yeah, like Doctor Who lines were going to work," scoffed Douchebag Carl.

"I just said hi..." said Doc, blushing enough that she could see it in the street lights and above his mask. She felt bad for him. She didn't think he'd been intending to hit on her, and she actually didn't mind if he was. But she was here for money, not a man.

She stomped her foot, the Doc Martens making a heavy clomp on the ground. Then she gave Fireball an open handed gesture attempting to indicate that he should move it along.

"OK," said Fireball, eyeing the blank spot in the circle in irritation. "I guess the other new talent decided not to show."

There was a heavy roar of an engine and something edged onto the street, driving slow and showboating. It was an ugly ass dune-buggy looking piece of shit with an exposed motor, built like the owner thought *pandemic* meant *Mad Max*.

Douchebag Carl groaned, clearly recognizing him. "Fireball," he complained. "I know this guy. He's an asshole."

"If I didn't let assholes race none of you would be here,"

said Fireball.

"Don't say I didn't warn you," Carl said sourly.

The dune buggy had a large number seven painted on the side. Not in a cool way, but like someone had just grabbed some house paint and slopped it on there. Kendra shook her head at the lack of pride in presentation. The driver was a forty-ish looking white guy with a bushy beard wearing motorcycle leathers and no mask.

"I guess we should be glad he's got pants on and not just the chaps," said Mike.

"That's cuz he's only a closet level fag," said Douchebag Carl. "He's not out yet."

Mike looked over at him, as if trying to gauge how offensive Carl was trying to be.

"What?" asked Carl with a shrug. "It takes real balls to go full pride parade."

A snicker ran around the circle, but was smothered by a wave of murmurs from the fully masked crowd. New guy did not immediately strap on a mask and walked bare-faced toward Fireball and the circle. The crowd parted like the red sea, keeping a solid six feet back.

Next to the string of black SUVs by the locked park gates, Kendra could see the betting pool go quietly into action. The hand-signals crossed the multiple language divides of Tagalog, Ukrainian, Russian, piss-poor English, regular shitty English, Cambodian, and Spanish. Even from a distance, Kendra could read that currently bets were being placed on if the new guy would even get to race.

"You have to put on a mask," said Fireball, patiently. "If you do not have one, one will be provided for you."

"I ain't wearing no pussy mask," said the new guy. "Live free or die." He crowed loudly and pivoted slightly, peacocking for the crowd. Kendra began to think Carl was right about the new driver and that made her nervous. Carl shouldn't ever be right about anything.

"Listen up, Plague Blankets," snapped Fireball, "you may live free, and you may die, but you are not allowed to take me with you. Put on a fucking mask."

"They don't work!" yelled Plague Blankets. "Only chinks and niggers get the 'Rona and I ain't fucking wearing one."

As the racial slurs rang out over the crowd began to get quiet and the space between Plague Blankets and everyone else perceptibly widened. Kendra glanced over at Stacy and Mike. They both had similar blank expressions that probably meant they had heard those slurs before and weren't impressed.

"You will wear one or I will call the HazMat team," said Fireball.

"Fuck you. I'm going to race."

"You can take the mask off in your car, but you have to wear one out here," said Fireball. But he was already snapping his fingers.

From out of the crowd, two men in full yellow PPE suits and gas masks like Kendra's appeared. They both carried shotguns. Kendra could tell the difference because Matt had a Wolfenstein while Hazard carried a sawed-off classic Beretta 20 gauge.

"You ain't gonna fucking shoot me over a mask," taunted Plague Blankets, turning toward Hazard, who was closer. That turned out to be a mistake because Matt bopped him on top of the head with the shotgun.

Plague Blankets grunted angrily and turned toward Matt preparing to fight, but Hazard thumped him in the gut. Plague Blankets doubled over, looking like he might puke. Hazard and Matt pushed and bullied him back to the car. Eventually, he drove away with a lot of screaming and unnecessary engine noise. The crowd visibly relaxed as the engine noise died away.

"He's right though," said Ferrari Jim. "There's no evidence that masks work."

"Fucking bullshit," barked Fireball. "That is because of the discrepancy in mask quality. So fuck you."

"We don't actually know one way or another," Doc said. "The virus is so new that we don't have any studies on mask efficacy."

"Thank you," Ferrari Jim said, as if this proved his point. Doc's eyebrows furrowed in confusion.

"What?" Fireball snapped.

"I'm just saying," said Doc, looking nervous at Fireball's intensity.

"Yeah," Fireball said. "Say it again. We don't know what?"

"We don't have a comprehensive study yet," Doc said. He glanced apologetically at Jim, who had folded his arms across his chest and was glaring at him. "That means we haven't gathered evidence yet for this *specific* virus. But we have a lot of evidence that masks work on other viruses, so the odds are masks are good for this one too."

"OK," said Fireball, looking like he was memorizing that as a talking point for later. "Good. You are allowed to stay."

"Was that in question?" asked Doc, looking around nervously.

"It's always in question," said Stacy. "It's Fireball's world, we're just racing in it." She batted her eyelashes at Doc, head cocking one direction while she curled her ponytail end around her finger. Kendra was impressed at Stacy's ability to flirt over a mask. Doc looked like he wasn't sure if he should back up further or appreciate the move.

"Oh. OK," said Doc. "Cool?" He looked around the circle for support.

Mike and Jim, who still looked pissed, rolled their eyes in unison, and Kendra tried not to fog up her mask by laughing. Carl adjusted his crotch because he was a douchebag and Stacy flipped him off.

"What?" asked Carl. As if he didn't know.

"Shut it, all of you," said Fireball. "Time for match-ups." He dumped a slew of papers from a Crown Royal bag out on the pavement. "Anatoliy goes first."

Anatoliy stepped on a piece of paper then bent down and picked it up.

"Carl," he said holding it up to show the name scrawled on it.

"Stacy," said Fireball, pointing at the girl who was standing next to Anatoliy. Stacy pulled on a pair of driving gloves and then bent over and picked a name.

"Doc," she said, waving cheerfully at Doc as she displayed the paper that just read: NEW GUY 1.

"Mike," said Fireball pointing.

Mike bent down and grabbed one of the remaining slips of

paper.

"You and me, hot stuff," said Mike, holding up the paper that had Kendra's name on it.

"Great," said Fireball, making notes on his clipboard. "We're now at odd numbers thanks to Carl's asshole friend."

"Not my friend!" yelped Carl, fully outraged.

"So I'm moving Jim ahead to the second bracket since he's last week's winner. First round brackets: we'll do Anatoliy and Carl, then it's Kendra and Mike, then Doc and Stacy. Winners from Stacy and Kendra's races will go up against each other, Anatoliy races Jim."

"Hey!" exclaimed Carl. "I could win."

"You could," said Jim, "but you're not going to."

"Then Jim races whoever comes out of the other bracket."

"Hey!" said Anatoliy in turn. Fireball ignored him. Kendra thought that was unfair—Anatoliy really did have a chance.

"Everyone races twice. All winners get the standard cut of the pool," continued Fireball. "Don't come complaining to me later. It is what it is."

Like they didn't know that—Stacy was right about it being Fireball's world. Fireball had the backing of the Puyallup Tribe by marriage and the Original Loco Boyz by affiliation. Nobody wanted to fuck with either of those, so they shut up and took the cut he said they could have.

"But there is a bonus from our sponsor," added Fireball.

"We have a sponsor?" asked Jim skeptically.

"Papa Steg," said Fireball and everyone groaned.

Papa Steg ran the betting pool and was always trying to

incentivize drivers into being more exciting. Kendra thought that sooner or later Papa Steg was going to incentivize someone right into killing themselves.

"Fastest time under seven minutes gets seven hundred bucks," said Fireball. Jim snorted in derision, but inside her mask Kendra bit her lip. This quarter's tuition hadn't gotten any cheaper even if she was now taking all of her classes online, and now she had to pay for rent since her on-campus living subsidy was no longer in effect. Seven hundred bucks would put a significant dent into her pile of bills.

Anatoliy, with the Mountain Dew green Honda, and Carl, with his shitty bondo-gray Charger covering a custom motor, pointing south on Pearl Street.

Pearl was technically a state highway and a four mile straight line from Pt. Defiance Park to Fircrest. There were a few hills here and there and one traffic cam, but that just kept it interesting. Fireball did straight drags as qualifiers; the fastest cars went on to the extended rally race. To even be competitive Kendra had modified sweet little Minnie to be able to hit 125mph in a quarter mile. After the latest bump up, Kendra thought Minnie might be able to make 185, but she wasn't sure she wanted to test it on the side streets. Tonight's rally shot straight up Pearl, janked around through the neighborhood to avoid the traffic cam, hit the freeway and dumped off onto a corkscrewing off-ramp that was great for drifts. Then it was back up through the corner section of Fircrest with the retirement-age, trigger happy cops and back down Pearl to the start.

It was a ten-mile round trip, and Kendra thought she could do it in under seven minutes, even with the side street slowdowns. Of course, for any of Fireball's races, if you went more than ten minutes it was assumed you'd crashed yourself and died or your car had blown up.

Seven and half minutes later, Anatoliy was back and Carl limped in behind him, having grazed a jersey barrier somewhere and thrown off his alignment. The betting pool liked that fine and the Ukrainians in attendance started pumping some sort of Die Antword techno remix. Kendra got Minnie to the starting line and did a little strutting around the car, bending over to give the hood a polish. Mike hollered something filthy about Kendra's ass and Kendra brought her hand up to her gas mask and blew a kiss.

"Anytime!" yelled Mike and Kendra laughed.

Fireball changed up the rally routes frequently, but Kendra had driven this neighborhood since she was fourteen and sneaking out with her grandma's beat up Chevette. There was a wicked pothole on 30th and a speed hump on Highland, neither of which showed up on Google maps. She was willing to bet she could ace Mike out on those obstacles alone.

Fireball put spotters on the course to live stream the racers to a closed online group. It made the races more exciting for the audience at the starting line and kept the racers mostly honest. Some drivers seemed to think it as a safety net, but Kendra didn't know why. Fireball didn't give assistance to stranded drivers—he was running a drag race, not a towing service. At most, she thought he might anonymously call for an ambulance if someone biffed it too hard. He wasn't evil after all, just a dick.

The speed hump was indeed a killer and Kendra was back in the same seven and a half minutes as Anatoliy. She checked the clock when she got out and saw that she was within seconds of the Ukranian. She'd been sandbagging it, and she was willing to bet he was too.

Next up were Stacy and Doc. Doc offered a good sportsman elbow instead of a handshake and Stacy looked at him like he was an idiot. Meanwhile, some of the guys in the crowd started a chant about Stacy that wasn't child-friendly.

"Ignore them," bellowed Kendra through her gas mask.

"I'm fine," said Stacy, raising her chin and giving her a death stare. Stacy wanted to play jailbait, but Kendra knew it made her nervous when the adults started taking her too seriously. However, Stacy was never going to admit that she couldn't hack it on the street grid.

"Yeah! You got this!" yelled Kendra, through the mask.

Stacy smiled at her, or at least Kendra thought she smiled by the way her eyes crinkled over the mask.

"See you next race!" she chirped and Kendra gave her a thumbs up.

But at seven minutes twenty-five seconds, Doc's Nissan GT-R roared past the Antique Sandwich Company, with the Art Nouveau lady sipping tea on the sign, and slid into the finish leading Stacy's Tesla by a solid three seconds. The upset caused a flurry of work in the betting pools and Kendra felt a wash of nerves. She liked Stacy, but Kendra also knew Stacy and her driving. Doc was an unknown quantity. She didn't like unknowns.

Jim and Anatoliy lined up next. There was a lot of showboating that went into getting two cars to the line. The Ukrainian contingent was out in force tonight. Anatoliy was popular. And Kendra saw several traditionally dressed girls, their hair covered in scarves, calf-length skirts paired with high-heels, all standing in a knot a lit bit away from the crowd swooning over him.

The race kicked off and the Ferrari and the Honda roared up the straight away in a thunder of noise. Kendra grabbed her phone and pulled up the livestream. Moments later she had video of the two cars taking the turn into the neighborhood. Anatoliy avoided the pot hole and edged out Jim, but Jim skated up a driveway and cruised the sidewalk avoiding the speed hump. Which was what she'd done during her race. Apparently, she wasn't the only one who'd been in the neighborhood before. Or he'd cribbed it off her. The next three check-ins showed Anatoliy and Jim neck and neck. It all came down to the final straight away. She didn't bet on the races she took part in, but she would have put her money on Jim. The Ferrari just had more horse-power. Which he showcased in a final push, sliding across the finish, and taking a victory lap around the traffic circle in front of the park. The Ukrainians groaned in disappointment. Kendra checked the clock. Jim had brought the time to beat down to seven minutes and eight seconds. Kendra knew she could do better. She had to, if she was going to get Papa Steg's seven hundred bucks.

With the race cleared, Kendra and Doc took the line. Doc's style of Nissan was generally known on the grid as a Godzilla, and up close she saw that he'd given it a little iridescent scale pattern over the silver paint job. She liked Doc's style.

Fireball's flagger walked to the line. He liked to pick girls that looked good on camera, but Kendra thought high-heel sneakers were dumb.

The flag dropped and Kendra hit the gas. Doc was right there with her. He'd ditched his fez and mask, and although it was hard to tell through the glare on the windows she thought she'd been right—he was cute. Up the hill, past the pharmacy, she pushed it hard, cutting Doc off and forcing him into the pot hole. She slid into the neighborhood and then slammed to a halt as coyote trotted out into the street.

"Son of a bitch!" she yelled as the coyote froze in front of her and Doc went sailing past. Furious with herself, she dodged around the canine and followed Doc, pushing Minnie to the limit. They hit the right and then the left and came back onto Pearl sliding through the turn.

They were running parallel to the freeway now. An overpass crossed over 6th Ave just before 6th intersected with Pearl. A wide grassy area with low shrubs that ran up the berm to the edge of the overpass was to the left and a strip-mall was on the right. Kendra thought Fireball had a spotter stashed somewhere around here, but she didn't see anyone. Not that she had a lot of time to look around.

Doc was a half-block ahead and Kendra growled to herself. But before she could shift, she saw a flash of headlights and then the dune buggy piece of shit roadster with the number seven slopped on the side roared out of a nail salon parking lot, heading straight for Doc.

Doc swerved and the GT-R bounced the curve, slalomed across the grass, over the shrubs and drove half-way up the rise of the overpass before sliding back down again. The dune buggy, a passenger hanging out the top, whooping and hollering, barely made the corner, heading up 6th Ave. Kendra watched, in what felt like the slow motion of a horror movie, as Plague Blankets turned back toward Doc and the passenger stood up in his seat and pulled out a shot-gun. There was a boom and Kendra flinched although she couldn't tell if they'd hit anything. Doc was spinning his wheels—the front end was crunched—she thought the front axle was cracked.

She yanked the emergency brake as she headed into the intersection. The car turned and slid and she ended pointing back toward Doc. Kendra reved up and went up the side-walk ramp. Doc was scrambling out of his car as number seven paused firing and seemed to re-target on her. She had the window rolled down as she skidded across the grass.

"Get in!" she yelled and Doc dove head first into the passenger seat through the window. Kendra threw the car into reverse and put the pedal down, following the same path she entered on. The dune buggy, unprepared for her reversal, over shot and sailed past her. Doc slammed onto the floor as she flipped a one-eighty onto the street. She had one block to go before the free-way on-ramp.

Doc managed to right himself as she floored it. Plague Blankets was on her tail and the speedometer said she was hitting 135 as she arrived on the freeway. She had about one mile of unimpeded asphalt and then it was off again. By the time she got to the exit she would be doing at least 160.

Doc hauled himself into the passenger seat and reached for the seat belt. He managed to get the belt across himself by the time she slid into the off-ramp. The drift was intense and she knew she was riding on the very edge of control. They came onto the street and ran the street light without a second thought. She wanted to check the time, but she didn't dare look away from the road. There was a sudden lessening of road noise and she realized that Doc had shut the window.

"Thanks!" she yelled.

"Are you still racing?" he yelled back.

"Yeah!" She realized that neither of them had their masks on and also that her impression from the starting line had been wrong. Doc wasn't just cute, he was full on hot.

Then there was sharp bang and Minnie's back window cracked.

"Fuck!" she yelled and took the left turn faster than she intended. She had a little over a quarter mile until the right turn back onto Pearl and then it was a straight four mile shot back to the start. Four miles, no obstacles, one traffic cam. She just had to time the light. She done the math when she was seventeen, but she'd never had a car that could make it or the empty streets to test it. But then, there had never been a pandemic before. All she had to do was hit the first green light and then make sure she was doing an average of 138.

She slid into the intersection and stopped in the middle, staring north along Pearl, waiting for the light to turn green. Out Doc's window she could see Plague Blankets barreling down on them.

"What are you doing?" yelled Doc. "You need to go!"

"One-thirty-eight," she said, breathing out as she readied her foot on the pedal. Later, she might freak out, but right this second, she *knew* she could do this. The passenger in number seven, stood up, poking out the top of the dune buggy, the shotgun in his hand.

"Go, go, go!" yelled Doc, his foot stomping on an imaginary gas pedal. On the third go, the light turned and Kendra hit the gas. Minnie leapt into motion, surging with power, tires squealing to find traction. The traffic cam was at an intersection a little over half-way down the stretch. It had taken thirty seconds to go one mile; she had less than half a second to do the equation on how fast she needed to be going... fuck it. She poured on more gas. The answer arrived a second after she hit the hill.

"One-fifty-one," she said announcing the answer just as she realized that she was only at 147. The light with the traffic cam was deep yellow as she squeaked through and Kendra laughed as her peripheral vision caught the flash of the camera, knowing that it had caught Plague Blankets and number seven. Five to seven business days from now he was going to get *such* an expensive ticket.

"You are fucking insane," yelled Doc, but he was grinning. He was probably right, but this was also the best race of her life.

There was another bang and Minnie's back window shattered. Kendra flinched and the car swerved in response to her touch. Doc ducked down and Kendra crouched over the steering wheel, trying to correct without over-correcting. One more mile to go.

"We just have to get back to Fireball," she yelled. The HazMat team, not to mention all the fucking Ukrainian's, would be able to deal with Plague Blankets. Probably. She hoped.

She dropped down the hill past the pharmacy; Plague Blankets was still on her tail. She bombed into the Ruston town limits and aimed for Point Defiance, wishing that for once the Ruston cops—who were always conveniently around to give tickets on Sunday afternoons—would be there. But they weren't. There was another blast from Plague Blankets and Kendra felt something whistle by her ear. She jerked her head and for a moment she was looking out the driver's side window.

As if in slow motion, Kendra took in the Antique Sandwich Company sign with the ornate lady sipping tea, and the metal bench shaped like an octopus that doubled as bike rack at the side of the building, and then she saw, parked next to the bike rack, Fireball's enormous Ford truck. Only it wasn't parked—even as she passed it, it was already in motion.

Kendra yanked her eyes forward and saw the finish line. She hit the brakes and slid across the finish line as a boom of steel on steel echoed like an explosion behind them.

There was absolute silence when Minnie finally came to a stop and Kendra stared at her white-knuckle grip on the wheel. Out the window she could see the race clock.

Six-minutes-twenty-eight-seconds.

"Thanks for the ride," said Doc, in a near whisper.

"No problem," Kendra replied.

"I really like you," said Doc, clearing his throat, "and now that we're exposed to each other… um… I was wondering if you would you like to be part of my quarantine bubble?"

She turned to look at him in disbelief. His bow-tie was askew and his hair was adorably disheveled. She would one-hundred-percent be running her fingers through that later. "Are you asking me out?"

"Yes," he said.

"Oh. OK."

"Was that a yes?"

Her car door was yanked open and Ferrari Jim looked in at them. Stacy and Mike weren't too far behind him. Anatoliy was standing with the Ukranians. They all had their guns out and were looking up the street. The betting pool was in some sort of melt down.

"Holy shit guys! Are you OK?" demanded Jim.

"Doc wants to get into my pants," said Kendra.

"Yeah, we know," said Mike. "What the hell happened out there?"

"Fireball rolled a seven," said Kendra.

Saving Mrs. Hapwell
John M. Floyd

"What I can't figure out," Nate said, as he lay in the dirt behind a clump of cactus near Rosie Hapwell's house, "is why you married that idiot in the first place."

Before Rosie could reply, another bullet whined off a rock three feet away. Both of them ducked their heads and crawled to the dry wash where Nate had left his horse.

When they were safely out of sight she said, breathing hard, "I had to, that's why."

"You what?"

"How else was I gonna get out of Lizard Flats?" She pulled off one of her shoes, turned it over, and poured out a stream of sand and dirt. "You was in jail at the time, if I recall."

Nate pondered that awhile, then said, "Well, I'm here now."

Rosie's face softened. "I know you are, honey. It's a noble thing, too, after all these years, that you rode out here to see me in my exact hour of need, to save my life."

"Well, I rode out here to see you, that's true. Can't say I knew your life was in danger, though."

She scowled. "It weren't, until about ten minutes ago. He just went crazy, is what he did."

As if to emphasize that statement, two more shots rang out from the porch of the house thirty yards away. Nate's horse, Blue, tied to a dead tree at the bottom of the wash, whinnied and pulled against his reins. After a moment Nate seemed to remember he had a gun of his own, and on an impulse he raised his head above the rim of the gully and took a potshot at the house. Just as he was aiming for a second shot, the gun jumped from his hand as if it were alive.

Nate slid back down beside Rosie, his eyes wide.

"Did you see what he did? That fool shot my gun right out of my hand!"

"A lucky shot," she said, lacing her shoe up again. "Earl can't hit the side of a barn."

"He hit my *gun*, Rosie!"

"Nathan, he's got glasses *this thick*. It was lucky, that's all. He can't see us down here, and he can't hit us unless he comes closer."

"I'm comin' closer!" a deep voice shouted, from the direction of the house. "I intend to kill you, Rosie, and if that's Nate Callahan I saw out there with you, I'll kill him too."

Nate and Rosie looked at each other a moment. The situation, it seemed, was about to get worse.

"Let's get outa here," he said.

"How do we do that?"

"On old Blue, that's how. He's standing right there."

"Both of us?"

"Sure, both of us."

"You told me in your letters he won't let a woman ride

him."

Nate's face fell. "That's right. He won't."

"I'm comin' to kill ya!" Earl Hapwell shouted.

"Well, we better do something," Nate said.

Rosie thought a moment. "You go, Nathan. You done proved your love and your bravery. You ride off and save your own self."

"I can't do that," he said. Then he brightened. "I know. I'll send Blue off without us. Since Earl can't see good, he'll think we're getting away. When he chases the horse, we'll run off the other way."

"Oh, honey," Rosie purred. She was overcome with emotion. "You'd really stay here with me and die?"

"Maybe we won't die. I told you, he might think we rode off." Nate was untying his horse from the tree as he spoke.

"Yeah, and he might not, too. He might come right down here and shoot us."

"Well, it's our only chance." Nate turned Blue loose and slapped him on the rump. He went charging off, and Nate and Rosie huddled in the shadows to wait.

A minute passed. Nothing happened.

"Did he go after your horse?" Rosie asked.

Nate listened. "I don't think so."

"That means he'll come kill us, then."

"I expect so," Nate said. He thought hard for several seconds. "How far does this gully go?"

"It plays out right around that corner," she said, pointing, "and the other end curves back toward the house. The only way out is west, toward the flats, and if we do that he'll see us. He can't see good, but if he sees us at all he'll chase us, and then we're deader'n two fence posts."

For the first time, Nate looked really glum. "I think we're dead anyway."

They were both quiet a moment.

"You know," Rosie said, "this is really romantic, you stayin' here to die with me and all."

Nate just went on looking glum.

"In fact, it's crazy," she said suddenly. "Listen to me, Nathan. You can still save your self. There might be time for you to get your horse back here and ride off."

"How would I do that, even if I wanted to?" he asked.

"Didn't you write me once that Blue will come runnin' when his owner whistles?"

"That was his other owner. Not me."

"He won't come when *you* whistle?"

"I can't whistle."

Rosie nodded sadly. "Me neither. Never learned how."

They fell silent again. Just as they were beginning to think Earl Hapwell might have forgotten all about them, he appeared at the edge of the wash, ten feet away. He had his rifle, and he looked mad as hell.

"Gotcha," he said. "You two better say yore prayers."

"Wait a minute, Earl," Nate said, standing up with both hands in the air. "What do you want to kill us for?"

Earl gave that some thought, then admitted, "I don't really want to kill *you*, Nate. If you can find yore horse, you can go on and leave. It's her I'm set on killin'."

"But why, Earl?"

His face darkened. "Cause she did an unforgivable thing, that's why."

That stopped Nate for a second or two. He had never heard Earl say a five-syllable word before. In fact, Nate didn't think he'd ever heard *anyone* say a five-syllable word. He got the meaning, though.

"What'd she do that was so bad?" he asked.

Earl frowned a moment, as if reliving the horrible deed, then said, "I told you to get yore horse and leave, Nate. I meant it."

"Not till you tell me what she did that's so bad you want to shoot her. If it's bad enough, I'll leave."

"You swear?" Earl asked him.

"I swear."

Earl hesitated, then said, "She turned off my football game."

Nate blinked. "She what?"

"She turned off my ballgame. Then she throwed away the remote."

It was suddenly very quiet in the gully.

"Was it halftime?" Nate asked.

"Nope. Fourth quarter."

"Was it a one-sided game?"

"Ten to nine," Earl said.

Another silence. Earl stared at his wife and his wife stared at Nate and Nate stared at the ground in front of him, deep in thought.

Finally he looked up at Earl.

"Can you whistle?" Nate asked.

Lockdown's a Killer

Julie Richards

The neighbourhood wears the eerie silence of lockdown like the hush of a 40-degree summer's day. Sitting in the garden, I notice that most of the familiar sounds that would normally punctuate a Wednesday, like the staccato of target practice at the nearby gun club, are absent. Even the peak-hour traffic is subdued with only the occasional throaty roar of a tearaway motorcycle and the odd reprimand of a horn. A whisper of breeze nudges the leaves on the pumpkin vines, sending ants scurrying and butterflies to flight. Such are the simple things, the rhythms of which cannot be undone by the humblest thing on the planet, as we have been undone.

I've always enjoyed growing vegetables – particularly pumpkins. I'm not sure why. There's something satisfying about tracking the vines as they scramble over the vegie beds and escape into the shrubbery, and then peering into the branches of grevillea to see the vines strung with pendulous orange fruit. They're prolific growers. Too many for me. I could share them with the new next-door neighbours. Might be a nice gesture in this strange new world.

I'm not quite sure what the new neighbours are all about. I call her Dark Glasses because she seems to wear them all the time – even inside. I only know because I got their parcel delivery by mistake. When she opened the front door, I could see myself mirrored in polarised lenses. She didn't take them off, even though it was obvious that I was trying see around them. Over the top of her shoulder I could see a dresser crowded with teddy bears – bears in uniforms, bears in dresses and bonnets; and even one with its arm in a sling and a bandage across its head, leaning against a photograph. 'Crikey!' I said, 'Talk about give a whole new meaning to *there's a bear in there.*' Maybe I was a little too cheerful, or maybe I came across as just plain nosy because she didn't answer. I'd hoped the comment might initiate a response, but staring into those lenses made me feel I like I was talking to myself, and it was somewhat unnerving.

I also noticed that she had placed teddies in every window facing the street. I've put one in my front window now. Apparently, this is what you're supposed to do to amuse young children during lockdown. I only put mine up because obviously Dark Glasses collects teddies and I thought maybe she would like it.

You know, a while back I couldn't have told you who lives in half the houses around me. But now, people emerge like newly minted butterflies from their lockdown cocoons. Often it seems like a conga line outside my place as the women take their permitted exercise in the hug of Lycra, scarves snaked around their necks, and the men, gradually disappearing behind beards as the days crawl by. There's a new daytime soundtrack to the neighbourhood too – the rhythmic pad of joggers' soles on footpaths, snatches of Bluetooth conversation, the hoarseness of dogs straining at leashes, the whir of bike wheels and the nag and skitter of children. I hear the children count with delight the bears as they pass next door, and then, with obvious disappointment, add my meagre contribution to their tally.

Lockdown life. Lives penned up behind walls. I wonder about these lives and those who live them. Well, there's so much time to spend wondering these days isn't there? And of course, there's time for all the bored people to knit up conspiracies of forbidden love, lies and accusation; time for them to feel the grate of habits once tolerated. I imagine the resentment oozing like a wound, making relationships sicken. Time without structure. Everywhere, routines collapsing into decay.

But lockdown also lets me eavesdrop into the daytime lives of my neighbours. With our homes pressing against the boundaries of our small suburban blocks, we live cheek-by-jowl. Through open doors and windows (well, with this last hurrah of warmth everything is open to air the house isn't it), I hear the coughing, the sneezing (eww, corona?). I hear the silly, whiny voices put on to secure the cooperation of pets and children. Household appliances, like beeping kettles, yield mundane secrets (I know how many cups you drink a day now), and the yammer of a TV – seriously, you have it on that channel *all* day?

Ahh, and now I hear the rhythmic whack of plastic golf balls into a driving net. It's Dark Glasses' partner. Perhaps he's working on his swing in readiness for a great post-lockdown golf comeback? Whack. Whack. Whack … then that unmistakeable sound of glass as it fractures.

'Shit!' someone yells.

Tears, followed by a spill of excuses … 'I didn't mean it – honestly. I would never …'. Then a jumble of words and expletives in pursuit. Something about effing teddy bears?

Silence. Long silence. I'm urged to action. I fetch my pruning saw and release a pumpkin from the vine.

On the footpath, in front of next door's, there's a freshly drawn rainbow and someone has chalked the words 'Everything will be Okay' and other little reassurances in bold, bright colours. They're popping up everywhere I walk. It's like a sort of lockdown graffiti.

The neighbours' front door opens and I find myself smiling at my reflection in the polarised lenses. She organises her face into a return smile. Well, it's more of a grimace really. I hold out the pumpkin towards her. 'They're a very versatile vegetable and this variety has few seeds and a skin that's easy to peel.' I sound like the back of a seed packet or an excerpt from a cooking program. The pumpkin is heavy. She doesn't move to take it. Looking over her shoulder I notice the teddies are different. Two have toppled over and another is on the floor. She follows my gaze.

'The dresser's too crowded. I accidentally knocked them off on my way to the door.'

'Sorry. I didn't realise you had to rush.'

I try to thrust my arms farther out towards her, hoping the movement will jog her memory about the gift of the pumpkin. It's getting heavier by the second and the smile on my face is beginning to wane under the strain. Her hand comes into view from behind the door. It's wrapped in a tea towel. I nod towards her hand.

'I hope I didn't cause that by making you run to the door.'

'I broke something before. I was cleaning it up when you rang the bell.'

I signal towards the dresser. 'I can pop it on there if you like – to save you carrying it, seeing as you've hurt your hand.'

She moves across to block my view. I squat and place the pumpkin reverently on the porch. 'Okay. I'll just leave it here then.' Standing up, I back away, turn and leave. Out of the corner of my eye, I see her bending towards the pumpkin. There's no called-out 'thank you'. Just the sound of the door closing. Stepping onto the footpath, I challenge the 'Everything will be Okay' with a stern 'will it?'. Right now, feeling the burn of rebuff, I just want to scuff the words out. I hope for rain tonight.

It doesn't rain. Standing on my back deck, I watch the International Space Station fly over – very important lockdown post-dusk viewing so I am told. Okay, can tick that one off the list. I think about tomorrow, and how each lockdown day dawns heavy as stone and hauls its way across our end of the planet. So much time but still I can't seem to get anything done. Everyone else has probably learned a language, a musical instrument, or finished a PhD by now. I can't even accomplish a routine. My Facebook feed is drowning in platitudes. Apparently, there's a kindness pandemic. Somebody has joined me up to the group. Perhaps next door reported my pumpkin donation. I wonder what would happen if I told the kindness pandemic group that right now, I really just feel like punching people in the face?

It's very quiet tonight next door. I think about the pumpkin. Did she actually pick it up? Or did she just pretend to, to make me feel better? Nah. She's not that sort of person – or is she? Perhaps it's just a sign of the times but, for some strange reason, I just have to know the pumpkin's fate. I cut a second pumpkin from the vine. I mean, there's plenty and they keep for a long period, so they could probably use another. Yeah, I know. It's just a pretence ….

The beam from my torch lights up the decked path to their front door. The pumpkin is gone. I guess I still qualify for the kindness pandemic then. I ring the bell. The torch catches the glint of a window teddy's eye. There's something strange about it. It's the in-patient teddy but its arm is out of the sling and torn away at the shoulder. The head bandage is gone and stuffing dribbles down its front. The front door opens slowly.

'Yes?'

This time, it's him.

'It's just your friendly neighbourhood pumpkin lady! I thought you might be able to use another one. They've been very productive this year.' I stop before I start to sound like a gardening program host.

'Oh. Okay. On the step is fine.'

'Is your partner's hand okay? She had it wrapped in a tea towel earlier.'

'It's fine. Thanks.'

'Were you able to fix what was broken? I couldn't help but hear it smash. You know … it's … it's hard not to overhear with everyone living so close and all the doors and windows open during this nice weather…'

'No. Couldn't fix it.'

The gap between the door and the doorframe begins to

narrow.

'What a shame. Gosh, I hope it wasn't a family heirloom.'

Somewhere inside a door slams shut.

'Gotta go,' he says hurriedly.

The door closes. A deadlock clicks. I place the pumpkin on the porch and leave.

*****

In my dream, I hear glass shatter, but it's the banging – like someone pounding on a door – that yanks me from my sleep. My door? No, not my door. A ricochet of red and blue lights plays across my bedroom walls. No. Definitely not my door. Uh oh ….

I emerge onto the street. I see lights snap on in surrounding houses but the house next door sits a shadowy hulk against the street, all light extinguished, as if resisting discovery. The front window is broken. The garden is strewn with teddy bears and a framed photograph – older people, like someone's parents. They hold teddy bears with first-prize rosettes pinned to them. The front door, half off its hinges, reveals a maw of hallway and I can just make out two people bending over a mound in a puddle of light on the kitchen floor. The mound doesn't stir despite their loud urging. I can't make out the name. I can't make out the shape. Someone says 'dead'. Someone else says 'I'll call it in.' I hear footsteps behind me and a voice urging me off the property.

The policeman toes the pumpkin aside to clear a path as he ushers me back to the street. Another begins to deploy a roll of crime-scene tape. I'm asked if I knew the people next door at all or if I'd heard anything unusual. It's lockdown, I say. I've heard a lot of things that I don't usually hear but I didn't hear this. And no, I don't even know their names. I just bring them pumpkins. How lame. I don't even know why I said that last bit.

They're bringing someone out. It's Dark Glasses – minus her glasses.

I want to pick up one of the bears and give it to her as a comfort, but I've seen enough crime shows to know that I mustn't touch anything at the scene and anyway, I can't reach them from the footpath. Dark Glasses yells out to me.

'Hey lady! Thanks for the pumpkin. Only needed one after all. And they'll need a pretty big evidence bag for that mother.'

She tramples teddy bears and gives those beyond her immediate reach a kick. The last thing she steps on is the photo and she has to do a fancy side-step to achieve it. She grinds the glass into the photo and in a tone that's a cross between triumph and relief, yells 'No more fucking bears!', and I am suddenly glad that I was never permitted to look into those eyes.

As I walk home, my torch plays over the chalked message on the footpath. It's still telling me that everything will be okay. Bullshit it will! Tomorrow, I'll bring out the pressure cleaner and that'll fix it once and for all.

The Usual Unusual Suspects

Jesse Hilson is a newspaper reporter working in the Catskills in New York State. His work has appeared or will appear in *Maudlin House, AZURE, Pink Plastic House, Pulp Modern,* and *Close to the Bone.* His novel *BLOOD TRIP* will be published by *Close to the Bone* in April 2022. You can follow Jesse on Twitter using the handle @platelet60 .

Gabriel Stevenson graduated from the University of Puerto Rico more years ago than he would care to admit, and has since wandered wherever Uncle Sam sends him. He currently lives in Delaware with his wife and children. His short fiction has appeared in 2020's *Best Indie Speculative Fiction,* the *J.J. Outré Review* and *Frontier Tales.* He can be found on Twitter @JibrilStevenson.

Maddi Davidson is the pen name for two sisters, Mary Ann Davidson and Diane Davidson. They've published numerous short stories, several mystery novels, and a non-fiction book.

Brandon Barrows is the author of the novels *Burn Me Out, This Rough Old World, Nervosa,* and has had over fifty published stories, a selection of which are collected in the books *The Alter In The Hills* and *The Castle-Town Tragedy.* He is an active member of Private Eye Writers of America and International Thriller Writers.

Robb White has published several crime, noir, and hardboiled novels and published crime, horror, and mainstream stories in various magazines and anthologies. His crime story, 'Inside Man,' was selected for *Best American Mystery Stories 2019*. A recent series features private eye Raimo Jarvi and includes *Northtown Eclipse*. His novel *When You Run with Wolves* was cited as a finalist by *Murder, Mayhem & More* for its Top Ten Crime Books of 2018. *If I Let You Get Me* was selected for the Bouchercon 2019 anthology. Find him at https://tomhaftmann.wixsite.com/robbtwhite

Regina Clarke lives in the ancient terrain of the Hudson River Valley, after many years of exploring other places. Twenty of her stories have been published online (and two in print). Her novel *MARI* was a finalist in the ListenUp Audiobooks competition and two dark (not quite horror) short stories — *Calliope* and *Stopover* — were featured on The Strange Recital podcast in Woodstock, NY. Her short story *A Magician's Wish* received Honorable Mention by Writer's Digest and her story *A Matter of Time* won the Reedsy writing contest. You can see her books and story page at her website: www.regina-clarke.com, and read more of her work at Wired for Storytelling.

Martin Zeigler writes short fiction, primarily mystery, science fiction, and horror. His stories have been published in a number of anthologies and journals, both in print and online. Every so often (okay, twice), he has gathered these stories into a self-published collection. In 2015 he released *A Functional Man And Other Stories*. More recently, in 2020, a year we will all remember with fondness, he released *Hypochondria And Other Stories*.

Besides writing, Marty enjoys the things most people do. And besides those, he likes reading, taking long walks, and playing the piano.

Marty makes his home in the Pacific Northwest.

K. G. Anderson is an American technology journalist and fiction writer who currently calls Seattle, Washington, her home. Her short stories appear in anthologies, magazines, and podcasts including The Mammoth Book of Jack the Ripper Stories, Weirdbook, and StarShipSofa. When not out gardening in the Seattle rain, she's in the kitchen making tomato sauce and tossing pizza dough. Find her online at http://writerway.com/fiction

Andrew Hook is a much published UK writer who works in a variety of genres, but specific to crime he has had two novels published featuring the same character, Mordent — *The Immortalists* and *Church Of Wire* – Telos Publishing — and has had crime short fiction in *Crimewave*, *Crimespree*, and *Needle magazine*, amongst other places. He is a member of the *Crime Writers Association* and organises events for the East Anglian Branch.

Ed Nobody is a writer from Ireland who wants to write daring, engaging stories not restricted by traditional genre conventions. He has published several short stories in magazines such as: *Lovecraftiana*, *Strange Science Fiction*, and *Dread Machine*. He has two novellas under consideration and a novel in the works. @EdIsNobody on Twitter.

Jody Smith is a horror author who lives in small town Ontario, Canada, who likes animals and TV. His gory, splattery horror novella, *Who Will Save Your Soul?* will be available in early 2021. https://dancingflamebooks.wixsite.com/my-site

Michael Grimala is a professional journalist at the *Las Vegas Sun*, where he has won two *Nevada Press Association* awards for feature writing. Recently has had a short story—*A Trunk Full of Illegal Fireworks*—published in the July/August 2021 issue of *Ellery Queen Mystery Magazine*.

W. T. Paterson is a three-time Pushcart Prize nominee, holds an MFA in Fiction Writing from the University of New Hampshire, and is a graduate of Second City Chicago. His work has appeared in over 80 publications worldwide including *The Saturday Evening Post*, *The Forge Literary Magazine*, *The Delhousie Review*, *Brilliant Flash Fiction*, and *Fresh Ink*. A semi-finalist in the *Aura Estra* short story contest, his work has also received notable accolades from *Lycan Valley*, *North 2 South Press*, and *Lumberloft*. He spends most nights yelling for his cat to "Get down from there!"

James Blakey's fiction has appeared in Mystery Weekly, Crimson Streets, and Over My Dead Body. His story *The Bicycle Thief* won a 2019 Derringer Award. He lives in suburban Philadelphia where he works as a network engineer for a software consulting company. When James isn't working or writing, he can be found on the hiking trail—he's climbed thirty-eight of the fifty US state high points—or bike-camping his way up and down the East Coast. Find him at www.JamesBlakeyWrites.com.

Emilian Wojnowski comes from another planet, which is why he feels bad on Earth. A philologist and translator by education, a hobbit by nature and appearance. He is constantly looking for peace, lost time, and books. Emilian has never drunk alcohol but fears the future all the time. His name can be found in such literary places as *Intrinsick, Curiosities, Amon Hen, Ghost Orchid Press,* and Graham Masterton's official website. Emilian's *Ditch Digging* has appeared in CRIMEUCOPIA – We're All Animals Under the Skin.

Andrew Darlington has been regularly published since the 1960s in all manner of strange and obscure places, magazines, websites, anthologies and books. He has also worked as a Stand-Up Poet on the 'Alternative Cabaret Circuit', and also has a phenomenal back catalogue of published interviews with many people from the worlds of Literature, SF-Fantasy, Art and Rock-Music for a variety of publications (a selection of his favourite interviews have been collected into the 'Headpress' book *'I Was Elvis Presley's Bastard Love-Child'*).

His latest poetry collection is *'Tweak Vision'* (Alien Buddha Press), and a new fiction collection *'A Saucerful Of Secrets'* is now available from Parallel Universe Publications, and a Scientifiction novel *'In The Time Of The Breaking'* (Alien Buddha Press) was published in January 2019. Catch up with him at http://andrewdarlington.blogspot.com/

Having grown up in Normal, IL, **Lawrence Allan** is Midwestern as fuck, and loves heroes who use humor as cover for their emotional trauma. His work has been published by *Shotgun Honey*, *Daily Science Fiction* and in the award winning crime anthology *WRONG TURN*. He is currently querying his first novel Big Fat F@!K Up. He lives in Los Angeles.

Ricky Sprague's work has appeared in a wide range of publications including *Mad*, *Cracked*, *Nickelodeon Magazine*, *Mystery Weekly*, and *Ellery Queen Mystery Magazine*. Upcoming projects include *GUT-SHOT*, a graphic novel from *Short, Scary Tales* based on his friend Ed Gorman's short story "Stalker" and illustrated by Jussi Piironen, short stories in the *Mystery Weekly DIE LAUGHING* collection, *Smart Rhino Publications' ASININE ASSASSINS* anthology, *Moonstone's* Domino Patrick story collection, and color art for Chris Wisnia's *DORIS DANGER* graphic novel from *Fantagraphics*. Hopefully his Kolchak novel, *DAY OF THE DEMONS*, will be completed soon for *Moonstone*. Also, he is an occasional guest on the *Movies From Hell* strange/horror/esoteric film appreciation podcast.

John M. Floyd's work has appeared in more than 300 different publications, including *Alfred Hitchcock's Mystery Magazine, Ellery Queen's Mystery Magazine, Strand Magazine, the Saturday Evening Post*, and three editions of *The Best American Mystery Stories*. A former Air Force captain and IBM systems engineer, John is also an Edgar Award finalist, a four-time Derringer Award winner, and the author of nine books.

His short story – *The Judge's Wife* – appeared in the Murderous Ink Press anthology series, CRIMEUCOPIA – *The Cosy Nostra*, and *Redemption* in CRIMEUCOPIA – *Dead Man's Hand.*

Julie Richards is a London-born writer living in Melbourne, Australia, who believes that 'writing chose her' rather than vice-versa. The author of 41 educational resource books, Julie has also published articles, short fiction and poetry in various anthologies, literary magazines and newspapers. A workshop facilitator and industry speaker, Julie also spent eight years teaching journalism, creative non-fiction, research, and editing. Julie also volunteers as a pro bono editor because she wants to make a difference and believes that such work is about outcomes not income. And yes, she really does love to grow pumpkins!

16 stories ranging from the 14th to the 21st Century, all from women authors whose forte is crime.

Featuring *Karen Skinner, Hilary Davidson, Pauline Gostling, Linda Kerr, Kate Miller, Tiffany Lindfield, Lena Ng, Ginny Swart, Sandrine Bergèss, Michelle Ann King, Amanda Steel, Kelly Lewis, Paulene Turner, Claire Leng, Madeleine McDonald and Joan Hall Hovey.*

Paperback Edition ISBN:
9781909498198
eBook Edition ISBN:
9781909498204

Paperback Edition ISBN:
9781909498235
eBook Edition ISBN:
9781909498228

A Crimeucopia Family Gathering

17 writers take us on Cosy journeys - some more traditional, while others are very much up to date.

Eve Fisher, Alexander Frew, Tom Johnstone, John M.Floyd, Andrew Humphrey, Joan Leotta, Gary Thomson, Eamonn Murphey, Matias Travieso-Diaz, Madeline McEwen, Lyn Fraser, Ella Moon, Gina L. Grandi, Louise Taylor, Judy Penz Sheluk, Joan Hall Hovey and Judy Upton.

Paperback Edition ISBN: 9781909498242
eBook Edition ISBN: 9781909498259

The five writers in this Anthology have proven track records in both the Western and Crime genres, and are old hands when it comes to telling compelling stories.

Paperback Edition ISBN: 9781909498280
eBook Edition ISBN: 9781909498297

9 781909 498266